GAYLORD			PRINTED IN U.S.A.

FOUR STEPS
TO THE ALTAR

**Center Point
Large Print**

FOUR STEPS
TO THE ALTAR

JEAN STONE

CENTER POINT PUBLISHING
THORNDIKE, MAINE

This Center Point Large Print edition
is published in the year 2007 by arrangement with
The Bantam Dell Publishing Group.

The text of this Large Print edition is unabridged. In other
aspects, this book may vary from the original edition. Printed in
Thailand. Set in 16-point Times New Roman type.

ISBN-10: 1-58547-953-5
ISBN-13: 978-1-58547-953-5

Cataloging-in-Publication data is available from the Library of Congress.

TO WENDY,
WITH THANKS

1

"Marry me, Lily."

It was early in May, a year when spring had come deliciously early to the Berkshire hills of Massachusetts, teasing the landscape with purple crocus and yellow daffodils, plumping tree branches with expectant buds, warming the earth with the promise of a new season, another chance at another beginning.

It was early in May, and it was the end of the day, the end of another wedding that Lily and her second-wedding-planning partners had created, this one a Sunday evening event between a nurse and a carpenter who lived in Albany and had met at a school play when their kids were in first grade. It was a second wedding for the nurse, a third for the carpenter.

If Lily Beckwith married Frank Forbes, it would be his second, her fourth, which wouldn't matter, because hardly anyone got married only once anymore.

Still, she would have to say no.

She zipped the quilted case that held the silver hors d'oeuvre trays they'd used for the crab cakes and spinach quiches. She moved it to the stack of things that Frank had offered to load into his truck and return from the reception at the country club to the rental store. He was generous like that. Always around to help the small bunch of enthusiastic women who took on too much work because it was such fun.

"Frank," Lily said softly, "I don't know what to say." She'd known him a year, well, less than that, actually, since she'd come back to West Hope, where she and her old college roommates had opened Second Chances, proclaiming themselves the be-all, end-all, know-it-all experts for second-time brides. They'd leased a shop in Frank's building on Main Street, and Lily had moved into the apartment upstairs. Because Frank was a man, and because he was single, it was inevitable that Lily quickly had snared him. It was also inevitable, she supposed, that he now felt secure in popping the question. She should have expected it, should have been prepared. Instead, she lowered her eyes. "Will you let me think about it?"

He laughed good-naturedly. "We can do a prenup. I'll keep my meager antiques business, you keep your late husband's vast fortune."

He was trying to lighten the mood, Lily thought. He had no idea things would not be that easy. She shook her head. "But I've already been married a few times."

"I don't care if you've had a few hundred husbands. I'd like to be the few hundred and first."

He was a dear man, Frank Forbes. He was gentle, kind, steady, and strong. He was good-enough-looking, not too short or too tall, not dashingly hand-some, but he had sturdy, broad shoulders and sincere brown eyes and a sweet, receding hairline. He'd make a great husband, partner, mate. And he loved her! Lily had felt sure of that from the start.

"You do love me, Lily," he said, taking her hand, his

callused, workingman fingers threading around her soft, delicate ones, smothering her large pear-shaped pink diamond, the ring she'd bought one day on a whim.

It was the pink diamond—not the previous marriages—that was the real problem.

If Lily married Frank—or anyone—she would lose her inheritance from poor, dead Reginald Beckwith, her most recent husband. As much as Lily cared about Frank, would he—would any man—really be worth fifty million? Not that she'd ever see the cash, certainly not the way Reginald's beastly sister, Antonia, rationed Lily's allowance as if it were chocolate and Lily, a diabetic.

Fluffing her wispy blond curls, Lily resumed her role as a coquette. "Don't be a goose, darling. I simply need a bit of time. You understand, don't you?" She stood on her tiptoes and kissed his forehead. "Now, I must go check on the girls." Then she flitted away, butterfly that she was, too embarrassed to admit to Frank that, short of going to Antonia and distastefully groveling, Lily simply couldn't marry him. It just wouldn't work, economically speaking.

She sucked in her cheeks and tried to tell herself that was okay.

2

I f the old bastard asks about John Benson, I'll say we haven't spoken for a while, that I've been busy with friends, launching their new business." Andrew stood at the mirror that hung over the bureau in the bedroom of his small cottage. He straightened his open shirt collar and adjusted the shoulders of his khaki twill blazer. He hoped it was okay not to wear a tie.

"The Dean of Academics at Winston College—the 'old bastard,' as you call him—might not even know John," Jo replied.

He turned to look at her, the vision of loveliness camped out in his bed, where she regularly was whenever Cassie slept over at her friend Marilla's. (Though Andrew had tried to tell Jo that Cassie was very hip for twelve years old and would be cool about them sleeping together, Jo had insisted, for propriety's sake, on not giving his daughter "too loose" a message about love and sex.) So sometimes Jo and Andrew stayed here, sometimes at Jo's house, where they would all live once he and Jo finally were married, which was just weeks away, though it seemed like decades. He leaned down and kissed her full, sexy mouth and wondered not for the first time how he had gotten so lucky. "Thanks for the encouragement, but even the new pope knows John Benson."

When Jo laughed, her green eyes crinkled and her

whole high-cheekboned face glowed. She tucked her taupe-colored, slept-on hair behind her ears, then kissed Andrew's cheek. "Winston College was lucky to have you as a professor once. They will be lucky again."

Andrew groaned, sat on the side of the bed, and tugged on his right sneaker, then his left. "Are the sneakers too . . ."

"Too what? Too you? No. They're perfect."

He felt her gaze on him as he began tying the shoelaces.

"You really are nervous, aren't you?" she asked.

He double-knotted each lace, the way he'd taught Cassie to do for good luck. "I want to be able to support my new wife in the style to which she has become accustomed."

She said that wouldn't take much, then they both laughed and he took her hand.

"Yes," he said. "I'm nervous. I need my old job back. Call it a man-thing about having a decent paycheck. But I'm afraid John has cut the strings that got me there the first time." The first time had been nearly six years ago, when he'd moved from New York City to West Hope, when he'd gone from being an international television journalist to a small-town college professor so he could raise his young daughter in the peace of the country. John—media mogul, Winston College alum, and hefty benefactor—had been a mentor to Andrew back then, had wanted to help him heal the wounds of a ripping divorce. Time, however, had changed a few things, and John was no longer an Andrew Kennedy fan, and vice versa.

Jo covered his hand with her other one. "You will be fine. You don't need John Benson. And if the college doesn't want you, you can still be a wedding planner. Maybe I can talk to the others about giving you a raise."

He reached for a pillow—his pillow that was next to her—and bounced it off the side of her head. She grabbed it and pretended to throw it back at him, just as he shouted "Uncle!" and leapt from the bed. He returned to the mirror, squared his shoulders again, and combed his tawny, never-in-place hair with his fingers.

"You'll come to the shop when you're done?" Jo asked.

"No."

Jo raised her lovely, lean, naked body up on one elbow. His heart did the little dance that it did whenever she revealed that she had her clothes off, the same little dance that made him feel like a teenager with just one thing on his mind.

"No?" she asked.

He shook his head, tucked his car keys into his pocket. "I'm going to stop at the hardware store and check out the plans for our new house." The new house was not exactly a new house, but a family room and a first-floor master bedroom suite that they were going to add on to Jo's house so it would be big enough for the three of them—Andrew, Cassie, and Jo.

"And then you'll come to the shop?"

He leaned down and kissed her. "And then I'll come to the shop. In the meantime, please stay right here in bed. It will help me relax to think that while I'm in the old bastard's office, your beautiful body will be rolling around in my sheets."

Jo decided to wait there an hour. Not that Andrew would know if she'd showered and dressed and gone off to work, but the thought of him sitting in the dean's stuffy office, smiling because he was thinking of her in his bed, was part of Andrew's charm that she could not resist. Playing along with it made her smile too.

But instead of "rolling around" or being tempted to go back to sleep, Jo slid into that heavenly state where you can make dreams happen, where you can always get the endings that you want.

She pictured Andrew, coming home from the college, tossing his briefcase into the corner of their new family room, meandering toward the fireplace, telling her about his wonderful day, that his most difficult student had mastered writing a press release, that the year's first edition of the school newspaper was on deadline and awesome, that the old bastard dean had said Andrew was doing a fine job and the college was fortunate to have him on their roster.

She saw Cassie, watching *American Idol* tapes in the "old" living room—the original room of the original house that Jo's grandfather had built for his bride seven decades ago—giggling with her best friend, Marilla, as the girls tried on makeup and revamped

13

each other's hair with braids and extensions and who knew what else.

And Jo felt her spirit, floating contentedly on her happiness cloud, drifting around the warm, cozy kitchen (it would be her turn to be the domestic goddess for dinner), making healthy chicken soup for her family because last night had been Andrew's turn and he'd cheated by ordering pizza.

She smiled and wrapped Andrew's covers more closely around her, warmed by the scent of their lovemaking last night, eager to start their great life together. Only three more weeks until May 27, the date they had chosen for their wedding, for Jo Lyons, 43, to wed Andrew David Kennedy, 43, both of West Hope, Massachusetts, or so the local newspaper notice would read.

One day at the shop, Lily had suggested they have the article published in the *New York Times*, what with Andrew, once known as Andrew David, a recognized face in many living rooms during the evening news, and Jo one of the partners in Second Chances, an up-and-coming business in a field where glamour and hype definitely mattered.

But Andrew and Jo had said, "No way," simultaneously, that this was their marriage, not a publicity stunt.

Lily had been annoyed. It was bad enough, she'd complained, that Jo was going to wear a petal-pink shantung suit, a Chanel knockoff. It was bad enough that there would be only two attendants, Jo's mother to stand up for her, and Cassie for Andrew in lieu of a

14

"best man." It was bad enough they had invited only sixty or so people and that the reception would be on the lawn of the Stone Castle, down by the lake and the dock and the rickety rowboat where they'd apparently fallen in love.

These things were bad enough, according to Lily, for the marriage of two wedding planners. But no publicity? Positive horrors.

Elaine, however, had understood, and Sarah had commented on the ridiculous tradition of publicly announcing the bonding of love, as if the bride and groom were the winners of the July 4th town raffle or the grand opening of an appliance store out on Route 7.

Jo turned onto her side and thought about how happy she was. For so long she had been so aimless, so empty, living in Boston, her career-driven days a sad substitute for her lonely nights. If it hadn't been for Brian—for the fact that he had come back to her, for the fact that, once again, she succumbed to his magic elixir that he dared to call "love"—Jo would not have lost everything, would not have returned to West Hope, would not have built a new business with her old friends, would not have met Andrew. It occurred to her that if Brian's trial ever got under way, if she had the chance to face him in the courtroom, she should thank him for jump-starting her life.

Her cell phone rang, snapping her back to the present. Could Andrew's interview be over so soon?

But the caller wasn't Andrew, it was Sarah.

"I wondered what time you're coming to work."

Jo looked at the clock. "Sorry. I'm running late. I should have called." As with Cassie, there was no need for the others to know that Andrew and Jo sometimes slept together all night. Luckily, cell phones still provided an anonymous "cover" as to the whereabouts of the persons on each end of the line.

"No problem. But I'm already here and I forgot to pick up daisies at Dennis's Flower Shop. I need to figure out how many will fit into the backdrop for the Gilberts' wedding." The wedding was going to be yellow and white and would be outside in a meadow. Sarah had designed a lattice wall that would frame the wedding party and would be adorned with as many daisies as she could weave through it.

"I'll pick up a few dozen. Will that be enough?"

"It should be. Thanks. And tell Andrew I'm sorry if I interrupted anything." She said good-bye and hung up before it registered with Jo that Sarah had surmised exactly where Jo was and, apparently, the reason she was late.

So much for the anonymity of cell phones.

She clicked off the phone, pulled herself out from under the covers, sat on the edge of the bed, and laughed at her old-fashioned self.

"What's so funny?" Cassie suddenly asked from the hall and appeared at the open doorway of Andrew's bedroom before Jo realized that she wasn't alone after all, or before her reflexes were quick enough to cover her nakedness.

3

Maybe if Lily just came right out and asked Antonia if she would cut off her allowance if she married Frank, she might get an answer she wouldn't have expected. Maybe Antonia would be so happy for Lily that she wouldn't begrudge her the lifestyle that Reginald surely meant for Lily to have whether or not she found happiness again.

Well, she supposed, as she sat in her small kitchen drinking morning tea, that was one theory.

She looked out the window, across the town green at the old town hall that now housed Antiques & Such, Frank Forbes's business that had been started by his father and kept alive by Frank. It was out of character—hers, anyway—to even consider living with a man who owned only one home, had a real job, and had never been to Europe, not even once. A man who took care of his aging father and his ailing mother, and whose business specialized in New England antiques, the price tags of which were hardly those of Tiffany's or Louis XV.

Lily's cache of former husbands—one moved back home with Mama, one decided he was gay, and the last, poor Reginald Beckwith, had been two decades older than Lily and had the misfortune to simply die— had the combined wealth of a small nation. She'd enjoyed it "while she had it," Aunt Margaret would have said, having parlayed what little Lily had netted from her first two, short-term marriages into clothes and spas and sparkly trinkets necessary for the mission of landing husband number three.

But now she'd landed back in West Hope, where she and Jo and Sarah and Elaine had met at college, Winston College, all those years ago. West Hope had never been a bastion of jet-setters, so what did Lily expect?

It would be much easier if she didn't, well, love Frank, she supposed.

She blinked and squinted across the street as Frank's pickup truck pulled into the parking lot. No doubt he'd already returned the things to the rental store from last night's wedding; no doubt he was getting to work early because he was conscientious, as well as everything else.

Conscientious, if not rich.

"Oh, Lily, dear Lily," she whined, addressing herself in the third person as she always did when her behavior stumped her, "Aunt Margaret would not be pleased."

Aunt Margaret had been Lily's father's sister, the free-spirited, party-loving woman who people said Lily took after—except for the bale of sweet-potato-colored hair piled on top of Margaret's head.

Lily and her parents had shared a two-family house with Margaret on the Hudson River across from West Point. It was there that Margaret often found Lily sitting at a window, a schoolbook inverted on her lap, her gaze fixed on the west side of the river, her thoughts caught in daydreams of parades and cadets. Lily's father, an army captain who had logged three tours in

18

Vietnam and in between taught something classified at the academy, was her idol, and someday she planned to marry a boy just like him. In return for her devotion, he laughed and called her Princess, his adorable child with the curly, white-blond hair.

Between her debutantish mother and playful Aunt Margaret, Lily learned early on that "pesky troubles" were best left to others to handle. Ladies, instead, should only concern themselves with giddy, happy things, not dark, unpleasant worries such as would Daddy come home from the war or not.

Like Lily's parents, Margaret doted on her, helped her immerse her young self in parties and in meeting the "right" boys. A right boy, after all, could make all the difference in the world, according to Aunt Margaret, who'd seen her share of right and wrong ones.

When Lily was in high school, she went to every West Point cotillion dressed in organdy and pearls and a glittering tiara. When it came time for college, she chose Winston College because it was not terribly far from West Point, and only two hours from home.

But just before Lily's high-school graduation, when the lilacs offered the promise of a sweet-scented future, Lily's parents—not one or the other, but *both*—were killed in an accident on the east side of the Bear Mountain Bridge. A drunk driver swerved toward them and smashed them head-on. Their bodies were flung onto the steep embankment; their station wagon went *splat* on the rocks, ending up—she'd overheard one police officer say to another—like a tuna-fish can that had been squished for that new process called recycling.

It hadn't taken a war to steal her daddy from her, or her mother for that matter.

Lily's guilt was all-consuming. Surely she'd been as much at fault as if she'd been behind the wheel of the drunk's car herself.

But she rallied her lessons about dismissing pesky troubles, buried her emotions, and managed to go on. It was years, however, before Lily could face crossing a bridge, any bridge. And to this day, the sick smell of lilacs reminded her of horror and of death and of all things too painful to feel, and made her wonder what had ever happened to Cadet Billy Sears.

Her friends—not husbands one or two, not Reginald, and now not Frank—had no idea that Lily had any anguish at all. Or that there had ever been a sweet boy named Billy, her first love and first lover, who she had erased from her day-to-day, so-busy mind.

The tea was cold now; she really must get downstairs to work and stop dwelling on the fact that she'd lived without real love most of her adult life. With a short sigh, Lily pushed Billy to his special place inside her heart. But as she got up from her doll-sized table, Lily thought of Frank. . . . If Billy Sears had been her first love and those in between had been, well, survival tools—she hoped dear, deceased Reginald would forgive her honesty—then perhaps Frank was her real second chance.

Staring back out the window across the town common to Frank's store, Lily suddenly wondered if she might invent a reason to go into New York—special baubles for wedding attendants, exotic fabric for one of Sarah's creations, a distinctive silver samovar for Elaine's catering needs. Because if Lily went into the city, she could see Antonia. Then maybe, just maybe, Lily might dare concoct a plan—short of downright asking—whereby she might end up with Frank Forbes and her share of the Beckwith money too.

"What did she say?" Sarah was asking Jo when Lily emerged an hour or so later in the shop, dressed in a modest beige light wool suit and wearing sensible Roberto Del Carlo low heels.

"Nothing," Jo said as she slumped onto the chair, dropped her head onto the desk, and draped her arm over the back of her neck. "It was awful."

"What could possibly be awful on a Monday morning?" Lily questioned. Her mood had elevated ten Bloomingdales' floors since she'd cooked up her new mission. Lily always had been better at taking action than sitting at a table feeling sorry for herself. "The nurse and the carpenter were wed in grand style yesterday," she chirped. "Our portfolio bulges with more pictures every day, and I need to make a quick trip to Manhattan."

No one responded, as if she'd been an unwelcome interruption.

"That's nice," Elaine said finally, "but right now Jo has a problem."

Lily didn't want to deal with problems that day, not

21

hers or anyone's. But she shifted on her Del Carlos and asked, "What problem?" because they were her friends and because she knew they would want her to.

"Andrew's daughter walked in on Jo when she was naked," Sarah said.

Lily blinked. "Oh," she said. "Pooh."

"It's worse than that," Jo added. "I was in Andrew's bed."

Cassie was twelve now, they all knew that. Wasn't twelve old enough to understand what love and lust and sleeping together was about? "Well," Lily replied, "it's not as if you're not getting married in a few weeks. It's not as if Cassie's not old enough to know about these kinds of things."

"I know," Jo said. "But I would have preferred that it hadn't happened. Especially the way it did."

"What did Andrew say?"

"He doesn't know. He has his interview at the college this morning."

"He wasn't even there? Well, I wouldn't worry about it if I were you. It could be worse. She could have walked in while you were having sex."

Silence revisited the room. Lily's eyes darted from Jo to Sarah to Elaine, then back to Jo. "Well? What? All I'm saying is there could be worse things. Now, who wants to go to New York?"

Sarah said she had daisies to weave and Jo said she wanted to wait for Andrew, but Elaine seemed excited that Lily wanted to go.

"I saw cedar grilling planks and Italian copper cook-ware online, but I'd love to check them out before I buy." She put her hands into the pockets of the jeans she wore—not $19.99 discount-store ones but Dolce & Gabbanas. "Could we go to that fabulous place at Columbus Circle?"

Lily smiled at the way Elaine said "fabulous." What had begun as a makeover a few months ago had ended in a total transformation: her vocabulary, her hair, her looks, and her *style* had moved up a self-confident notch. The fact was she'd gone from a homemaker (Elaine had corrected people when they called her a *housewife,* because her husband, Lloyd, was an *ex* and she was no one else's *wife*) to the founder and manager of McNulty's Catering, the catering arm for Second Chances. She was happily assisted by her father, who'd been in the restaurant business for about three hundred years, and by the youngest of her three kids, a teenage daughter who, six months ago, barely had spoken to her mother. Despite being surrounded by "family," Elaine was clearly, confidently, the one in charge.

Lily suggested they drive rather than rely on train schedules or be at the mercy of the sole limousine service in the West Hope area. She surprised everyone by saying they should take Elaine's minivan, when she, more than once, had refused to ride in it because it was so Mom-like and Lily was so-not. She said it would be easier to transport purchases back home, but her real reason was if Antonia spotted the vehicle, she wouldn't think Lily was being frivolous with her allowance.

Halfway from West Hope to the city, Lily made a phone call that assured her Antonia was in, that she would be in—no great shock, because Antonia was always in except on Thursday ballet night or Saturday evenings at the opera. The sixty-something-year-old woman wouldn't miss those events, because they gave her a chance to do what she loved best—playing dress-up in ancient fur stoles and dowager ball gowns and wearing the dusty crown jewels from one of her many safes.

Regrettably, Lily once suggested that Antonia donate the gowns to the costume departments of off-Broadway theater projects, that perhaps it was time for the woman to treat herself to something new. Alluding to such squandering, Lily should have known, invited a coarse comment about how buying new clothes would mean spending Beckwith money with which Antonia had been entrusted, she being the only true Beckwith left.

The Beckwiths—Reginald and Antonia's great-grandfather, specifically—had garnered a fortune from typewriters in the late 1800s, then later amassed more through adding machines. Reginald used to laugh and say his ancestors had been in letters and in numbers.

Lily had liked Reginald very much; he made her laugh. She hadn't loved him, though, a fact that had often made her sad, though he'd said he didn't mind, that he loved her enough for both of them.

She explained all this to Elaine as they continued

their journey south from the Berkshires. She did not, however, say why she was going to Antonia, other than it was for "family business." No sense having Elaine make her feel even more guilty than she already felt about not marrying Frank because he didn't have money, or, at least, not enough.

"I'd invite you to lunch, but Antonia is so weird. I'm not even sure if she'll offer me any," Lily said as Elaine rounded the corner onto Madison Avenue and pulled up in front of Antonia's apartment building.

"Not to worry," Elaine said. "I've always wanted one of those hot dogs from a cart. What time shall we meet?"

"I'll call you on your cell phone. I'll try to finish early enough so we'll have time to peek in a couple of antique shops on Third Avenue. Maybe we can find some clever things for the Randolph/Barton Victorian wedding or a serving dish or two for Jo's." She said the last part flatly, still annoyed that Jo and Andrew would not let her turn their wedding into a Hollywood production.

Elaine nodded and wished Lily good luck with her family business, and Lily gulped and got out and waved good-bye to the minivan. She took a deep breath, held it a moment, then turned and walked into the entryway of the building and asked the doorman to please announce her to the other Ms. Beckwith.

4

L ily remembered when she had a butler. His name was Lawson, and his father had been one of the children who survived the *Titanic* disaster. Lawson had been with Reginald since Reginald was a teenager and he, not much older. He had personality, for a butler, and style—*panache,* Reginald liked to say.

Simpson, Antonia's expressionless butler, had neither personality nor panache. He escorted Lily into the front room of the apartment that had belonged to a Beckwith for five generations, a legacy that would end with Antonia, because neither she nor Reginald had begat other Beckwiths, which was no doubt Lily's fault.

Lily sat down on the horsehair sofa. She closed her eyes to the Renoir over the mantel and told herself to stop being so negative, because her beastly sister-in-law was capable enough of that on her own.

"You're late," Antonia bristled as she marched into the room. She wore a blue satin robe that had a thick boa of fluff edging the low neckline, which did not conceal the puckery flesh that defined her aging, deflating breasts. The wattle of her throat was covered by a stack of several strands of pearls, and her mouth was outlined by fire-engine-red lipstick.

Whenever Lily saw her, she was reminded of Aunt Margaret's instruction: "No woman over twenty should leave the house without wearing lipstick." She might have changed her mind if she'd ever met Antonia.

"It's nice to see you," Lily said, standing up and extending her hand. She was not surprised that Antonia's fingers barely touched hers, or that her skin felt like the autumn leaves in West Hope: crackly and dried up. "The traffic was impossible."

Antonia parked her squat body on a chair across from Lily, and Lily returned to the horsehair. She studied the pale eyes and pale skin and cap of white hair and waited for the woman to speak.

"That's one of the reasons I never left this damn city," Antonia said. "I don't have the patience for traffic." She did not drive, of course, had never driven. Why would one, when a chauffeur was always at one's disposal?

Before Lily could say, *But you love it here in New York,* or make another comment that would be sarcastic, Antonia added, "What brings you in, anyway? Is that little business of yours in financial trouble?"

Lily forced a smile, wondering how Antonia could be so nasty when her only sibling, Reginald, had been so merry. She tried not to wonder why it was so often true that the good were the ones who died if not young then at least first. "Second Chances is doing quite marvelously. We're actually having to turn people down."

The woman made a sound that was something like a grunt.

"We handled the wedding of two dancers from the

27

Boston Ballet last month," Lily continued, thinking that Antonia might show a little interest. "It was very beautiful. The bride wore a plain white satin sheath and her hair was laced with flowers and she twirled up the aisle into her groom's arms."

Instead of showing interest, Antonia stood up. "Please come to the point, Lily. Why are you here?" She strode to the tall bow windows and pushed aside a panel of heavy velvet drape. Not even Reginald had been able to convince his sister to have the room updated, modernized.

Lily folded her hands on her lap. "I had to come into the city and I thought I'd stop by for a visit. Perhaps this isn't a good time." She stood up, smoothed the front of her beige suit.

With her eyes fixed out the window, Antonia said, "It's finally spring, isn't it? That dreadful old winter is over." She sighed.

Lily supposed that was the closest Antonia could come to being halfway civil to her, to making small talk that didn't involve money or the lack of it. Having lost her brother nearly two years ago had not softened Antonia. All of which affirmed what Lily had surmised: There was no way Lily's allowance would continue if she married Frank.

Glancing at her watch, Lily decided she'd stay a half hour longer, in memory of dear Reginald, which would leave plenty of time to catch a cab over to Columbus Circle, where she could meet Elaine early and salvage the day.

Andrew arrived at the shop just after noon and dropped a stack of paint chips on the corner of Jo's desk. "It stunk," he said and flopped into the chair next to her.

She suspected the interview, not his visit to the hardware store, was what had stunk. "What happened?"

"Blogs," he said. "I've been out of teaching only a year and the whole world has changed. 'Do you plan to incorporate the importance of blogs into your journalism curriculum?' I think it was a trick question, to see if I knew what he was talking about, if I was hip to advancements of the world. I wanted to say we live in West Hope, not Timbuktu, for chrissake."

Jo smiled and leaned across her desk. "So do you plan to incorporate blogs into your curriculum?"

He laughed. "As soon as my daughter tells me how they work."

Jo toyed with the reds and the yellows of the paint chips. She didn't want to talk about Cassie or tell Andrew of her embarrassment just yet. "How did it really go? Did the 'old bastard' give you any indication if they'll take you back?"

He shook his head. "But he did make a note when I told him I'd been working with four Winston College alums."

"He probably saw fund-raising dollar signs."

"Count on it. But then he made sure to tell me that the English comp professor took my place as head of the newspaper, and they divided my classes among others in the department. He'll let me know if anything comes up. I won't hold my breath." He shrugged, then eyed the paint chips. "So should we do the family room in red or yellow?"

Jo didn't know how to be supportive without sounding condescending. To say, *Oh, Andrew, I'm sure the college wants you,* seemed thin and unrealistic. After all, how would she know? So she simply smiled and said, "Yellow. Let's go with the yellow and maybe we'll buy deep-blue furniture."

"And save the red for our bedroom?" he asked with a wink.

"Very funny. But actually, Sarah might like this red as a guide for the Randolph/Barton wedding. You know, the Victorian one."

Andrew laughed. "And Cassie wants purple for her bedroom. Not lavender. Purple. I told her I'm not sure how you'll feel about that."

Jo stood up and brought the paint chips to the front windows where the spring sunlight spilled in. She wondered how difficult it was going to be to help Andrew raise his daughter. Twelve years old today was so different from when Jo had been a girl. "I saw her this morning," she said, holding the yellow chips against the light, not looking at him.

"Cassie?"

"Yes. She left second period and walked home from school. Apparently, she forgot her homework." The lemon shade was pretty, but the buttery one seemed cozier, not that Jo really cared about paint right at that moment.

"So she knows you were there overnight," Andrew said. "You're not upset about that, are you?"

She dropped her hand that held the paint chips and looked out the window. "A little. She walked in as I was getting out of bed. I didn't have on any clothes."

Andrew laughed. "Well, at least that confirms to her that I have good taste."

The muscles of her jawline quickly tightened. "Andrew, it was awful. I grabbed at the sheets, awkwardly trying to cover up, while Cassie simply stood there."

He stood up and went to her. "Honey," he said, his arms encircling her waist, "I told you not to worry. Cassie is crazy about you. She's glad we're getting married."

But Jo wasn't as sure of that as she'd been in the beginning. What if she didn't measure up to Cassie's expectations for a mom? Then what would they do?

"Did you drive her back to school?" Andrew asked.

Jo shook her head. "It happened so quickly. She was there, then she was gone." The truth, however, was that Jo had been so embarrassed, she hadn't thought to ask. More proof of what a lousy stepmother she'd be.

"Why don't you leave early today," Andrew suggested. "Pick her up at school. Take her to the hardware store and help her pick out paint in a reasonable color."

If Jo shared her fears with Andrew, he might have second thoughts about her too, about the union of the two two—no, the *three*—of them. So instead of bela-

31

boring the issue, Jo nodded slowly. "Sure," she said, faking a smile. "That's a great idea."

"As a reward," he said, planting a soft kiss on her neck, "tomorrow we can go to the town hall and get our marriage license."

Marriage license. Two words Jo had long ago stopped believing would ever apply to her. This time her smile was genuine. "It's not too soon?"

"Nope," he said. "I checked. When we get it, it's good for sixty days. I want to have it in my hand before you change your mind."

As if there would be any chance of that.

5

I f Brian hadn't left her, Jo would not have moved back to West Hope, and her mother probably wouldn't have married Ted, the town butcher, and moved into the new condos out by Tanglewood, and Jo wouldn't have moved into her childhood home, which she and Andrew would now be renovating for their new life together.

If it weren't for Brian, she also wouldn't be parked outside West Hope Elementary, which was now the Middle School, too, waiting for Cassie.

She wondered if Cassie would have preferred the "pre-Andrew" Jo, the savvy businesswoman with a downtown Boston address and an awesome condo that overlooked the Charles. Of course, even Jo's former life had been dull compared with the life of Cassie's mother, Patty O'Shay, the once-famous cover girl, who'd become world renowned for her bright turquoise eyes and thick, shining dark hair, both of which Cassie had inherited.

Did Cassie—despite having rejected a recent chance to go live with her mother—quietly resent Jo? Did she harbor a divorced kid's secret dream that one day her parents would get back together, the way Jo had once hoped her parents would have done? Jo had been nine when her parents split up; Cassie, much younger. Jo had "lost" her father; Cassie, her mother. Would those things make a difference?

She looked around the playground, the one-story brick school that had been new when Jo went there. She tried to remember being in sixth grade. It had been in the mid-seventies, a time of big changes. She recalled that her teacher, Miss Topor, had been pretty and smart and had a warm, wonderful smile, and that at the spring picnic at Laurel Lake Park, when Denny Barstow got a piece of hot dog caught in his throat, Miss Topor performed a new phenomenon called the Heimlich maneuver. The piece of meat shot from Denny's throat, and the entire class stood and watched, silenced by their teacher's heroism.

Jo also remembered that was the year her grandfather gave her a digital watch for her birthday—a new invention that had her classmates mesmerized, except Cindy Lee Farnsworth. Cindy Lee said her mother had wanted to buy her one when they went shopping at G. Fox in Hartford, but that Cindy Lee declined, saying she thought they were ugly and were meant for boys. (Cindy Lee hadn't liked Jo since the fifth grade, when Carl Miller, the hunkiest boy in the school, wrote Jo's name on the cover of his notebook.)

Later that summer Nixon resigned and everything tumbled. By the time Jo started seventh grade, the world was quite different, indeed.

She gazed at the beige door that she knew was locked now and realized there was little innocence left. Then the bell rang—the shrill sound was oddly the same—followed by a short pause, then the commotion of footsteps clattering toward the outside. The door burst open and a swarm of kids—little, big, blond, brunette, skipping, and meandering—appeared. It wasn't long before Jo spotted Cassie, though she blinked to be sure it was really her.

When she'd seen Cassie this morning, Cassie had on a pair of jeans and a short denim jacket embroidered with sequins. Now she wore a way-too-short denim skirt and a pink, form-fitting top that rode high over her navel, exposing several inches of her flat young belly.

Jo got out of the car. "Cassie?" she called.

The girl looked at her, turned her head quickly away.

"Cassie?" Jo repeated, walking closer toward her. Around them, kids scattered, including Cassie's best friend, Marilla, who wore a matching denim skirt, equally short, and a yellow top of similar exposing proportions.

Slowly, Cassie turned back to Jo. That's when Jo saw

the heavy black eyeliner and the silver-flecked blue eye shadow.

Jo decided that later she'd surely receive an award for not gasping out loud, for staying cool under duress. "Your dad thought we might like to go pick out paint for your new room."

Cassie blinked, looked away again. "Sorry. I promised Marilla I'd go to her house to study for our biology test tomorrow."

Jo scanned the lot. "Marilla seems to have vanished."

With a shrug, Cassie said, "I can walk to her house."

"I can give you a ride."

"It's right down the street." But Cassie didn't move, didn't step away.

"Cassie?" Jo asked, sensing that this moment could redefine their relationship, could propel her into stepmother heaven or hell. "I think purple will be a really great color. Can we go later this week?"

The girl shrugged again. "Sure," she replied, then flashed her dark-lined turquoise eyes. "I gotta go."

Jo said okay, and walked back to the car, her heart racing as if she'd just given the Heimlich to a kid herself, as if she had spared Cassie from a confrontation worse than death.

Now all Jo needed to decide was what to share with Andrew and what to ignore for the sake of a (hopefully) greater good.

Lily and Elaine found an exquisite antique lace tablecloth that would look stunning on the altar at the Victorian-themed wedding. They also found a lace runner for the mahogany sideboard that would serve as a buffet table and three gleaming, tiered, silver dessert serving dishes. Whether or not Sarah used the pieces to decorate the Randolph/Barton reception didn't matter. They would be added to the Second Chances growing "prop room," as Lily called the storage space they now rented from Frank on the second floor of his antiques shop in the former town hall, across from Sarah's boyfriend's office.

God knew there would be no point in using them for Jo and Andrew's "teensy-weensy wedding," Lily had commented, and Elaine had shushed her, right there in the store.

Elaine had also bought the cedar grilling planks, a set of breading trays, and a sushi press. She'd skipped the copper Italian cookware, which she deemed too expensive, but bought several dozen parchment coasters, though she wouldn't reveal what they were for.

Before heading back to West Hope they stopped for a late lunch in a small restaurant Lily had never been to.

When the waiter delivered their dim sum and tea, Elaine moved aside the chopsticks, picked up her fork, and asked, "So what's the real reason we're here?"

Lily smiled and gazed around the high-ceilinged, mahogany-woodworked room at the sunset-orange walls and the fabulous artwork in shades of deep red. A burnished gold light fixture shaped like an inverted cone was suspended from a thin cord over each ebony table. Red linens and a minimalist glass-cylinder centerpiece that held three long-stemmed wildflowers completed the urban-contemporary look.

"The real reason we're here is to check out this restaurant. I read about it in *New York* magazine."

Elaine's gaze followed Lily's. "Yes, it's very pretty. But what I meant was, what's the real reason we came into the city?"

Lily glanced at Elaine, scooped up her chopsticks, and plucked a tangle of glass noodles from a spring roll. "I told you. Family business."

"You can't stand Antonia. You've made it clear that any 'business' you need to do with her, you do on the phone. 'No audience required,' I believe is what you've said."

Lily smiled. Sooner or later, she supposed, good friends know all your business. Especially old friends, who've witnessed your life cycles, the good and the bad, the up and the down.

"I'm not trying to pry, Lily. I just want to be sure everything is okay."

The waiter stopped by and poured more lemon water. Lily wished she had ordered wine. "Everything's fine," she replied with a swift nip of the noodles that she then dropped into her mouth.

Silent chewing ensued. Then Elaine said, "Bullshit."

Lily laughed out loud. "Lainey, you are full of surprises these days. You used to be so . . . ."

"Compliant," Elaine said. "Milquetoasty."

It was true, of course, but Lily hated to say that.

Instead, she leaned forward and whispered, "Can you keep a secret?" because, what the heck, she simply had to tell someone.

Elaine smiled. "I've kept more secrets than anyone would imagine."

Taking a small bite of her lunch, Lily chewed slowly, then swallowed and dabbed the corners of her mouth with her napkin. "Frank Forbes proposed to me."

Elaine dropped her fork. "Proposed? You mean, he asked you to marry him?"

"You know very well what it means. We're in the marriage business, aren't we?"

"Oh, Lily, how exciting. When's the big day? Shall we plan a big wedding? Oh, wait, not until after Jo and Andrew's, okay?"

Lily held up her hand. She averted her eyes from her pink diamond. "Stop right there. I haven't said yes yet."

Elaine leveled her eyes on Lily. "Why not? Are you playing hard-to-get?"

She shook her head. Suddenly the reality of her situation was embarrassing, even to her. "Because I'm not sure, that's why. Because I don't know if I want to get married again."

Silence returned. From the next table, Lily overheard the waiter ask if the party wanted dessert. Coconut ice cream on a slice of grilled pineapple, gingerbread drizzled with lemon curd, chocolate cake in a roasted pear sauce. She wanted to suggest that Elaine pay attention to the creative offerings of sweets, but she knew that wasn't what Elaine wanted to hear.

Lily set down her chopsticks. "Oh, all right," she said. "Promise you won't tell the others. Or that you won't judge me or lecture me or yell at me, okay?"

"Good grief, Lily, what is it?"

She let out a sigh. "If I marry Frank, Antonia gets to keep all of Reginald's money. Unless I can convince her that she shouldn't do that."

Lily supposed she should feel better now that she'd gotten her dilemma out there in the open, out there amid the orange walls and red artwork and inverted conelike lights. She supposed she should feel better now that she'd shared her predicament with a trusted friend. But as Elaine just sat there, staring in disbelief, Lily did not feel better. She felt embarrassed, silly, shameful, like a childish thief, her hand caught in Aunt Margaret's jewelry box, searching for the tiara that only good girls were allowed to wear.

6

Jo needed a night to herself. She needed a night to separate the Gilberts' yellow-and-white wedding scheduled for Friday from the Randolph/Barton's wedding Sunday from her own nuptials, which she'd had little time to think about other than to buy the pretty silk suit she would wear and to pick out a light plum-colored one for her mother and a color-matched yet more youthful style for Cassie.

She supposed she could make some time with what

was left of the afternoon. But after her failed attempt to connect with Cassie, Jo wasn't in the mood. So she did what she did best—she went back to the shop and back to work, her busywork, her refuge from her worries and from, she guessed, herself.

Luckily Andrew wasn't there. He'd left a note that said the builders called: they were going to pour the footings for the foundation of the addition to the house, and he wanted to watch.

Jo tossed his note into the basket, wishing she had as much energy to put into the wedding plans as Andrew had enthusiasm for concrete.

An hour passed, then two. Then, just as Jo was about to lock up for the night, in walked Lily and Elaine, arms full of shopping bags and boxes, road-weary smiles on their faces and chatter evidently on their minds.

"We found the perfect lace for the Randolph/Barton wedding," Elaine said.

"And beautiful silver dishes," Lily added, "that you might want if only you weren't having such a dinky reception."

Elaine said, "Lily, stop it," and Jo just laughed and said, "No matter how hard you try to humiliate me, I'm not changing anything."

Lily dropped her bags and pouted. "Just a little pouf?"

"No pouf," Jo said.

"At least let Lainey create a special menu," Lily whined. "Like ice cream on grilled pineapple?"

Jo shook her head, realizing now that Lily had made her smile. "It sounds absolutely awful," she said.

"What about edible name cards?" Elaine said, and Jo and Lily both turned to her.

"What?" Jo asked.

"What?" Lily asked. "You never mentioned such a thing."

"I've only seen them done once. It's best if the wedding's small." She rummaged through a bag. Jo wanted to leave but would not be rude to Elaine. Elaine finally pulled out a stack of parchment-looking coasters. "These are perfect," she said.

"Perfect for what?" Jo asked.

"To use as dishes for the name cards."

Jo looked at Lily, who said, "Don't ask me."

"Oh, never mind," Elaine said. "You have to see them all made up. They will be beautiful, trust me."

"Sure," Jo said, "why not."

Then Lily stepped forward, took the coasters, and said, "Edible name cards. Well, at least we can have them photographed for our portfolio. Get something worthwhile out of your wedding, other than pictures of your mother and new stepdaughter, lovely as they both might be."

It was the word *stepdaughter* that erased the smile from Jo's face. "I'd love to stay and chat," she said, "but I have to get home. They poured the footings today for the addition to the house." Which, of course, didn't matter; she just wasn't in the mood to discuss edible name cards, portfolios, or, most of all, step-

41

daughters. She only knew she wanted to marry Andrew without pomp, circumstance, or pouf. She only knew she wanted to shake her uncertainty over what to do, or not do, about Cassie.

She said good night and left the shop with Cassie on her mind. How would Cassie traverse the maze of puberty? How young was too young today to expect rebellious behavior? Jo supposed she could ask Elaine—Elaine, after all, had two girls who were pretty much grown up. How was Jo supposed to know? The world was so different than when she was young: She knew that kids now—at early ages—drank, got high, had sex. Some of them, anyway.

Would Cassie be one?

Should she talk to Cassie about birth control? Should she talk to her about her choice of clothes, her trashy makeup, the message she was giving boys without Andrew's knowledge? Didn't Cassie's father have a right to know? Or, for that matter, did Jo have a right to interfere?

Elaine would have helped, but Jo was too exhausted to turn around and go back to Second Chances and risk hearing more things about her wedding that Lily did not like.

As Jo turned the corner and drove past the bookstore, she had a thought. She put on her directional signal and pulled into a parking space. What she didn't know, maybe a best-selling author might.

Ten Ways to Love Your Stepchild.

Building Healthy Step-Family Relationships.
His Kids. Her Kids.

Jo stared at the books that sat on the kitchen table. Andrew and the builders had left by the time she arrived home. She'd called and said she needed time alone tonight if that was okay. He'd said sure, although he'd miss her, and what about those footings? They looked great, didn't they?

She'd said yes, the whole thing looked exciting. The truth was she'd barely glanced in the direction of the backyard, where her grandmother's clothesline once had been and now the family room and master bedroom would be taking its place.

They'd said they loved each other, then hung up, and Jo was left alone with the books.

His Kids. Her Kids. She sensed that being a stepmother was a task that would be more daunting than she had imagined. She'd never, after all, planned on being a stepmother. Once she had dreamed of having her own child, her own children. But the opportunities had passed along with the years, and now she was forty-three and it probably was too late.

Wasn't it?

She pushed away thoughts of soft baby blankets and hand-knit booties and picked up the first book, sensing that the research would not be as simple as when she'd needed to learn about wedding planning.

Scanning the table of contents, Jo suddenly remembered that it had been at this same table where she'd once sat with her mother, listening to Marion's awkward explanation about boys and girls and how babies were made. Grandpa Clarke had been out at a union meeting; Grandma had been in the living room, crocheting—eavesdropping, no doubt, in case Marion needed assistance. But Marion had done fine, filling in a few blanks that Jo hadn't yet learned in health class at school and correcting a few missteps she'd heard at various sleepovers. Marion, however, was a real parent, a real mother, who'd been raising Jo all along.

Closing her eyes, Jo tried to remember what it felt like to be twelve, when Carl Miller liked her but she didn't like him, because she liked Danny Peterson, who liked Alicia Barnes.

Jo smiled. She remembered going to Woolworth's with her friend Sandy, pooling their coins to buy Maybelline liquid eyeliner and an eyelash curler, then going to Albert Steiger's department store and trying on miniskirts that her mother would never have allowed Jo to wear.

Apart from the eye makeup that Jo and Sandy wore only to Friday night dances at the Y, rebellion had been confined to dressing-room giggles. If Jo had dared to buy one of those skirts, then wear it to school, Marion Lyons would have known about it before the end of first period. A teacher would have seen her and told another teacher who would have told the principal who knew Jo's mother from church or the library board or the July 4 parade committee and who would have called Marion and let her know. It had been like that in West Hope—small town, few secrets. Apparently

44

things were different today, or no one cared anymore, or mothers were no longer as strict as Marion had been.

Jo leaned back in the chair and looked around the kitchen, at the old cabinets that had once been painted white, then yellow, then blue, and were now white again; at the flooring that had once been hardwood, then red-brick-looking linoleum, then indoor–outdoor carpeting, and was now light-green vinyl.

Jo had grown up in the house in a whole different era, when life had boundaries and kids had rules. As much as she'd once longed to leave what she'd perceived as a stifling town, she knew that she hadn't turned out too badly.

She opened to Chapter One, thought about reading, then had a better idea.

Andrew scooped another spoonful of macaroni and cheese onto his plate as he tried to think of an effective way to bring up the issue that Cassie had caught Jo naked in his bed. It was the perfect opportunity, with just the two of them there. How long had it been since they'd had dinner without Jo? *Too long,* he thought guiltily. He was still Cassie's dad, and though they'd be a new family, he must remember to reserve time for Cassie alone, just the two of them, the way it had been for six years.

And they were great together! Father and daughter, her apple not falling too far from his like-minded tree. There was nothing they couldn't talk about, least of all

45

this. Hell, they'd had the birds-and-the-bees talk a couple of years ago, when Cassie informed him she knew everything. She'd always made these kinds of "delicate" matters easy on him, like when she'd been the one to say she needed a bra, or when she'd started her period and asked the school nurse to help her pick up some "things." And all that girlie stuff aside, Andrew had told Jo the truth: Cassie was crazy about her.

So why did he feel awkward now? Why didn't he know where to start?

He chewed slowly and decided to proceed in the tradition of rock stars and comedians and warm up his audience first. "It's really nice that Mrs. Connor still sends dinner over sometimes." Mrs. Connor was their next-door neighbor, who had saved Andrew's single-parent butt on more than one occasion, first as Cassie's grandmotherly babysitter, now as a responsible adult to help out with his daughter when he was held up or when Cassie needed a ride to or from somewhere. Though Mrs. Connor knew Andrew and Jo would soon be married and he and Cassie would move to Jo's house, she continued to supply a homemade dinner at least once a week. "She's going to miss us," he added.

Cassie shrugged a no-big-deal kind of shrug.

"It's good," he said. "The macaroni."

She nodded.

Well, he wondered, as the two of them nibbled away at his window of opportunity, he supposed he could say that Jo mentioned Cassie forgot her homework and

46

he could ask if she found it all right.

"So," he said, "did you have a good day at school?"

She looked at him and rolled her eyes. It was a move that always reminded him of Cassie's mother, the woman who'd dumped Andrew and Cassie and broken both their hearts.

She finished her broccoli, because Cassie was a rare kid who loved vegetables. She even had toyed with becoming a vegetarian when she'd had her first crush, on Sarah's son, Burch.

"I had my interview at the college today," Andrew said, then regretted that he'd turned the focus onto him.

"Cool. Are you going back to teach?"

"I hope so. I don't know yet. It's up to them." He ate more of the casserole and wondered if Mrs. Connor would give Jo the recipe. *Check that*, he said to himself, *I should get the recipe for myself. So I can make it when it's my night to cook.* He smiled, loving the potential of his new life, knowing it would be wonderfully different from the superficial years he'd spent with Patty.

Then Cassie's head turned to the black plastic cat clock whose eyes moved back and forth in time with the swing of its pendulum tail. "I have a biology test tomorrow," she said as she stood up. "I have to call Marilla. We didn't finish studying before her mother brought me home."

"Wait," Andrew said quickly and a little too loudly as he dropped his fork. He didn't want his chance to slide by. "You know Jo stayed here last night," he blurted

47

out. Well, he supposed, that was one way to do it: straight to the slightly embarrassing point.

Cassie's eyes didn't meet his. Had that ever happened before?

Andrew scowled. "Jo is kind of freaked about it, but I told her you'd be fine, that you know we're getting married and it wouldn't be giving you any 'wrong kind of message.'" He tried to smile a slightly conspiratorial smile, a just-between-them look to reassure Cassie that he might be marrying Jo but Cassie would not lose her position as his closest friend.

It would have helped if she'd just turn her eyes toward him.

Her silence lasted a heartbeat too long. Finally she said, "Sure, Dad, I'm cool with it." She remained standing as if awaiting further instructions, then Andrew said, "Oh. Well, good."

Then Cassie left the kitchen and Andrew stared at the remnants of dinner still on his plate and wondered why a small knot was now at the bottom of his stomach where the macaroni and cheese ought to be.

7

Jo knew that, because it was Monday evening, Marion's new husband, Ted, would be at his West Hope Men's Club meeting, and Jo's mother would be alone in the beautiful condo overlooking the tall pines and sloping lawns on the back side of Tanglewood.

Peering through the glass doors off the deck, Jo saw Marion at the new kitchen table. She seemed to be poking through her small metal recipe box, the same metal box Jo had seen all her life, the one that had helped produce everything from salmon loaf with a sauce of creamed peas to congo bars for the church fair. Jo watched her mother, now aging and content. She marveled at the fact that though Marion was ensconced in the pretty, tri-level home, the love and the goodness of things that "really mattered" appeared to have stayed intact. Jo wondered if she would stay the same once she married Andrew, once she became a stepmother to Cassie.

She drew in a short breath and knocked on the door.

"Tea," Marion stated once Jo was inside and seated at the table with the recipe box. "Where's the groom tonight?"

Jo smiled. It seemed she always did that now whenever Andrew's name came up. "Home with Cassie. I needed a night to myself."

Marion put a kettle of water on the stove, ignited the burner beneath it. "So here you are at your mother's. Not by yourself after all."

Marion was nothing if not astute.

Pulling the recipe box toward her, Jo flicked through the yellowed index cards, past recipes written in her grandmother's handwriting, past others typed no doubt on Marion's typewriter when she was at work as a clerk down at the town hall. "Mom," she said, "I'm trying to figure out how to be a good stepmother to Cassie."

Marion nodded, dropped tea bags into mugs. "You'll do it slowly, honey. You'll be fine. Cassie is a nice girl."

"She's twelve."

Marion nodded.

"I saw her at school today. I went to pick her up, but she wasn't interested. Mom, she was dressed in a ridiculously short miniskirt with her navel on display. And she had on eye makeup that I'm sure Andrew has never seen, let alone would approve of."

Marion nodded again; the teakettle whistled.

"Should I tell Andrew? Should I talk to Cassie? I feel like she's sneaking around behind his back, trying to look like she's twenty-one. How am I supposed to know how to handle this? I mean, what if Cassie gets angry and decides she doesn't like me?"

Marion poured the water, brought the mugs to the table, and sat down. "Stop trying so hard," she said.

Jo blinked, and Marion smiled.

"First of all," Marion continued, "Cassie isn't your responsibility, she's Andrew's. You don't have to be her mother; just try being her friend. Maybe she's going through a stage, maybe she's just doing ordinary growing-up things. Keep an eye on her. If you really feel this behavior is becoming a problem, then you can decide what to do. But right now, don't be a stool pigeon. Nobody likes stool pigeons."

Jo put her elbows on the table, rested her chin in her hands.

"Whatever is going on," Marion continued, "give

Cassie the time and the space to be herself. The way I let you be yourself."

There was no point in mentioning that Marion had not known about some of the ways in which Jo had been "herself."

Then Marion leaned across the table toward Jo. "You and Sandy weren't angels, I know that," she said. "I knew about the time you threw stones at that boy's bedroom window and broke it. What was his name?"

Jo nearly knocked over her tea. She felt silly, embarrassed, shy. "Danny," Jo said. "Danny Peterson."

"You had such a crush on him." Marion smiled.

Shaking her head, Jo asked, "Mother? How did you know?"

"Because the boy's father called. He saw the two of you running away through the bushes. It was dark, but he heard Sandy call out, 'Jo, slow down!' As far as he knew there was only one girl in all of West Hope who could have answered to that name."

Of all the problems between Jo and her mother—and there had been several over the years—Jo had never known, never suspected, that Marion would have kept this a secret. "You never told me you knew."

"No. I paid for the window and decided it was best not to mention it. You were mortified enough that the boy you were madly in love with was madly in love with someone else." Marion smiled, then added, "Alicia Barnes. Yes. I knew that part too."

Jo smiled. "Well," she said, letting her hands fall onto the table. "Thanks."

51

Marion covered Jo's hands with hers. "All I'm saying is, take it slow with Cassie. My bet is she already knows her boundaries. Keep an eye on the ball and an ear to the ground, but don't alienate her by asking for trouble."

Jo wondered when her mother had become so smart, and why Jo hadn't known that when she was twelve.

Lily had decided to act as if nothing were wrong, as if she were still in the "thinking" stages about marrying Frank, as if she still intended to give him an answer after Andrew and Jo's wedding, after the chaos quieted.

The truth was, she was mortified that she'd confessed to Elaine about the money and Frank and how reprehensible she really was at heart, and Elaine had made matters worse by saying, "If the money thing bothers you so much, Lily, why don't you just say no?"

Lily didn't know the answer to that question, any more than she knew what had made her think she could fight her narcissistic, shallow demons by calling Frank and offering to make dinner for him and his father and his mother, who was in the hospital bed in the living room.

Could one good deed really make up for all her self-centered ones?

Of course, Lily's idea of "making" dinner consisted of plundering Elaine's refrigerators for wedding-reception leftovers, which was why she now stood in the Forbes's kitchen having served spinach quiche and crab cakes and scallops wrapped in bacon.

"It's the thought that counts," Frank said.

"Did you make these yourself?" his father asked, devouring his sixth or seventh scallop.

Frank's mother, Eleanor—who apparently had the C word though no one discussed it, which was fine with Lily—only wanted toast with a bit of grape jelly. Lily placed it on a napkin with gold printing that read, *Jaimie and Stuart, April 1, 2006,* and brought it to the other room.

The woman's eyes stared at the wall next to the fireplace, as if she were counting pale hydrangea blossoms on the old beige wallpaper. Maybe she was simply listening to the *beep-beep* coming from the monitor beside her.

"Sit," Eleanor instructed, patting the edge of the bed.

Lily sat, careful not to bump the tubes that zigzagged from the IV drips into the woman's arm like cables from a DVD player into a television set. She'd met Eleanor twice before but had never seen her out of bed, had no idea if she was tall or short, plump or not, though she seemed soft-spoken, sweet.

"It's Lily, isn't it?" the woman asked, and Lily felt a snap of guilt that she'd spent so little time trying to get to know Frank's family. She was afraid of getting too attached, she guessed. Too attached, too committed, too exposed.

"Yes," she said. "It's Lily. Lily Beckwith."

Eleanor Forbes nodded, then she asked, "Are you

53

going to marry Frank?" Her voice was a mere whisper, either from her illness or so the men wouldn't over-hear.

Lily didn't know how to answer, so she said, "I don't know."

Eleanor touched Lily's hand. "He's a nice boy, my Frank. It's wonderful that he turned out so nice when his brother, Brian, turned out so . . ." Her voice trailed off and her eyes closed, and for a moment Lily wondered if she had fallen asleep. Or maybe she had died.

The monitor *beep-beep*ed.

"Mrs. Forbes?" she asked, looking down at the woman's thin hand that remained on hers, hoping beyond hope that the woman was still alive. Lily would say, *Yes!* she'd marry Frank, if that would bring Eleanor back to life.

The eyelids fluttered open. The kind face smiled. "You should marry him," she said. "You're not like Sondra, are you?"

Lily grinned. "No," she said, "I'm not like Sondra," having no idea, really, if she was or not. Frank so rarely talked about his former wife, and that was fine with Lily, because that meant there was nothing she had to live up to or make up for.

"He deserves a nice girl," Eleanor continued, as if Lily needed one more layer of guilt. She'd had so many layers excavated in recent days she now felt like a piece of Elaine's baklava.

The woman began to cough and Lily held her breath. "Can I get you some water? Some tea, perhaps?"

54

But Eleanor just shook her head and seemed to try to smile.

Lily stood up. Her knees were weak. Good grief, she'd never sat so close to someone who was so sick. She'd like to leave the house, run away, and not come back, not have to deal with the reality of the life and death that was evolving right here in this house. She'd like to handle this the way Aunt Margaret would.

But Lily was not Aunt Margaret, so she smiled and said, "I hope you enjoy your toast," hoping she didn't sound abrupt. "I need to check on Frank and your husband in the other room." She guided the woman's hand toward the wedding napkin, then went back to the kitchen, where Mr. Forbes was working on the quiche.

"So," Frank said, "this was a nice surprise."

Lily forced another smile, hoping it did not look fake, hoping it concealed the raw emotion she felt. "Yes, well, you have a lot on your hands. You have your own business to run, you have this house to run, and you've been helping us at the shop . . ."

"My pleasure," he said, and she felt the guilt twang again.

"But this is what friends are for, right, Mr. Forbes?" she asked.

The elderly man nodded and washed down his meal with black coffee that Frank must have made while Lily was with his mother. "Are you going to marry my son?" the elder Forbes man suddenly asked.

Frank said, "Dad . . ."

Lily stepped back and said, "Well, now, wherever did

55

you get an idea like that?"

"'Lily this' and 'Lily that.' That's all we ever hear. Just ask Eleanor." His old eyes danced and he winked at Lily.

"If you're trying to flatter me, Mr. Forbes, it's working." She opened a small box that Elaine had packed with butter cookies.

"So?" he asked. "Are you or aren't you?"

"Dad," Frank said again, then playfully shoved a cookie into his father's mouth. "That's enough."

Lily forced another smile, then picked up the trays and brought them to the sink, tears threatening her eyes. What on earth made her think she deserved to be with them, such a nice, stable family, such loving, kindhearted souls?

Andrew sat in the driveway, wondering why Jo wasn't home. He'd driven over unannounced, to collect a good-night kiss.

But where the heck was she?

He had a key now; he could go inside the house. But her car was gone; the place was dark. And so he hesitated.

She'd said she needed time alone. Had she meant that what she needed was time away from him?

Stop it, he told himself. *This is Jo. This is not Patty.*

He had his small surprise all planned. He was going to *rap-rap* on the kitchen door. He was going to smile and look "little boy cute" and charm her the way he'd once charmed millions of television viewers.

He was going to kiss her once, then leave. He'd read in an old *Buzz* magazine that that was a very sexy thing to do.

But he couldn't kiss her if she wasn't home.

Where the heck was she?

It was too late to be shopping, too late for much of anything in West Hope.

So he sat there another moment, wondering if he should wait, wondering if that would make her think that he'd been spying on her, that he was trying to smother her, *smother* being the word Patty had used when he'd complained she wasn't spending enough time with him and Cassie. *Smother* being the word she'd used to try to cover up for her late nights and secret forays with the Australian bastard she ended up running away with.

He looked up the street, then down the street, hoping Jo's car would come. There were no headlights, though.

If he sat here much longer, he supposed he would go nuts.

Instead, Andrew shifted the old Volvo into reverse. He hesitated a moment, promising himself that he would not make a big deal out of this by mentioning it to Jo, reminding himself that he could trust her, because she was not, was not, Patty.

Then he took a deep, deep breath and backed out of the driveway, wondering if and how he would survive this new commitment, and if love did this to everyone, made them totally irrational.

8

H i. I'm Teri Higgins. Can you handle a wedding with eighteen attendants?"

It was four o'clock the next afternoon. Lily was alone—abandoned!—in the showroom at Second Chances, *tap-tap*ping a pencil as she sat at Jo's desk, wishing the others hadn't left and taken with them their distraction, wishing something would happen to take her mind off thoughts of Frank and the Forbes family and Antonia and the Beckwith money, which had kept her agitated most of the night, the morning, and the whole damn afternoon.

Work, she supposed, would be the antidote that Jo would recommend.

But a wedding with eighteen attendants?

If Lily married Frank she wouldn't have that many attendants, because Lily didn't have many friends. Jo, Elaine, and Sarah kept her quite busy enough, when they were around.

Lily stood and welcomed the young woman. "We can handle anything," she said, not knowing if it was true. If the others didn't like it, it would serve them right for leaving her in charge. It would serve Sarah right for going over to the meadow to test the Gilberts' daisies; it would serve Elaine right for going next door to work on early food preparations; it would serve Jo and Andrew right for going to get their marriage license because, unlike Lily, they had no reason not to.

She guided Teri Higgins to the navy chairs and they both sat.

"I'm Lily Beckwith," she said. "My partners aren't here right now, but I'm sure I can help you. Now, what's this about eighteen attendants?"

Teri Higgins smiled. Her hair was simple and straight; her eyes were large and a nice shade of blue. Her face was scrubbed clean, its pinkness seemed quite natural. Lily stopped herself from squinting to determine how simply gorgeous she would look if she could spend a day gussying up at Laurel Lake Spa.

"I'm the kindergarten teacher at West Hope Elementary," Teri said.

Which, Lily supposed, would account for why she hadn't gone to Laurel Lake: She couldn't possibly have the time, let alone the cash. Hopefully the man she would be marrying could pay for Second Chances services.

"I was married when I first got out of high school," Teri continued. "I was divorced six months later. I hope that qualifies me as a second-time bride, because I really need your help."

"Well," Lily said, "yes, of course. Though we really don't ask for credentials. We like to think our business is more for mature brides than about the number of husbands under their belts."

Teri scowled a little.

"Mature," Lily said, "you know, over twenty-one." She twisted one of her blond curls and wondered if the woman would recognize her comment as a joke.

"Then I certainly qualify," Teri said with a half smile. "I'm marrying Joe Daley," Teri continued. "He's the fifth-grade science teacher. So it's all right that this is his first wedding?"

Did teachers make more in fifth grade than in kindergarten? "It's fine," Lily replied. "But you do know our services aren't cheap?"

Teri lowered her eyes. "I hoped we could work something out. When you hear the rest of my story."

Lily blanched. Did the woman want a wedding free of charge? She checked her watch. She might as well listen, she supposed. There was nothing else to do. "Why don't you tell me about your eighteen attendants," Lily said. "I guess we should start with that."

The young woman brightened. "They're my students this year. I hope it will be okay. They're only five, you know."

If she'd been drinking wine or tea, Lily supposed she would have sprayed it across the elegant showroom. Did she mean five years old? Eighteen five-year-olds in a wedding? One flower girl and one ring bearer often stretched the bounds of what was tolerable. But Lily didn't flinch. "Do you mean the attendants you've selected are only five years old?"

"Yes. Except the Dudley twins. They're six. They were adopted by Hannah and Ray Dudley. The twins are from Russia."

This was way more information than Lily could digest. She pressed her fingers to her temples; she felt a headache coming on.

"When do you want to get married?" Lily asked, hoping that by the wedding date the kids would at least be six, the Dudleys, seven.

"This spring. Actually, we've picked the first weekend of June."

"This June?" Her words squeaked out. Didn't the teacher know that June was only weeks away? Of course, Lily could not say yes. The first weekend of June simply was too soon. They were too booked between now and then, and Jo and Andrew's wedding would be the week before. . . .

"From what I understand," Teri said, "it's one of only two weekends each year that Tanglewood allows weddings."

Tanglewood? Now she wanted Tanglewood? Lily was about to laugh when the woman said, "It's because of one of the children. Tiffany Lupek. Tiffany had leukemia."

Lily felt the blood drain from her face. A five-year-old with leukemia. A bride without money.

"Ever since I told the kids I was engaged," Teri went on, "Tiffany had said she wants to see me as a bride. I'd like to give her this happy memory for when she's in the hospital, when she needs a pick-me-up. I'm sure you know what I mean."

For maybe the first time ever, Lily felt she'd been rendered speechless. Even overworked Sarah or all-business Jo wouldn't turn down this request, would they? She considered banging on the wall to ask Elaine's opinion but decided that would look unprofessional.

"Well," Lily said, "I'm not sure we can work it out, but I can ask around. Check the venue. Talk with my partners." She knew that Frank "knew people" at Tanglewood. She knew he was "connected" to most people in the Berkshires, because he was a good guy, he was one of them. She felt a tug of envy for the venerable life he'd had while she'd been merely playing at being a grown-up, never having done much of anything for anyone. She smiled at Teri Higgins. "I'll do my best."

The young woman returned the smile. "It would be so wonderful. But without your help, I'm sure I couldn't do it. Eighteen five-year-old attendants would be far too much to handle on my own."

Yes, well, Lily could understand that. She could not imagine handling one five-year-old, let alone a squadron. There were reasons why there had been no children from any of her three marriages. She'd told her husbands that she couldn't stand any little darling under the age of eighteen. She never admitted it was because she was too scared of being a mother, too frightened of building a perfect little family, only to have it disappear, go poof, in a single moment when a drunk driver met it head-on. There had only been one substitute for children—a noisy, sulfur-crested cockatoo in Lily's second marriage. Thankfully, when husband number two returned home to Mama, Tweety went with him.

She thought about Frank's ex-wife, how she'd walked out before they'd had any kids. He would have been a great father; he had such a patient, gentle nature. "You're not like Sondra, are you?" his mother had asked.

Lily quickly cleared her throat, wondering why on earth she was thinking about all that right now.

"Now, about your fee . . ." Teri continued, but Lily waved her hand.

"We'll talk about that later too. If we can make this work."

They would not charge her, of course. How could they? The others might be annoyed, but Lily could cover the costs from her allowance.

The pair stood up and Lily shook Teri Higgins's hand. But it wasn't until the kindergarten teacher had left the shop that Lily realized this wedding could help her procrastinate another week, help her turn her life into a whirlwind, so she wouldn't have to deal.

The children are keeping me so busy, she'd say to Frank if he pressed her for an answer to his proposal.

Eighteen fittings!

Imagine that!

9

"Tiffany Lupek has leukemia. How could I say no?"

A moment ago, Lily had stood head-to-shoulder next to Sarah (Sarah was so much taller, with black hair to Lily's blond, the two like salt and pepper, pale face and Cherokee). They had stood and oohed and ahhed over Jo and Andrew's marriage license, the paper that now certified they could be man and wife.

When the oohs and ahhs were done, Lily had told them about Teri Higgins and her requests. Now the three of them had turned to Lily, each with a cheerless look that said it was too late in the day for one of Lily's pranks.

"Well," Lily repeated, "how could I say no?"

"She's not kidding," Andrew said.

"Oy," Sarah said, as if she were Jewish and not half Native American.

"But we're so busy, Lily," Jo said.

"And you're talking about the week after our wedding," Andrew added, waving the license once again as if it proved they couldn't possibly comply.

If Elaine were there instead of preparing the decorations for the daisy wedding cake, maybe at least she would have stuck up for Lily. "Well, I said we'd try to make it happen, so I guess it's up to me. Not that any of you cares, but I've already decided to donate all our time. I'll pay the expenses out of my own pocket." It wouldn't be the first time Lily footed the bill.

None of them took her bait, none jumped in and said, *Oh, Lily, that's okay. We'll do it together.*

She jumped off the corner of Jo's desk where she'd been perched and said, "In fact, I can get started right now. I'll find Frank and have him help me enlist Tanglewood." With a quick wave good-bye, Lily chirped, "Toodles," and walked out of the shop.

As she crossed the street and then the town common,

none of them called out for her to come back; none said they would help. Lily wrapped her arms around her middle, lowered her gaze to meet the sidewalk, and wondered what on earth she'd done, and why, lately, she seemed to screw up everything she did.

Frank was working late; he probably had gone home first to make sure his parents had their dinners before he went back to the antiques store. Lily stood outside the old town hall, surveying the brick exterior that no doubt had once been red but now was brown—not unlike the way Tiffany Lupek had once been healthy but now was sick, or how Frank's mother had once been vibrant but now was not. Passages, Lily supposed, in brick and mortar, flesh and bones.

Lily knew she should be grateful for having been spared the trauma of tending to a sick child or aging parents. She might have had Aunt Margaret to take care of, but her aunt died without a fuss when she was seventy—though her boyfriend at the time thought she was sixty-three. When it came time for the death certificate, Lily had no choice but to spill her aunt's secret in the funeral home so the records would match and the insurance company would release payment for her "final" arrangements. Aunt Margaret had been stricken with a quick, fatal aneurysm while Lily was at a hot-mineral-springs spa somewhere in Bulgaria. Margaret never had to endure a slow, withering death, and Lily had not had to watch her skin turn brittle and translucent or see her eyes grow dim and disinterested in life.

Nor had Lily needed to worry about whether or not a person she loved was being well cared for, as Frank had to do now, which was why he was working late, burning the responsibility candle at both fraying ends.

Lily wondered if she should suggest that he get someone in to help or if that would be considered interfering. She had no real experience with protocol in families.

With a small sigh she ascended the worn concrete stairs that sagged a little in the middle from thousands—no, probably millions—of footsteps over a hundred years or more, the way she supposed an old mattress sagged when a couple had been married forever and spent their nights in sweet embrace, a couple such as Frank's parents before his mother had been moved into the living room and onto the rent-a-bed.

Frank was sitting in a dark maple chair that had a high, spindled back and casters on the bottom. His gaze was fixed on a computer screen that looked out of place on the antique wooden desk.

"I've come to rescue you from the perils of adulthood," Lily said as she pranced toward him.

He turned to her with a tentative smile. Sometimes Frank looked at her that way, as if he was unsure what to make of her. She wondered if he'd have more confidence if she ever managed to say yes, if they ever married.

"How's your mother today?" Lily asked as she leaned down and kissed the top if his cute, balding head.

"Tired," he said, removing his glasses and wiping his brow. "She loved seeing you last night. But now I'm worried about Dad."

Lily had never liked it when people referred to their parents as plain "Mom" or "Dad"—not as "*my* mom" or "*my* dad"—as if they had conceived everyone in the world. But Frank was in distress, so she wouldn't correct him. "Why?" she asked. "Did he eat too much last night?" She hoped she didn't sound off-putting or flippant. She didn't want to take her irritation at her friends out on the one who least deserved it.

"No," Frank replied, not blanching at her words. "But he hardly sleeps now, he's so worried about Mom."

Lily had been with Reginald, of course, during his brief illness. But she hadn't really worried; she'd let Antonia do that. She remembered now that Eleanor had begun to say something about Brian, then had drifted off. Families worried about one another, Lily supposed, when they were sick or in some sort of trouble. Few worried about the ones who assumed responsibility for the others. "It isn't fair that you have to be the one in charge," Lily said, her anger sparking once again. "It's not right that your brother doesn't have to help."

"He can't do much from jail, Lily." His tone took a slight edge.

"I know, my darling," she said, softening her voice. "But I hate to see you fretting so. It's frustrating because I know I can't help."

67

He took her hand and kissed it but didn't say anything.

"There is someone I have been asked to help, though." She spun around and dropped onto his lap. "A little girl with leukemia. Well, I'm not going to help her, exactly. It's her kindergarten teacher. Imagine, to be five years old and to be so sick."

"Lily," Frank said, "what are you talking about?"

He seemed a bit weary, but she was getting used to that. So Lily told him about the wedding and the eighteen five-year-old attendants and the fact that the bride wanted it at Tanglewood the first weekend in June. Then she asked if he might have some pull with the events people over there, because the notice was so short and surely they were booked.

For the first time since Lily had walked in, Frank broke into a smile. "You do have a way of cheering me up. Where do you get your energy?" Then she giggled and he touched her cheek and said, "I'll make some phone calls in the morning."

Though Lily was the one who needed the favor, it was nice that, because she needed Frank, he might feel better too. She'd never understood why that was how things often worked.

Then she kissed him on the mouth and he kissed her back and she ran her hands over his chest and he said he knew another way that she could cheer him up and she said she'd be happy to help out with that too.

It was after eight when Lily left Antiques & Such,

leaving Frank to finish up his work before going home. But as she closed the door behind her and headed for the concrete stairs, an enormous figure stepped out of the dusky shadows.

She gasped. Her heart fluttered in her throat.

"Lily?" a man's voice asked.

She recognized him then. Still, it took a second for her scare to settle down. "Sutter," she said. It was Sutter Jones, Sarah's Cherokee lover, the attorney who had moved his practice from New York to West Hope and, specifically, onto the top floor of the old town hall in a small office space he now rented from Frank. It was Sutter who had reunited Sarah with her mother, and brought immeasurable joy into Sarah's life. "You startled me. Are you working late like Frank?"

"West Coast business," he said.

She wondered if his voice was so deep because he was so tall, if the sounds of his words had to come all the way from the bottoms of his feet up to his mouth.

He nodded toward the window that glowed from the light of Frank's computer screen. "How's he doing?"

"He's okay," she said, "but it's difficult right now. His mother is so sick . . ."

Sutter, a man of only necessary words, simply nodded. It occurred to Lily that most people over forty, except her, probably understood what it was like to worry about someone else.

She nodded back, then said, "Well, good night," and went on her way, glad that Sutter hadn't arrived a half hour earlier and caught her making love to Frank on

69

the old Victorian settee that he'd bought from an estate up in Williamstown for half the price that he now asked.

10

I t wasn't much of a celebration when one considered the magnitude of what Andrew and Jo had done that day: gone to the town hall, sworn that they were of sound mind and legally free to marry each other, signed their names in the town clerk's big book, and accepted the piece of paper, notarized and sealed, that said they could, indeed, trust each other and become man and wife.

It wasn't much of a celebration, just meat loaf and peas and mashed potatoes, which Andrew made while Jo stayed late at Second Chances, tying up loose ends for the Gilberts' wedding. She always had so much more work to do than he did; it was embarrassing sometimes.

The evening might have been more festive, partylike, maybe even sexy, but Cassie and Marilla sat at the table too, passing plates and looking somber when they weren't giggling, the moods of adolescence swinging back and forth like the pendulum of their old cat clock.

When he'd showed them the crisp, newly notarized license and declared that he and Jo were "now fit to get married under the laws of the Commonwealth of Massachusetts as certified by the town clerk of West Hope," he knew he sounded like a goof. But Andrew was, after all, as proud of the certificate as he was of the fact he hadn't told Jo that he went to her house last night, that he hadn't relapsed into insecurity.

But while Marilla had feigned interest in looking at the license, Cassie merely gave it a sideways glance as she scooped another mouthful of peas.

The rest of the meal passed like the pendulum again, until they finished and Jo said, "The meat loaf was delicious."

"Thank you," he said. "I'm going to make a wonderful wife, aren't I?" He'd said it to get a chuckle out of everyone, but when no one laughed, he felt oddly uncomfortable. "It was a joke," he said and, God bless weird little Marilla, she giggled again.

"Thanks for dinner, Mr. Kennedy," Marilla said. "It was way better than my mother's."

It might have been a compliment if Andrew didn't know that the girl's poor mother was hardly a model for June Cleaver or Carol Brady.

"Well," he said, "it's Cassie's favorite." He'd made it to make up for their awkwardness last night, and maybe because his daughter might not have been as "cool" about Jo being in his bed as he'd figured she would be.

"Speaking of Cassie," Cassie said, "she needs a new outfit for May Fair."

May Fair was a school concert, dance, and all-around festival for sixth, seventh, and eighth graders, or so said the paper that she'd brought home. Jo had said it was tradition at West Hope, though now they had booths for laser tag instead of dunking teachers.

"I'd love to go shopping with you on Saturday," Jo said, and Andrew silently gave her ten points for putting effort into the bonding thing.

Cassie glanced at Marilla, then looked sullenly at Jo. "No offense, but Marilla and I planned to go to the mall tonight." She quickly turned to Andrew. "Can you bring us, Dad? It's after eight, but you won't mind coming inside, will you?"

The mall had levied a recent rule that kids under sixteen had to be accompanied by an adult after eight o'clock. They'd claimed it was to eliminate bad behavior, though Andrew had often seen adults behaving worse than kids.

"Well," he said, "I don't know about tonight, honey . . ." His eyes turned to Jo, searching for an answer. Maybe they could go together?

But Jo shook her head. Had she taken Cassie's comment to mean she didn't want to shop with Jo? "You take them, Andrew," Jo said good-naturedly. "There are lots of things I can do at home."

"You're sure you don't mind?" Cassie asked, offering thin consolation.

"I think we all should go," Andrew said. As eager as he was to keep his daughter happy, she wasn't always going to get her way.

"No," Jo said. "I can use the time to think about our wedding, now that the paperwork is finished." She smiled. It was a shallow smile, however, and left Andrew mildly annoyed. He hoped this kind of undercurrent wouldn't serve as the foundation of every situation that they'd incur as a family. If so, he'd need to find a way to convince himself that this was girls' stuff, that he shouldn't let it bother him.

Cassie stood up and said, "It's getting late, we'd better go."

Marilla began to stand as well, then looked back at Jo and abruptly asked, "Are you going to change your name?"

Jo blanched. It occurred to Andrew that he'd never seen her blanch. "What?" she asked.

"Change your name," Marilla repeated. "You know. Are you going to be Jo Kennedy instead of Jo Lyons?"

Andrew didn't even know that Marilla knew Jo's last name; then again, everyone knew everyone in West Hope. But what surprised him more than the question was the time it took for Jo to form an answer, and that when she did, she laughed before she spoke.

"Well," she said, "to be honest, I haven't thought that yet." She stood up and began to bring the s to the sink, and Andrew sat there, supposing that ing or not changing her name was another of things that should be no big deal but knowing it was, that it would be, to him.

11

B logs," Andrew said the next morning in the back room of Second Chances as he helped Sarah and Jo unpack two hundred forty minia-

73

ture yellow vases, which would be filled with three daisies each and given as favors at the wedding on Friday. He tried to sound upbeat and casual. He figured that talking about blogs was safer than asking Jo if she'd given another minute's thought to changing her name.

"Did Cassie explain how a blog works?" Jo asked.

"She and Marilla did." He didn't add that they'd discussed it at the mall, in bits and pieces while Andrew sat outside one dressing room after another waiting for the giggling girls to parade in front of three-way mirrors. He didn't add that it would have been more fun if Jo had been there too, especially when the girls disappeared into the lingerie store and left him alone on bench.

"I think we need a blog for Second Chances," h continued. "A place where brides can read about th latest trends in second weddings. All of you ladies take turns. Elaine can talk about food. Sarah about orations and themes. Jo, you can talk logistics. Lily can talk about anything she wants, becaus will anyway." He chuckled and plunked another dozen vases on Sarah's design table.

"It actually is a good idea," Sarah said. "Not that of us can fit one more thing on our calendars. Betwe my son and my mother and Sutter and this business, hardly even have time for my jewelry-making anymore."

"Which is why you could take turns. It would be more manageable plus offer a good cross section of

74

things to think about. Then the audience can share their thoughts and experiences." He said the word *audience* as if he were talking about television.

"Well," Jo said, "I'm not sure. Will it be accessed from our Web site?" The Web site—*second-chancesweddings.com*—had been Andrew's idea too, a few months earlier, when he needed to make up for all the chaos he'd created with the column he'd been writing behind their backs for *Buzz* magazine. The site had only been "up" for a month or so, but the e-mails were pouring in:

I've stayed close to my ex's sister. Should I invite her to my wedding?

Should we send announcements to friends who aren't invited?

Should I toss my bouquet like brides do at first weddings?

For the most part, Andrew had been answering the e-mails, which seemed rather asinine because what the heck did he know. But he was always the one who had the least to do, despite that he was now more involved than when he'd been only the receptionist, hired by Lily to sit behind the French-provincial desk and smile at potential customers who sashayed through the door.

Maybe he should include a "Dear Andrew" column. He cleared his throat.

"Of course it will be accessed from our Web site," he said as he ripped open another carton. "It's a good idea, Jo. There's no need to analyze it to death."

"Well, we should ask Lily and Elaine," Jo said. "Get their opinions."

He dove into the carton, pulled out three vases, and slammed them on the table.

Jo looked at him oddly. "It's just that if we give away too much 'free' advice, we'll cheat ourselves out of business."

"Or we could lock up a position as second-wedding experts," Andrew replied, his voice now bordering on testy. Maybe he was pissed about last night, after all. Maybe he was pissed about the night before. Maybe he was just plain pissed that he was a goddamn wedding planner instead of doing something manly like being a television journalist or teaching college, both of which he'd sacrificed for making a perfect meat loaf and marrying a woman who might not even take his name as hers. "Besides," he added, yanking out more vases and plunking them down with gusto, "it might actually be a good idea to get input from real second-wedding brides, instead of making things up as we go along."

At some point in the past few seconds Jo and Sarah had stopped working. They stood still, staring at him now, Jo with her green eyes, Sarah with her coal-black ones.

"I'll be in the showroom," Sarah said, "while you two figure out whatever your problem is."

"Andrew?" Jo asked once Sarah had left. "What's the matter?"

He lined up the vases like little soldiers ready to do

battle. "I went to your house," he said. "But you weren't home."

"Last night?" she asked. "I went home right after dinner while you went to the mall . . ."

Andrew shook his head. He had started on this path to self-destruction now; he might as well continue.

"The night before," he said. "I talked to Cassie about seeing you in bed. I wanted to tell you that she said she was cool with everything but that I have a funny feeling she's not."

"We both have that funny feeling, Andrew. It was pretty obvious last night."

He nodded. He did not want to be distracted from the things he needed to say. "So I went to your house," he said.

"And I wasn't there."

"Right," he said and aligned another row.

"Is that why you're upset? Why didn't you say something yesterday?"

"I thought I should forget it. But then these other things happened . . ."

"Wait," she said. "You're upset because I went to see my mother?"

Her mother? She'd gone to see her mother? Andrew knew now that he had become completely certifiable. Jealous and insane. "I didn't know where you were," he said. There was no need to mention he thought she had gone off with another man. There was no need to remind her about Patty, to remind her that he'd had a first wife in another time and place.

77

She went to him and put her arms around him. "Well, aren't you being just a little ridiculous?"

He supposed he should feel better, but for some reason, he did not. "Are you going to change your name?" he asked, the way Marilla had.

Jo stepped back with a laugh. "Good grief," she said. "Is that what's really bothering you?"

"I don't know," he said honestly. "But are you?"

He sensed her back arching, a cat staging her defense. "Andrew, I don't know. I haven't really thought about it."

"When did you plan to think about it?"

"I don't know. Soon."

He nodded. "Well, let me know, okay?" He tried to smile as he opened another carton, but something in his heart had shifted, and he didn't like the way it felt.

Andrew's parents had been very nice people who might have been happier if they didn't have a child. They'd both been physicians who devoted their careers to caring for strangers and struggled to make time for Andrew in between. Luckily, as he'd gotten older he had John Benson as a mentor, their penthouse-across-the-hall neighbor who'd taken young Andrew under his media-frenzied wing and introduced him to the world of TV and newscasts and expounded on Andrew's innate *presence* on and off the camera. People would listen to Andrew, John said. With gifted intelligence hovering beneath his handsome, home-spun good looks, Andrew had the rare gift that he could be believed. And it was believability, according to John, where true power lay. All he needed was the courage to use it.

All of which had been a hundred or more years ago, or so it seemed as Andrew kissed Jo on the cheek and said he needed to go outside and get some fresh air and exercise. "All those daisies," he said with a laugh, but stopped smiling once he was on Main Street.

Something, he knew, was terribly wrong, from the way Cassie was behaving to the doubts that he was having—even to the way he had just snapped over something as stupid as a blog.

Something was wrong. Did that "something" have to do with him or did it have to do with Jo?

No matter what she thought or did, the blog was a great idea. He had planned everything.

I learned about an awesome recipe for mushroom hors d'oeuvres, Elaine might write. Or she could talk about a recipe that used lots of almonds, which seemed pretty hot right now, or maybe a vegan something-or-other that everyone would like. Then others would write back with ideas of their own and communication lines would flow.

He knew it would work. Maybe he could get Lily to write outrageous entries about style or etiquette or something equally chic. Or she could tell him about such stuff and he could write it as if it were coming from her. It wouldn't be the first time he wrote "undercover."

Yes, he thought. The blogs would be fun. Surely Jo would see that.

He shoved his hands into the pockets of his denim jacket and walked past the luncheonette. He thought about the time Jo had been there on a date, when he'd gone inside and practically pulled her away from the guy because Andrew was in love with her but couldn't tell her then.

He loved her so much. Didn't he?

She was so strong, so smart, so independent. Those were attributes he loved about her, weren't they? Or was he just an old-fashioned chauvinist at heart?

He glanced in the window of the bookstore that seemed to have been there forever; he spotted the latest novels jockeying for visibility among the stacks of newspapers and high-gloss magazines. He thought about a woman who had called a few months ago and asked if the staff of Second Chances would write a feature column for a new magazine geared to the second-, third-, fourth-time bride. He wondered if the magazine had ever gotten under way. Would that be something he could do? If he had more productive things to do, more of a chance to use his brain, would he feel better about himself, about his life, about the woman he loved?

He passed the real-estate office that featured properties at inflated prices in hopes of snaring tourists/buyers from New York. He thought about the renovations to Jo's house. The foundation had been poured. There was no turning back now, was there?

Renovations. Blogs. A magazine. Would those things be enough? Would any or all of it help compensate for the fact that he really was a journalist? A man who might have been content to get his job back at the college but it didn't look as if they were going to agree?

And, if they didn't, what was he supposed to do?

Turning up his collar to the cool spring breeze, Andrew realized that was his problem. Not Jo, not his ex-wife or his daughter, not the blog. The problem was that Andrew David Kennedy had much more to offer than working with a bunch of women, great though they were, planning weddings, of all things.

He was bored, plain and simple, and he realized now that the future—even with Jo—might not be enough to satisfy his soul.

He raised his head and kept walking, not knowing what the hell he should do now, or who the hell he could talk to, or why the hell he just couldn't be grateful for all he had and forget that his life had been so much more so long ago.

12

Lily sat in Sutter's office overlooking the town common and saw Andrew walking up Main Street with his hands stuffed in his pockets and his head held high and rigid. She wondered where he was going and why he was not walking with his usual happy, sneaker-footed gait.

It occurred to her—not for the first time—that, like Lily, Andrew didn't really belong in the quaint little town. She'd often noticed how hard he worked at trying to fit in, from feigning interest in his daughter's riding lessons to pretending to like boating to growing scraggly vegetables in his backyard and telling himself they were 4-H award winners. But every so often, like today, Lily noticed that his stride reverted to the fast pace of a Manhattan-born-and-raised boy with his shoulders squared a little too stiffly for West Hope. This time seemed the worst.

She turned back to Sutter, who sat behind an old wooden desk, one Frank had resurrected—along with a number of wooden filing cabinets—from his antiques storeroom. The desk seemed small for a man of such broad shoulders and muscled girth, but the morning light that drifted through the dusty windows softened Sutter's chiseled copper face and made it seem as if he'd been sitting there forever doing the whole town's legal business, rather than solely reading Lily's papers.

Even Sutter's handsome, costly clothes and sophisticated demeanor did not seem out of place.

No, she thought, Andrew was the only one who seemed so much like Lily—city fish forcing themselves to adapt to the small pond of the country. Perhaps Andrew would fit better once he and Jo were married. Perhaps Lily would too, if she married Frank, if Sutter could find a tiny loophole in the prenup or in Reginald's will, which he was perusing now.

The big Cherokee man grunted "hmmm" and turned a page.

Lily repositioned herself in her chair, glad she'd

worn her beige, ready-to-wear Chanel suit (two years old now, but West Hope wouldn't notice), grateful she'd learned at an early age that what one lacked in assets one could make up for with an appropriate appearance. And an appropriate appearance could help one project a well-defined aura of confidence, an essential element when discussing money, or a lack thereof.

She'd had the brilliant idea after running into Sutter the night before. He was an attorney! He knew the law! He was the best kind of friend—a new one—who didn't yet know all her flaws!

Unless, of course, Sarah had told him.

But Sarah wouldn't do that, would she? No, she was too private, the way those creative types tended to be. Besides, she was too wrapped up in her family and her new love now. She hardly even mentioned her jewelry-making anymore. Which really was too bad, because if Lily was asked to reveal the most positive thing about her friend, she would say that Sarah Duncan designed silver jewelry as well as, if not better than, Paloma Picasso or Elsa Peretti. Of course, if Lily told Sarah that, Sarah would just laugh at her. The woman, after all, still wore her shining black hair straight down her long back and lived like a leftover hippie in a log cabin that was decorated like a teepee. It was doubtful she'd be pleased to be told she had an elitist sense of style.

Still, thanks to Sarah and Sarah's new live-in attorney-lover, Lily had gleefully stayed up long past midnight digging through her piles of legal papers, searching for anything that Sutter might be able to use in Lily's favor.

If only Reginald hadn't trusted Antonia. If only he'd had a clue that his sister was as beastly as Lily had tried telling him on more than one occasion, that Antonia was jealous because Lily had stolen his time and attention—and probably his love as well—from his precious spinster of a sister, who preferred a life of make-believe at the ballet and the opera to dealing with real people in real time.

"My brother left me in charge, as it should be," Antonia had announced after the reading of Reginald's will at the Beckwith attorney's office, which was enveloped in mahogany and leather and smelled like stale pipe smoke. "I'll decide what will be a sufficient allowance for you."

Lily's attorney—who had curiously been connected to the Beckwith fortune too—explained that, according to the will, Antonia was within her rights to set the limit. Lily and Reginald had been married only six years, after all, and it was typewriter-and-adding-machine, Beckwith money.

Antonia then shrewdly set an adequate amount just over a hardly contestable, "livable" line for Lily, but way less than she deserved. Still, Lily hadn't balked, because she feared that she might drown in nothing if she made too big a wave.

"Unless you remarry," Lily's former lawyer had explained. "Then all bets are off."

She'd thought that was a rather blue-collar remark

coming from a stuffy Beckwith lawyer, but at the time Lily truly was in mourning and could not imagine being married to anyone, ever again.

She should have known that was an uncharacteristic lapse in Lily-like judgment.

"Well," Sutter said finally, as he peeled off his eyeglasses, "you're right. You have a problem."

Lily looked out the window, as if one more glance at Andrew would help her feel less desolate, less like the only fish adrift. But wherever he was going, Andrew had disappeared from view, and Lily was alone.

"I'll lose everything," Lily told her friends over lunch after she'd left Sutter's office, after she'd finally broken down and told Sarah and Jo about Frank's proposal. "I know that sometimes I seem shallow to all of you, but I lost my parents when I was so young. . . . I know that money has helped to fill the hole. Okay, I know it's superficial, but money is my life. And, whether you understand or not, I'm terrified of not having it."

They were sitting in the back room of Second Chances—Jo, Sarah, Elaine, and Lily. Andrew had not resurfaced from wherever he'd gone.

Finally Sarah spoke. "Sutter offered no advice?" she asked, because, of course, she was in love with him and most likely thought that he could walk on legal (and every other kind of) water.

Lily shook her head. "Antonia is the executrix. Whatever she says goes. Oh," she said, holding her hand up to her forehead in a Scarlett O'Hara move that she simply couldn't stop, "what am I going to do?"

For a moment no one said a word. Then Sarah set down her vegan sandwich, which Elaine had made for all of them today, and said, "If you really want to be with Frank, why do you have to marry him? Antonia couldn't change anything if you just lived with Frank, could she?"

"I suppose not. But Frank is old-fashioned, Sarah. And I believe in marriage. We're not like you and Sutter." She was glad, at least, that she'd said "you and Sutter" and not "you and Jason," Sarah's former live-in lover, the father of Sarah's son. Still, if Sarah took any offense, she shrugged it off.

Then Jo spoke up. "I like Frank, Lily. It wasn't easy for me in the beginning, having him around because of his brother. But even though he's such a good guy—in fact, maybe *because* he's a good guy—you might want to think about whether marrying him would really be the right move for you. Forget about the money aspect. If it weren't for that, would you really want to be his wife? Do you really want to live here in West Hope forever, have the West Hope social circles become the fun part of your life?"

Well, of course Lily had thought of that a thousand times already but was too embarrassed to admit it. "Thanks for your thoughts, Jo, but I know that you can't be objective. Besides, I've always thought my social life would revolve around my best friends." She felt defensive suddenly, irritated that Jo's old boyfriend, Brian, had been, still was, Frank's brother, and that Brian was part of the reason Frank was under so much stress.

"Well," Sarah added, "it's not as if Frank is poverty-stricken. He has a long-standing business. He owns some commercial property. The old town hall."

And, of course, the building in which they all now worked. Lily sighed. "But he doesn't have millions," she said quietly.

"And when Antonia dies?" Jo asked. "What happens to the money then?"

"Nothing. I still get my allowance because it comes from the trust fund. The rest goes to charities. The ballet, the opera, maybe stipends to the household help."

Elaine poured more coffee from a red-and-white insulated jug. "I know what you should do."

All heads turned toward her.

"Be Antonia's new best friend."

Jo blinked and Sarah laughed and Lily moved her hand to her throat. "Hell's bells, Elaine. That's hardly realistic."

Elaine got off the stool that sat next to Sarah's drawing table. With coffee cup in hand, she strolled around the fabrics and the drawings and the wedding props that now adorned almost every square foot of Sarah's creative space. "I think it is realistic, Lily. You've complained about Antonia since you married Reginald. But have you ever tried to be her friend?"

"She hates me."

"She was threatened by you. Once. After all, you stole her baby brother. It doesn't seem to me that she's had much else in her life."

"She has the ballet and the opera."

"But not many friends."

"No. She always bitched that she had to take care of her brother because their parents were always traveling to one continent or another. They left Reginald and Antonia with their nanny and the servants."

"So Antonia felt responsible. And then, in later years, he married you and the bottom fell out of her world."

They were silent again.

"She doesn't have friends because she's not very likable," Lily finally said.

"Then maybe she needs you," Elaine added, "as much as you need her."

Jo had learned long ago to try not to intrude on another person's crisis, to not judge the reasons another person had for thinking a certain way or behaving in ways that she hoped she would not. Lily's problem was Lily's, and while they could try to ease her discomfort, they certainly couldn't convince her that she was being superficial, that maybe now was the time for Lily to grow up.

Jo was not Lily, so she could not possibly understand Lily's situation any more than she could fathom why Andrew was in the mood that he was in. Was he having second thoughts about their marriage? Was he getting anxious? He'd be much more anxious if she told him what she'd seen when she went to Cassie's school, if she told him that her instincts said Cassie might be headed for adolescent trouble.

Long after the lunch hour, long after the others had resumed their work, Andrew finally called.

"Hi," he said.

"Hi," Jo replied.

"I'm home," he said.

"Oh," she said.

"I have a headache."

"That's too bad."

"Yeah."

His voice lacked animation. Maybe he really did have a headache.

"Did you take something?" she asked.

"What?"

"Did you take something. For your headache."

"Oh. No. Not yet."

"Should I come over after work?"

"Sure. If you want."

If she wanted? What the heck was going on? "Maybe I should call first. To be sure you're not asleep." She picked up the papers on her desk, arranged them in a pile. Surely she was being foolish, surely everything was fine.

"No. Come over when you leave work."

"Shall I pick up something for supper?"

"Yes. No. Don't bother."

"It's no bother, Andrew."

He paused. "Well, okay, then. Chinese if you want."

"Will Cassie be home?"

"I guess."

"Andrew?" she asked. "Is everything all right?"

He paused, then said, "Sure. I'll see you later?"

"Yes."

There was nothing left to say then but good-bye.

After that, Jo turned back to the checklist for the Gilberts' wedding and realized that she was the one with a headache now.

13

When we started this business, we had no conception of the details—and the differences—in planning second weddings instead of firsts. We knew that things would be different, should be different, but we honestly did not know how different they would be.

We learned quickly.

Andrew sat at his laptop in the small study off the living room of the cottage, his and Cassie's cottage, the place they'd grown to love but soon would leave.

He had walked for more than two hours after he left Second Chances. He thought about Jo, about Cassie, about his future and his past. He thought about the years that he'd been a single dad, about the early times when he sat right there in the cottage, sleepless, worried sick, because Cassie didn't have a mom.

He thought about the time he'd gone to the

mother–daughter luncheon for the kindergarten kids. He'd been the only father there.

He thought about the time Cassie had come home from Mrs. Connor's and asked if he would marry Mrs. Connor so she wouldn't have to keep schlepping her My Little Pony suitcase back and forth between the houses when Andrew had to go into New York City for one reason or another. He'd laughed at the way Cassie had said "schlep" as if it were a standard word in a six-year-old's vocabulary. He didn't laugh at the suggestion that the seventy-year-old Mrs. Connor should become his wife.

As he walked he'd also thought about when Cassie was eight or nine and she'd given him a Mother's Day card because she said that she figured he was her mother *and* her father, wasn't he? The card was pink and had glitter on the cover and a small white ribbon tied in a bow. Andrew had put it in his drawer, tucked beneath his socks, until he'd gone to teach one day and a student noticed glitter on his shoes. After that he wrapped the card in plastic and moved it to the bottom drawer.

On his solitary walk, Andrew had thought of all those times and more, but mostly he thought how scared he'd been at first after Patty left, then how at some point—he did not know when—he'd slid into a place of comfort, just him and his daughter, as if she'd never had a mother, as if he'd never had a mate.

Sometime after an hour and three-quarters had passed, Andrew realized the recent thoughts that he'd been having were like the ones he'd felt back when he and Cassie first moved to West Hope.

He was not bored. He did not want to go back to New York City, back into television, back into the life of a semi-celebrity. He did not feel less a man because he could make an awesome meat loaf (in fact he was secretly proud of that).

The problem was, Andrew Kennedy was scared.

Scared of marriage.

Scared of commitment.

But mostly, scared of losing everything a second time around.

But it wasn't until he hung up from talking to Jo that it occurred to him he might not be the only "second-timer" with those kinds of feelings.

So he'd sat down at his laptop and begun to write the blog, to write with optimism and with information, to write with wit and charm, as if he was one of the women of Second Chances, administering advice.

He decided to write the opening installment as if he were Jo. Maybe the blog would recharge his spirit the way his *Buzz* magazine column once had; maybe it would lighten his mood if he pretended to be inside her head and not his own.

In the course of wedding planning, we've also learned that getting married a second (or third, or more!) time has more problems beyond the ceremonial or the emotional kind. There are many basics to address! Here are a few examples:

92

1. His place or hers: Where the heck will you live? It seems like an obvious problem, but at this stage of life, you both most likely have made some kind of home. Which one of you is more willing or able to make the move? The ideal situation is to start fresh. Begin with a new home that the two of you can create— one without memories of other spouses or lovers, the good or the bad—a place that will be yours with your new family. Andrew and I are lucky enough to be moving into what was my grandparents' home, the home where I was raised. But we are planning major renovations and an addition that will make it seem new, even to me.

He grinned again, hoping that was how she felt. The renovations hardly made the place "new," but at least Jo hadn't lived there with anyone except her mother and her grandparents. He winced at the reminder that though this was his second wedding, it would be Jo's first. Brian Forbes, thank God, didn't count for anything. Brian Forbes would never be lucky enough to live in Jo's house with her.

Then he thought about Cassie, and he quickly typed:

2. If kids are in the picture, this is an even bigger consideration. Neighborhoods, schools, and their "rooms" must be carefully thought out.

Cassie would like the new setup at Jo's. Though she'd be leaving her small, familiar room, she'd have two rooms upstairs—the largest bedroom and the next-largest for a study/TV/computer room. The upstairs bathroom would be all hers. Andrew promised not even to use it when he was in the third upstairs bedroom that would be his study. All in all, Cassie would have lots of room for all her stuff, though she'd be happiest, of course, if she got the purple paint she wanted.

Which led him to think of all the junk that he'd accumulated in the cottage and what he'd leave behind. Like what about the pots and pans he'd picked up at tag sales because when they'd moved out of the city he'd wanted no reminders of Patty's presence, not the towels that he hung on the bathroom racks, not the soufflé dish in which she prepared chocolate soufflé, the only thing that she knew how to make?

He shut his eyes and continued.

3. Who has the best potato peeler or stereo system or bathroom towels? As in example #1, you both probably have a complete kitchen, bath, and a bevy of stuff. We suggest you spend a weekend with your "intended" to go over these "essentials," and have a big garage sale, unless you plan on doubling the size of your house.

In less than three weeks he and Jo would be married and they hadn't done this yet. Even the new family room and master suite would not make the house able to accommodate two houses full of junk.

He sat back in his chair and drew in a deep breath. He reread the entry. Then he thought about the other issue weighing on his mind. Hesitating for only a moment, he wrote,

4. Will the bride take the groom's name, or will she keep her own?

He stared at the words that stared back at him. Why did this question seem like such a big freaking deal?

And then Andrew knew the answer.

Patty, Cassie's mother, had never taken Andrew's name. She had her *career,* she'd explained. She had her *image* to maintain.

So Patty had remained Patty O'Shay, international cover girl, independent woman, who needed nothing from her husband, not even his name.

He blinked, then saved the words that he had typed. He opened a new file that he titled *blog stuff.* As soon as the women agreed to this support system for second-timers, he'd have some opening material all set to go.

And who knew, he realized, maybe someone in the big, blog audience out there in the universe would strike up a dialogue on this name-changing thing, and he would finally be able to relax, and he and Jo would live happily ever after, after all.

14

With a little luck, Lily would get Antonia's answering service—a real woman named Claudia, because, as with most things, Antonia refused to go modern.

Lily sat on the pink-and-white-striped sofa in her tiny living room above Second Chances. She stared at the cordless phone she held in her hand and told herself she had nothing to lose. Antonia didn't like her—had never liked her—so an attempt to befriend the woman wasn't going to upset the family apple cart.

The first time they'd met was a disaster. Reginald had wanted to buy a yacht to use in the summers to traverse the Mediterranean, specifically the waters surrounding Sardinia, the small island off Italy that had entranced him since he was a boy.

Lily and Reginald were in the early stages of their relationship. They'd met through a "mutual friend"— the nail technician who buffed Reginald on Thursdays at three o'clock and did Lily's acrylics on Thursdays at four. The woman convinced Reginald to wait one afternoon, saying she knew a young divorcée he might like. By five-thirty Lily and Reginald were having drinks at the Pierre. No one ever knew that Lily had been the one to instigate the introduction, that one week earlier she'd grilled the nail tech about her customer list, then presented her with a most generous tip.

Reginald didn't tell Lily about his sister until their fourth date.

"She raised me," he'd said, and Lily thought that was wonderful because the closest she'd ever come to having siblings had been Jo, Sarah, and Elaine, and she hadn't met them until college.

He told Lily happy tales of trips to Europe on grand ocean liners in the early 1950s; his mother had been afraid of airplanes. The ships were luxurious and slow—in the daytime Antonia played checkers with him in the card room, at night the rhythm of the waves rocked young Reginald to sleep, while his older sister sang soft lullabies, imitating the soothing voices of Rosemary Clooney and Julie London.

Lily hadn't known who the singers were, but she could tell the trips represented fond times in Reginald's memory.

"Antonia never married," he said with sadness. "But I've been lucky that instead she's watched over me."

Lucky, indeed.

She's too young.

She's too flighty.

She's only after our money.

Although Lily never heard Antonia say any of those things to her brother, the sentiments were plainly etched between the lines that formed on the woman's forehead when Reginald at last introduced them.

He brought Lily to the family home on Madison Avenue because, even then, Antonia rarely went out, except for Pavarotti or Baryshnikov or whoever the woman deemed their reasonable facsimiles. Maybe she was afraid of the New York City streets the way her mother had feared airplanes.

They'd had tea and cookies. The words were sparse: Where had Lily gone to college? Where was her family home? Where did she have her coming out?

She'd considered saying she went to Wellesley and her family was from Oyster Bay and her debutante ball was at the Waldorf because the Plaza had been undergoing renovations.

Instead she told the truth and watched the woman's jawline tighten and her red-painted lips grow pale. And any doubts that Lily might have had about marrying a man two decades her senior quickly dissipated. Instead she looked upon it as a personal challenge, her greatest triumph to be won.

She never, however, dreamed that she'd wind up sitting on the tiny, little-girl-like sofa in her tiny, little-girl-like apartment, with the security of her entire future resting on the whims of the woman she'd provoked.

"Lily?" Antonia Beckwith spoke as if she wanted to add, *Lily who?*

Lily clutched the white, handmade, "plush" angora rabbit that she kept on the back of the sofa, her huggable alternative to a common teddy bear. She gritted her teeth. "Yes, Antonia. How are you?"

"No different than when I saw you two days ago."

Two days ago? Had it only been two days?

"Yes, well . . ." Lily began to stammer, hating that she'd lost her edge, her confidence, when dealing with the woman now that Reginald was gone. She cleared her throat, tried to summon her most authoritative voice. "When I saw you Monday I meant to ask you something, but it slipped my mind." No matter how hard she tried, Lily sensed that, compared with the ancient woman, she still sounded like a little girl. "I'm sure you're frightfully busy this season. . . ."

"And I've already selected my charities for the year."

Lily clutched the plush rabbit more tightly and shut her tired eyes. "Oh, Antonia, this isn't about money!"

"What, then? I certainly can't help you with your business. I never married, after all, not even once."

Reginald used to blame himself for that, for being a burden to his older sister, her "charge" of sorts because their mother was so delicate and incompetent and Antonia never trusted the nannies to raise her brother as she could.

"When she might have been out dating, she was reading to me instead," he told Lily.

Lily wanted to suggest there might be other reasons why Antonia never had a man, but it would have served no purpose, then or now.

"Actually," she said, hoping that her grimace would not travel through the phone lines, "I'm sure if I needed your help, you'd have a great deal to offer. Your experience with the opera and the ballet . . . well, it might give our brides new ideas for their weddings."

"Weddings do not interest me," Antonia replied.

Sucking in a small breath, Lily remembered Elaine's words: "You stole her baby brother. . . . Maybe she needs you." But the silence that followed Antonia's last comment reminded Lily that Reginald's sister was just fine without the likes of Lily or the reminder that she'd lost the only person she had loved.

"What do you really want?" Antonia interrupted Lily's thoughts.

She gripped the left ear of the rabbit. "Well, as you mentioned when I saw you, it finally is spring. I thought you might enjoy a trip out to the country." She scrunched her eyes this time, feeling her nose, her cheeks, her forehead crinkle.

Silence again, this time laced by the faint white noise of an old person breathing. And then Antonia asked, "What country?"

Not one in Europe, Lily wanted to say. *Not one you get to by a grand ocean liner.* "The Berkshires," she said. "West Hope."

"Do you mean where you live?"

"Yes. I thought you might like a vacation. It's so beautiful up here. Reginald loved it when we came for one of my college reunions." She wasn't sure she should have added the part about Reginald.

Antonia laughed. (Was that a laugh?) "I hate the country," she said. "Bugs. Mosquitoes. Encephalitis. Lyme disease. Thank you, but I shall be most happy to decline."

Decline?

Decline?

100

Lily, of course, couldn't let her do that. Partly because she needed to befriend her, partly because she couldn't let her gain the upper hand again.

Her stalwart resolve returned. "It's only May, Antonia. The bugs aren't even out yet. There's a lovely inn on the outskirts of town that I think you'd really enjoy. It's a magnificent Italian villa with a wonderful palazzo."

"I couldn't possibly come. My calendar is very crowded."

Crowded, Lily knew, with those ballet nights and the opera.

It had been worth a try, but clearly this was not going to work. Lily sighed. "Well," she said, "perhaps next month." Or next year. Or never.

When Antonia did not respond, Lily simply said good-bye. Then she held on to the rabbit and looked out the window toward Frank's antiques shop and knew she couldn't marry him unless an unexpected miracle dropped out of the sky.

Thursday rushed by like the spring-thaw waters of the Housatonic River. With the two impending weekend weddings, Lily barely even had a chance to gloat when Frank phoned Friday morning to say he had secured the Seranak House at Tanglewood for the kindergarten teacher's wedding.

Jo nodded and Sarah stifled a small groan and Elaine said she was relieved to learn that Tanglewood allowed only their caterer to do the food for private events.

Lily didn't take any of it personally.

At noon their caravan conveyed the last of the people and the props to the lovely meadow Jo had found where the Gilberts' wedding would be held. The setting overlooked the scalloped edges of the mountains that were vivid green now, with winter far behind; the perfect afternoon included a warm sun that belonged more to July than May. Lily took credit for the weather from the bride and groom.

The tables were set up under a big white tent; the head table displayed a lavish wedding cake that Elaine had coated with a pretty yellow fondant, then painted with white sugar daisies and adorned with sugar ribbons and delicate-looking sugar-lace.

"Has Elaine designed your cake yet?" Lily asked after their work was complete and she stood with Jo, facing Sarah's wall of daisies, watching the early wedding guests arrive.

"No," Jo said. "We've been so busy."

"Make time for yourself," Lily said. "It will be your wedding, after all."

"My first."

Lily nodded, keeping her wedding smile in view. "All the more reason to get on it." She did not mention again that Jo shouldn't have downscaled her nuptials to the teeny number that she had. Lily had begun to realize that she wasn't in much of a position at this point to be handing out advice, at least not to a friend.

"Lily?" Jo asked suddenly. "Do you think I should change my name?"

On the other hand, if her advice was requested . . .

"Change your name to what? To Andrew's?"

"Yes. Of course, to Andrew's. What do you think?"

Lily had taken each of her three husbands' last names because that was how things always had been done. Besides, it wasn't as if she worked or had a career or had made a name for herself as anything but someone's wife. But Jo was different. Jo Lyons had an identity, from West Hope to Boston anyway.

Watching as the waiters put finishing touches on the tables (Elaine had continued the yellow–white color theme by preparing entrée choices of white fish, rice, and corn, or fettuccini Alfredo with early yellow squash, both of which would have a bright contrast color of red blush from the orange loquat accents), Lily said, "It's really up to you, Jo."

If Jo was surprised that Lily did not spring forth with an opinion, she didn't say.

"However," Lily added, because she supposed she simply had to, "changing one's name requires a lot of tedious paperwork."

"I'm not afraid of paperwork," Jo replied, and Lily merely shrugged because she didn't know what else to say.

The wedding guests filled the rows of white chairs; behind the wall of daisies a harpist sat, unseen, now sending melodic tunes drifting on the air.

"Today the Gilberts, Sunday the Randolph/Bartons," Sarah said as she joined Lily and Jo. "From happy daisies to heavy Victorians."

"The lace you picked is hardly heavy-looking," Jo said.

Lily didn't, however, say that the venue was quite dreadful. The ceremony would be held in the bride's grandmother's late-nineteenth-century house, replete with dried hydrangea blossoms that stood in tall vases on marble-topped, curved-footed end tables. Bulky draperies adorned tall, dark-wood-framed windows; the furniture was upholstered in a kind of deep-red velvet and looked as uncomfortable as Antonia's horsehair.

It was a dismal house, not unlike Antonia's, despite that it was in the country, not the city.

Antonia. The woman who would determine the course of Lily's life forever, it appeared.

Lily moved slowly from her friends. She straightened the silverware at the head table by the pretty yellow cake that Elaine had made for a bride who was not wealthy, a groom who was not rich. What was wrong with Lily that she couldn't be content to be like others, that she couldn't be content just to be loved?

Was it still because of Billy Sears these many, many years later?

"Lily?" It was Jo, who had walked up behind her. Jo, who had put the past behind her and let herself be loved, whose only problem now seemed to have to do with what her name should be.

Lily quickly wiped a tear that had formed in her eye and smiled. "I'm fine," she lied. "Just a moment of overflowing joy for our divine little business and the happiness we bring to others."

Jo didn't say a word, just slipped her arm around Lily's small waist and guided her back to where Sarah stood, so they could witness the phenomenon called love that was out of Lily's reach.

15

Saturday was as busy as Thursday and Friday, with the day before a wedding as crazy as the day itself. At least being busy left little time to foster doubts that Andrew was having second thoughts about marrying her, or that Cassie had decided she didn't want her for a stepmother.

He'd said everything was fine, that he'd just been feeling scared. He said Cassie would be fine too, they just needed to give her a little time. He said that he would talk to Cassie when the weekend crunch was over; he said that he would ask if maybe she was scared as well.

If everything was fine, Jo wasn't sure why she stood alone at her kitchen window Saturday night, staring at the cement foundation that soon would hold the new addition to the house, the new addition to her life.

She was alone because Andrew had agreed to chaperone the May Fair festival. Jo had not been invited. He'd said he knew that she'd be too busy with the weddings.

Jo wondered if Cassie had suggested that. She wondered if the girl was pleased her father would be there, and if she'd worn eye makeup.

Turning on the tap water, Jo poured a glass and downed a couple of aspirin. Halfway through her swallow, she heard a car door close. Andrew?

The knock, however, didn't sound like his.

She moved to the door, and drew back the sheer curtain. Instead of Andrew standing on the porch, she saw Frank Forbes.

"Frank," she said when she'd unlocked the dead bolt and let him come inside. "This is a surprise. Is everything okay?" She'd just left Lily at the shop, so she knew there was nothing wrong with her. Then Jo remembered Frank's mother. "Oh," she said. "Please. Sit down. It's not your mother, is it?"

He shook his head and sat at the kitchen table. "She's still the same. Hanging on to life. I wonder why we do that?"

When they were young Jo thought Frank was much too serious. In the last year she'd come to realize that as Brian's older brother, Frank had taken on the role of the responsible, trustworthy son, the one who'd tried to compensate for all his brother's screwups. She wondered if she had indirectly made Frank's life more difficult by loving his errant brother, by enabling Brian to get away with being such a jerk. "Would you like some tea?" Jo asked. "Or a drink?"

"I'd love a beer," he said. "If you have any."

She poured him one of Andrew's "designer" beers, the kind, he'd joked, that were made for savoring, like wine, not for swilling in front of a big-screen TV, as if he'd ever do that, unless to watch the news.

She'd often wondered if Brian had lived like that when Jo wasn't around. He certainly wasn't doing it now in his eight-by-ten-foot cell.

Hating that Frank's presence made her think of Brian, Jo tried to sound cheery when she said, "So, to what do I owe the pleasure?" She set the beer down on the table and sat down across from him.

Frank sipped his beer with thought-collecting slowness. Behind his glasses his eyes narrowed. It occurred to Jo that if his mother was okay, he must have come to talk about his situation with Lily. She'd have to find a way not to reveal the real reason that Lily wouldn't say I do.

She smiled. "It's amazing how busy we are at the shop. And it's so wonderful—and so hard to believe!—that Lily has become quite an astute businesswoman." Perhaps a boost to Lily's credibility would help, in case he'd come to share any doubts about her. "The wedding yesterday was terrific," Jo continued, "thanks in great part to Lily. And tomorrow we're doing Gladys Randolph and Jim Barton's wedding. Do you remember Jim from high school? I think he was in your class." Of course Frank hadn't come to Jo's to listen to wedding small talk. She shifted on the colonial-blue seat pad between her and the chair, one of four her mother had selected a dozen years ago when she'd redecorated the kitchen, more things Jo would dispense of once the renovations were fully under way, which Frank surely hadn't come to discuss either.

"Lily is an amazing woman," Frank said, setting down the bottle, ignoring her comment about Jim Barton. "I asked her to marry me, you know. She hasn't said yes yet."

"Has she said no?"

"Well"—he smiled—"no."

Jo cupped her glass and turned it to the left, then right. "Lily's personality can be deceiving," she said. "She looks like she's an airhead. But she's really not, you know. She's methodical and caring and she always tries to do what's right, what would please other people."

He nodded. "I know. Which is why I love her. She's not at all like my first wife, Sondra. Did you know her?"

"No." Sondra, like Frank, had been three or four years ahead of Jo in school. "Didn't she move to Colorado?" Jo had heard the gossip from her mother, who always wrote letters when Jo had lived in Boston, keeping her abreast of all the big and small West Hope news. When Sondra Forbes up and left her husband of ten years, it, sadly, had been front-page fodder.

"Dumped me, that's what she did," Frank said. "She said this place was boring and so was I."

Having been dumped by Brian, Jo was sure that she knew how he'd felt. "I'm sorry," she said.

He took another swig. "I worry that Lily might do the same. After all, Sondra was born and raised here; if she needed to escape, how can I expect that West Hope will hold Lily Beckwith?" Then he shrugged. "But I suppose we can't go through life worrying, can we?"

Jo shook her head.

"And now you and Andrew are getting married, and I'm really happy for you, Jo. You certainly deserve some happiness after what Brian did to you."

She sipped her water, did not respond, wished he hadn't mentioned his brother's name.

He cleared his throat and added, "Which is the reason that I'm here."

It took a second for Jo to realize what he'd said. Before she could reply, he added, "I was in Albany today or I would have come to tell you sooner. The fact is, Jo, I heard from Brian's lawyer yesterday. The trial date's been set. For the third week of May."

Jo squeezed the glass that rested in her hand. Brian's trial. The time had come. The time she had dreaded since he was arrested. Since the detective Frank had hired found Brian hiding out in Switzerland, since he'd come back to this country and she'd filed the complaint.

The time had come. "Oh," was all that she could say.

And then Jo realized something else: Frank had said the trial would be held the third week of May. Days before her wedding to Andrew.

When Lily answered the phone on Sunday morning, how was she supposed to know the caller would be Antonia? She'd thought it might be Frank, who'd been out of town yesterday at a big auction up in Albany. She thought he might be wondering how Lily was doing and if the "girls" needed his help to haul props or anything to and from the Victorian-wedding venue. She thought he might be phoning to apologize for not calling her last night, even if he hadn't gotten home until late.

No matter what, she didn't really like that she was thinking like a wife.

"I changed my mind," Antonia said loudly before Lily was fully awake, before she could grasp that it was not Frank, before she could comprehend what the woman said. "Tomorrow will be fine, if that gives you enough time."

Tomorrow? Lily thought. *Enough time for what?*

"We should be there by noon," Antonia continued. "You'll need to make a reservation for my driver. And one for Pauline."

Reginald used to say that Pauline was Antonia's "faithful servant," her "Jackie of all trades," the number one of which was taking care of Antonia the way Antonia had taken care of Reginald. Apparently the Beckwiths never learned to take care of themselves.

"We have a wedding today," Lily heard herself say. "I have to work."

"And I said we'd be there tomorrow. I've decided to see if what you said is true, if spring is actually nice up there in the mountains."

She could have corrected Antonia and said the Berkshires were hills, not mountains, but Lily was too startled. Besides, it was too early in the day for confrontation.

110

"So you're coming for a visit?" Lily asked.

"I was invited, wasn't I?"

Lily rubbed her eyes. "Yes. Yes, of course. It will be very nice." Then she listened as Antonia rattled off her "accomodation requirements" and instructed Lily to call back with the arrangements and directions.

Even second-time brides should have a wedding theme, Andrew typed above the sounds of the rock group Green Day that emanated from Cassie's stereo upstairs. It was Sunday morning, the next wedding wasn't for a few hours, and Andrew figured he had time to sit in the small study off the living room and prepare another blog entry—this one would be from Lily. He'd decided he would keep creating messages until his collection was impressive enough so he could show the others and they would all agree that a blog would be exciting. Fun. A credibility bump for Second Chances.

He smiled as he considered the word *bump:* a TV word, a ratings word. Would the media business ever completely leave his blood?

"Not hardly," he said with a short laugh.

At least he could do this for now. Tomorrow he would sit down with Cassie and talk about her expectations for Jo. Tomorrow he would sit with Jo and find out if she was going to take his name or not.

Tomorrow, after this nutsy wedding weekend was complete.

Until then, he could at least prepare to share his

thoughts with cyberspace. Hell, maybe he was better with an audience that was invisible, like in his TV-reporter days.

Ah, yes, he thought again. *The media. The world of news that has become the world of hype.*

Then he thought again about the magazine that the mystery woman had called about. The magazine that was going to be designed to focus on second weddings. Who the heck was she? He remembered that Jo had taken the call. She might have written down the woman's name and number. Jo was organized like that.

He started at his cell phone, which sat next to his computer. He hadn't heard from Winston College yet; he knew he might not. What harm would there be in tracking down the woman? A job was a job, and though he loved Jo and her former college roommates, it might serve everyone much better if he didn't count on wedding planning to meet his career needs. He could write about it instead. At least he knew how to write. At least he knew how to persuade an audience to pay attention. And he'd learned a few things about the business side of magazines when he'd been railroaded into helping Irene when John was "indisposed."

Without another thought, Andrew jumped up from his chair and shouted, "Cass! I have to go to the shop for a little while!"

But Cassie's stereo was too loud; she no doubt couldn't hear him. So Andrew threw on his light jacket and took the stairs two at a time. He knocked on

Cassie's door, then pushed it open when she didn't answer.

And there she was—or rather, there *someone* was—sitting at the small vanity he'd bought when Cassie turned ten. The reflection in the mirror looking back at him could no way be his daughter. His daughter did not have such heavily black-lined eyes, did not wear jewelry in her eyebrows or dark purple lipstick on her lips.

"What the hell are you doing?" Andrew screeched.

Cassie sighed and turned the music down. "What?" she asked.

"Are you going to a costume party?"

She set down a thick wand of some junk that she'd been putting on her lashes. "Dad," she said, "be cool, huh?"

"Cool?" He glanced around the room. How long had it been since he'd been in Cassie's room? He always tried to give Cassie her privacy, her space. Apparently, he shouldn't have.

Posters of sweaty rock stars dressed in black were Scotch-taped to the ceiling, another one . . . oh, God, a poster taped over her bed was of Patty, Cassie's mother, posed on what he assumed was an Australian beach, wearing nothing but a skimpy bikini.

He pulled his eyes from the image, but motioned to it with his thumb. "Where the heck did that come from?"

She blinked. "I bought it the other night. In the underwear store. She's everywhere, Dad."

Yes, Patty had always been "everywhere."

113

"Cassie," he said, slumping onto the unmade bed. "Cassie, honey, what are you doing?" His head was spinning now; his ears seemed to be buzzing.

"It's Sunday, Dad. I'm going to the mall."

What might have been a skirt was tossed across the bedspread. It was black with silver studs stapled along the side seam, which was half the distance from Cassie's waist down to her knee. Had she bought that at the mall, too? Surely she hadn't worn it to May Fair.

Had she?

Had he been so busy with his head in his self-centered clouds that he hadn't paid attention to Cassie and Marilla in the backseat of his car? Who he'd let go off by themselves because he was a trusting chaperone? One of the cool dads? A guy who hadn't even known that his daughter had bought a risqué poster of her—God help him—mother?

He snatched up the skirt. "You're not wearing this."

She sighed again, turning off the stereo.

Andrew's insides rolled as if a bowling ball had been dropped in his stomach and was racing down the alley.

"Dad," she said, "don't make a big deal out of this."

Strike. The pins went down.

"Cassie, honey, what's happening?"

"Nothing's happening, Dad. I'm going to the mall. That's all."

He felt Patty's turquoise eyes burn into the back of his now-aching head. "No," he said. "No, you're not."

"Dad, come on. I'm a little old for you to start telling me what to do."

So that was the problem. He'd never been the right kind of father. He'd tried too hard to be cool. He'd never disciplined Cassie, never drawn up rules. But he'd never felt he had to. Until now. "I can," he said. "I will."

Her hand moved toward the stereo. Her better judgment seemed to change her mind.

"Honey," he said, trying with all his might as a father and as a friend, "is this because of Jo? Don't you like her?"

Cassie turned back to the mirror and began to pluck the silver rings from her eyebrows. "I know she's been spying on me, Dad. I figure she's trying to get me into trouble."

The bowling ball was back. "What are you talking about?"

Cassie stood up abruptly; the vanity stool tumbled to the floor. "Look, Dad, I know she's going to be my stepmother. But she'll never replace her." She pointed to the poster behind Andrew's head. But he didn't have the courage to turn around and look at it again. Instead, he kept his eyes fixed on his daughter, at the black around her eyes that now drizzled down her face as tears plopped down her cheeks.

Andrew stood up and reached out to her. "Cassie. Honey . . ."

But Cassie turned and bolted from the room, leaving him standing there, with Patty staring at him, the two of them accompanied by a bunch of rock stars in the bedroom that had once belonged to their little girl.

16

Unlike Friday, Sunday was rainy. Lily fully expected that a damp chill would seep into the big Victorian and emit an aura and a scent of an earlier, mildewed time. Something reminiscent of *The Addams Family*, perhaps.

Cre-e-e-e-eak came the sound as the thick oak front door opened to greet her.

She donned her best public-relations wedding smile and hoped it wasn't little Pugsley on the other side. Or maybe it was Antonia, who would no doubt feel at home.

It was neither Pugsley nor Antonia, but Sarah.

"You're late," she said. "I've almost finished decorating."

"I was delayed," Lily replied, "by an urgent family matter."

Anyone but Sarah would have asked what happened and if everyone was okay and was there anything that she could do to help. Not that she wouldn't help anyone who asked. But Sarah didn't pry, and Lily was too distressed right now to talk about it anyway.

She stepped into the foyer and let out a small cry. "Sarah! What have you done?"

Sarah smiled her slow and humble smile. "Do you like it?"

Lily moved past her and went into the parlor, where the ceremony would be held. "Good heavens," she said. "This isn't the same place."

"But it is," Sarah said. "It only needed a few touches."

A few touches? The house had been transformed from a dingy crypt into a softly glowing, romantic haven. The furniture had been removed. In its place small rows of chairs—enough to seat the fifty guests—stood before the altar. At the beginning of each row, Sarah had tied magnificent cream-colored lace bows, each accented by a plump, vanilla rose.

The altar was equally lovely. Sarah had placed one of the lace runners that Elaine and Lily had bought across the top of what was a cherry-stained huntboard with fine cabriole legs. Lily smiled at the way her knowledge of antiques had grown since meeting Frank, since being in his life.

Frank.

"Oh," she sighed.

Touching a petal in the sweet bouquet of vanilla roses that sat in a low brass vase atop the altar and the lace, Lily wondered for the hundredth time what she was going to do when Antonia arrived the next day. What would she say to Frank? What would she do with Antonia? Surely she could not introduce the two of them.

Your dead husband's sister? Frank would ask, and have every right to question why Lily had never mentioned her, because she never had. What would have been the point?

Is he your lover? Antonia would ask, fishing for fur-

117

ther information about whether or not Lily planned to marry him and reinstate the Beckwith money where it belonged.

"Well?" Sarah asked, jolting Lily from her trance. "Do you like it?"

"Like it? It's pure heaven, Sarah. You've done a wonderful job." Without another word, she sat.

"That's one of the children's chairs," Sarah said. "Be careful not to mess it up."

It was then that Lily noticed that the chair was smaller than the rest, though it suited her just fine. Children's chairs had been another of Sarah's innovations: Second weddings, she had reasoned, usually had lots of kids.

Lily counted the small chairs. It seemed that this time there would be four.

At the kindergarten teacher's wedding, there would be eighteen, not his or hers, but they would be there nonetheless. Children, after all, symbolized life and love and innocence.

Lily and Billy Sears had planned on having children. "Lots and lots and lots of kids," she'd said as they'd huddled under a blanket beneath a big tree by the river, watching the sun set behind the stoic skyline of West Point. They had made love twice already and had used condoms so the kids wouldn't arrive too soon. There would be plenty of time for that, after Cadet William Sears had graduated and been given his commission, after he and Lily married beneath the crossed swords at the chapel, after they had tossed aside the white and silver wrappings of their bounty of wedding gifts and set up housekeeping, just the two of them and the babies they longed to have.

"The girls will be as cute and sweet as you," Billy had said.

"And the boys as handsome and as smart as you," Lily had replied.

But life had stepped in and scattered the sand castles of their dreams, and children had not come.

Reginald had wanted to adopt. It had been the single time Antonia was on Lily's side. "The last thing we need," Antonia had said, "is for someone else's children to get their hands on the Beckwith fortune." It was bad enough that Lily's hands were on it.

"Sarah?" Lily asked now. "Didn't you ever just want to do it? Get married, have a bunch of kids, do the whole 'establishment' thing?"

Sarah straightened one last bow and laughed. "Sometimes you scare me, Lily." She'd made it very clear that, while weddings were good for business, they were not for her. Not even for her and Sutter, because she didn't feel the need. Picking up her scissors and a few leftover roses, Sarah said, "Jo's upstairs helping the bride get dressed. I'll be in the kitchen helping Elaine with the hors d'oeuvres."

Lily nodded with disinterest.

"As long as you're going to stay there," Sarah added, "you might as well answer the door if any of the guests arrive."

A moment later the door chimes rang. Lily hesitated,

then stood up and went to greet the people she did not know and would never see again, wishing all the while that Sarah could transform her life the way she'd changed the house.

Jo didn't know what she'd expected. She had, after all, known that sooner or damn-well-later Brian's trial would take place, that she would have to enter a courtroom and come face-to-face with him again. That she would have to sit on the witness stand and tell the world what he had done to her.

She knew it would happen, yet in these past months with Andrew, she'd managed to detach from the remnants of Brian's mess.

As much as Jo had known that sooner or damn-well-later the trial would take place, she'd chosen to erase it from her Brian-weary mind.

"This is the most beautiful wedding dress I could have ever imagined," Gladys Randolph said.

Jo had stopped counting how many times she'd heard that from the brides of Second Chances. She smiled. "We're so glad you like it." They were upstairs in the master bedroom of the hundred-plus-year-old house that Sarah had made magical for Gladys Randolph and Jim Barton's wedding day. With Jo and Gladys was Gladys's sister, Linda, who was the maid of honor. Linda wore a celery-colored dress trimmed with the same ivory lace that graced the bodice of Gladys's antique-satin sheath. Gladys was not usually a very pretty woman; today, however, she was a lovely bride.

"It's going to be an awesome day," Linda exclaimed, then kissed her sister on the cheek. "I've barely slept, I'm so excited. You two are finally getting married!"

Jo pinned a small mantilla on Gladys's short-cropped, golden-rinsed hair. Jo knew the story well. Gladys and Jim had been childhood sweethearts. When they were in the eighth grade, the Randolphs moved to the Midwest. Gladys and Jim both grew up and married other people, had kids (she three; he, one). Eight years later her marriage ended; twelve years later, so did his. Then they each joined the same Internet dating service.

"If that's not true love, then nothing is," Linda had said the first time she and Gladys went into Second Chances and Gladys told them how she and Jim Barton had gotten back together. Elaine nodded and Sarah smiled and Lily wept. And Jo was more convinced than ever that love usually happened at the most unexpected times.

She hoped that love wouldn't abate as quickly, once she told Andrew about the trial. She hoped he wouldn't be as nervous as he'd been when he went to her house and she wasn't home.

"How much more time?" the bride asked, and Linda said, "Twelve minutes. Twelve minutes until you are the happiest bride in the entire world."

Until the last few days, Jo had thought *she* would be the happiest bride in the entire world. *She.* Not Gladys Randolph or Lucy Gilbert or a kindergarten teacher.

But now . . . . between Cassie's odd behavior and

Andrew's apparent angst, was the trial another omen?

What if the testimony lasted beyond the wedding date? What if it interfered with their honeymoon? Andrew would have a right to be very angry. They were only going to Martha's Vineyard for a few days— the business was too busy to take more time than that—but what if . . . ?

She knew there were at least two other women who'd been scammed by Brian. At least two others who would have to tell their stories too. How long would that take?

The back of her neck tightened. She placed the long-stemmed ivory roses in the bride's hands; she adjusted the pearl-dotted ribbons that were tied around the flowers and flowed gracefully to the hem of the antique satin dress.

"Every bride is the happiest," Gladys said.

"Of course! It's the best day of her life and everything is perfect."

"Even when it's raining?"

"Absolutely! Look how beautiful you are!"

Jo fruitlessly rubbed the tension in her neck. Linda was right: Gladys was beautiful. Because even the plainest, most ordinary woman was beautiful on her wedding day, and every wedding turned out perfect.

Unless . . .

She watched as Gladys took a last, scrutinizing look into the mirror. And it was then that Jo knew she could not marry Andrew after all. Not yet, anyway. She needed for Brian's trial to be over and done with. She had to have a clear and happy mind. She needed for Brian Forbes to be out of her life for good.

17

"Y ou have to help me," Lily implored her friends as they sat in a red vinyl booth at a coffee shop on the outskirts of town. The Randolph/Barton wedding had been joyful and complete; the women had approved the work of the cleaning crew and discharged them from the Victorian; luckily they hadn't needed Frank or his pickup truck, because Lily hadn't wanted to face him right then. What she needed was her friends. What she needed was to go somewhere with them to talk.

"I'm beat," Sarah had said.

"Me too," Elaine had added. "And it's still raining. I just want to go home and take off my shoes."

Lily stepped up the urgency in her voice. "Please. I need you. All of you."

Jo asked Lily if it could wait until the morning. Lily said no, the problem would only be worse by then.

So they had agreed, because that's what they always did for one another.

And there they sat, among a sparse Sunday evening crowd: a few pastel-clad nurses apparently having ended their weekend shift at Berkshire Medical Center; a smattering of long-haul truck drivers evidently getting a jump on their weekend treks to Chicago or Detroit.

Elaine ordered an omelet because she, the caterer, hadn't eaten all day.

"I did as you ladies suggested," Lily said. "And now Antonia will be here tomorrow. I have no idea what to do with her. Or with Frank. Or with myself for that matter. I don't even know how long she's planning to stay."

Tired, glazed eyes looked back at her.

"And she's bringing her damn entourage. Her driver. And Pauline, her personal assistant. Amazingly, she's leaving the butler in New York." She folded her arms. She rocked slightly back and forth. "Whatever shall we do?"

"We?" Sarah asked.

Jo set down her mug. "Frank went to that big auction in Albany. Maybe Antonia's driver could help him haul the things he bought."

Lily blinked a quick, sharp blink. "I can't do that! Jo! I can't introduce the two of them!"

Jo shrugged. "Sorry. It's just that with everything that's going on . . . you know, with Frank's mother sick and him working so hard, well, I thought he might like the extra help."

"I think the objective is to keep the 'in-laws' separated," Sarah said.

"Well," Elaine said, "we have all those edible place cards to make for Jo and Andrew's wedding. Maybe we could ask Antonia to help. Or her personal assistant? It's not too soon to make them, then freeze them."

Lily sensed a pinhole of hope. Elaine might have come up with a great idea. "Terrific," she said. "Maybe that will work."

But it was Jo who shook her head. "No," she said, "it's not a good idea."

"Of course it is!" Lily shrieked too loudly, and the nurses and the truck drivers turned their heads toward them.

Jo lowered her eyes and spoke just above a whisper. "It's just that I think we'd better hold off on doing things for my wedding."

The stares then moved to Jo, who sat, tears welling in her eyes, as she slowly related the news of Brian's trial and how she couldn't marry Andrew in the middle of it all.

"She can't do this," Lily said to Elaine. She was driving Elaine back to the shop because Elaine had left her van there and ridden to the wedding in Sarah's truck. "We have to stop her, Lainey. We have to convince her that it's still okay for her to marry Andrew. And it's not just for the press we'll get. It's not because we have everything all planned."

Elaine turned her head out the window of Lily's small Mercedes. "Maybe it's us," she said. "Maybe none of us is destined to be someone else's wife. At least not right now. Maybe we're just supposed to see to it that other people marry. Others, but not us."

Lily felt her eyes grow wide. "Elaine McNulty Thomas, don't even think such a thing."

125

"Well, why not? You can't figure out how you can marry Frank; Sarah never wanted to tie the knot; and now this thing with Jo and Andrew."

"And you and Martin?"

She turned back to Lily. "What about us?"

"You're seeing each other again, aren't you? Are you going to make it to the altar?" They'd planned to marry last autumn. It had been the reason the women came back together in the first place, to be Elaine's bridesmaids for her second time around. But Elaine had called it off, and she and Martin had broken up. Now they were back together, though she didn't talk about him much.

"I won't be marrying Martin," Elaine said.

"Oh, good grief, Elaine, why not? One of us just needs to get this marriage thing over and done with."

"I won't be marrying Martin for one good reason," Elaine said, looking back out to the street. "It's because he hasn't asked me."

Lily laughed. "Well, for godssake, girl, why don't you ask him?"

"It's not that easy, Lily. I love Martin, I'm not ashamed of that. But I'm not the same woman I was a year ago. I'm independent now. If get married, I'll risk losing that, won't I?"

Lily was tired of trying to dissect everyone's love life, hers included. So she simply stepped on the accelerator and wondered if the women of Second Chances were the only middle-aged women on the planet who simply couldn't get it right.

126

"You can't do this," Andrew said to Jo as she stood in his kitchen, tears coursing down her cheeks.

"I have to, Andrew. We don't know what's going to happen. How can I testify against Brian one day and marry you the next?"

"How can you not? You love me, don't you?"

"Please. Try to understand."

He shook his head. "I can't. The invitations went out weeks ago. Invitations to your friends. Your mother's friends. People you've known your whole life. And the honeymoon's all planned. That perfect place out in Gay Head . . . it was your choice, remember?" He moved to the kitchen window. He stared out at the cellar hole, the thing that was supposed to have been the foundation for their new life. "You can't just change your mind, Jo. You can't do what Elaine did."

"I haven't changed my mind, Andrew. Not about you. And I'm not doing what Elaine did. We'll just postpone it. Pick another date. Something in September maybe."

He supposed he should put his arms around her. He supposed he should go to her and kiss her and tell her everything would be all right. But the thought of Brian . . .

"Maybe September or maybe never?" Andrew asked, his anger winning out over his senses. "Are you sure that's not what you'd prefer?"

"No, Andrew. I want to marry you. Just not right now. Not until—"

He held up his hand. "Never mind. I know. Not until

127

Brian Forbes isn't in the picture. God, Jo, just please tell me you're not still in love with him."

It was difficult to tell if the look in Jo's wet eyes was one of fury or of disbelief. As much as part of Andrew wished he could take the question back, wished he never had demanded such an answer, he waited, while she stood, staring.

Instead of answering him, though, Jo just turned around and went out the kitchen door, leaving him standing there, having just lost the second most important person in his life.

18

L ily was going to tell Frank she would be frightfully busy for a few days, or at least that's what she decided she'd say to him. She could spend time with Antonia each day, then sneak off early to meet Frank at his store and they could make love or just cuddle on the settee in the back room. Surely it would work. Besides, it wasn't as if Antonia would stay for any length of time.

Would she?

While dropping off Elaine, Lily looked across Main Street to Antiques & Such. No lights were on. Frank's pickup wasn't in the lot. He must be home, tending to his mother and his father.

"I'll see you tomorrow," she said to Elaine. "I'm going to run over to the Forbeses'." It was getting late, but Frank once said his mother's illness had no timetable. Maybe he was still awake and would like some company.

Elaine waved and Lily drove away and five minutes later she pulled into the driveway of the home where Frank was raised, where he'd returned after his divorce, not counting the many nights he spent in the back room of his store.

As Lily had expected, the house was lit and welcoming. A car she didn't recognize was also in the driveway. *Oh, good,* she thought, as she got out of her car. Frank always seemed to like introducing her to his family's friends.

"Sondra," Frank said as they stood in the living room next to the hospital bed where his mother watched with curious eyes, "this is Lily."

It took only a moment for Lily to get the picture, to place the woman's name and her long brown hair, oval face, and eyes that might be blue or green depending on the light. Or at least that's what Frank had said one night when he and Lily were sharing bits and pieces about each other's past.

She was not unattractive. She did not seem unpleasant or aloof. She was, however, Lily knew, Frank's former wife, to whom he'd been married for something like ten years.

"It's nice to meet you," Sondra said, extending her hand to Lily. Lily couldn't tell whether or not Sondra had been told the importance of a woman called Lily in Frank's life these days.

"Likewise," Lily said, shaking the cool, dry hand. She suddenly remembered she hadn't seen the front side of a mirror since nine o'clock that morning. Her linen skirt must be wrinkled and her hair a frizz ball from the rain. Her personal dilemmas had uncharacteristically usurped her sense of looking good, or, at least, respectable.

In the awkward moment that followed, Lily supposed Frank might have said, *Lily is my fiancée,* if Lily had said yes, if she hadn't been so scared to lose a little cash.

Instead, he said, "Sondra heard Mother is sick. She came back east to see some of her relatives and decided to drop in."

Lily nodded and said, "How nice." She turned from both of them and stepped toward the hospital bed, as if she knew Frank's mother other than the few words that they had shared. "How are you feeling tonight, Eleanor?" She said "Eleanor," as if she always called her that and not Mrs. Forbes.

The dry lips smiled. "I'm fine, thank you, dear."

"I didn't expect to see you tonight," Frank interrupted. "Sondra and I were about to go out for a bite to eat. Would you like to join us?"

Most women, Lily supposed, would say, *Oh, no, I won't impose. You two go ahead.*

But Lily was Lily, not most women, so she said, "Sure, that would be nice."

She regretted it, of course.

They went in Sondra's rental car, because Lily's

130

Mercedes was built only for two and Frank's pickup wasn't offered.

Frank rode in the front with Sondra; Lily sat in the back alone. She watched the backs of their heads and tried to picture them together as man and wife. Sondra sat tall in the driver's seat. She had large, dominant shoulders that were well-defined even under a shapeless khaki raincoat. Lily suspected that, when they'd made love, Sondra had been the one on top.

Other than hearing they were going to the Stone Castle because it had always been one of Sondra's "favorites," Lily couldn't decipher much of the former couple's conversation. The wipers squeaked across the windshield, camouflaging their words, which Lily thought were spoken lower than they should be under the circumstances.

Martha Holland greeted them warmly at the castle. If she thought it odd that the three of them were together, she didn't show it. Lily was glad, however, that she'd made Antonia's reservations at Wheatleigh, not there. The way her luck had been going, Antonia et al. would have decided to saunter in tonight.

"So," Sondra said to Lily once they'd perused the menus and ordered wine, "here I am, back in West Hope."

"Here you are," Frank said.

Lily merely smiled. "How are things in Chicago?" she asked.

Sondra half-smiled back. "It's Colorado, actually. Things in Colorado have been fine. Until recently, that

131

is. I had a wonderful job at a big bank. Then the lay-offs came. Well," she said with a low voice, "it wasn't as bad for me. Some people with families . . . Well, none of us expected it."

"That's how layoffs are," Frank said, his face a serious mask. "It's always difficult."

"The severance packages weren't as good as when Global Paper went out of business."

Frank looked at Lily. "Global Paper is based here. A lot of residents worked there until a few years ago when their parent company shut them down. Too many new regulations. Too much money needed to bring the old mill up to the new safety codes."

Lily nodded as if she cared. She wondered if Frank and Sondra had these boring kinds of conversations when they'd been married. If so, it wasn't hard to understand why things hadn't worked.

The wine arrived. They sipped and ordered dinner. Then Sondra half-smiled again at Lily. "Frank tells me you have a little business here in West Hope."

Lily laughed and matched her half smile. "It's not so little anymore. We began it as a hobby, for something fun to do. I guess we've done too good a job, because we're now turning people away."

"Mmm," Sondra said, her gaze moving from Lily over to Frank. "Second weddings. Have you handled many where the bride and groom were married to each other the first time around?" Her amusement now was played out with a simpish, silly grin.

Lily's spine stiffened from the bottom to the top.

"Actually, no," she said. "Our research shows that reweddings are very few and not at all successful." The Second Chances research, of course, showed no such thing. In fact the Benson wedding—their showpiece—might have been considered a "remarriage" even though the couple had never divorced. *Whatever,* Lily thought with a sigh, aware that her biggest concern now—in addition to juggling Antonia—would be to do some fancy maneuvering if she intended to keep Frank.

"Is Cassie there?"

The phone had rung and Andrew had quickly grabbed for the receiver, hoping it was Jo, hoping she'd come back to her senses. Instead, it was a boy.

"She's doing her homework," Andrew barked. "She can't come to the phone."

The boy laughed and said, "I only want to talk to her a second."

"Sorry. Those are the rules." The boy's voice was deep enough to hint that it had already changed. Andrew preferred Eddie—Cassie's first "real" boyfriend, who still was a tenor. Unfortunately, she no longer liked him.

"Well then," the boy said, almost sarcastically, "when she's *finished,* tell her to call Victor."

Andrew hung up without saying good-bye. He found it irritating that boys had recently begun to call his daughter. He found it equally irritating that today, sixth- or seventh-grade boys seemed so cavalier about calling girls they liked.

As with most things, it wasn't like that when he was a kid.

He sat back on the tattered sofa, remembering Melissa Langlois.

They'd been in junior high; Melissa—the most beautiful girl in the whole school, maybe in all of Manhattan—was in his homeroom.

He'd called her several times, each time not without a prelude of sweating palms and pacing of the penthouse, rehearsing over and over the words that he would say.

Hi, Melissa. It's me, Andrew Kennedy. Did you do your history homework yet?

No.

Hi, Melissa. It's Andrew. Have you studied for the English test?

No.

Hey, Melissa. It's Andrew. Want to screw?

In spite of his current anguish, Andrew felt a small smile. *Women,* he thought.

Then his smile vanished as he realized his daughter wasn't yet a woman, was she?

He closed his eyes and wondered how the heck he was supposed to know how to handle things with Cassie when he couldn't even get his own life straight.

19

Lily and Frank sat for a long time in Lily's car
after Sondra had dropped them off then continued on her way to the nearest Super 8 Motel.
She'd been hinting, Lily knew, to stay in the Forbeses'
big colonial, but Frank had said it would be too dis-
ruptive for his mother.

"Believe me," Frank said, "I had no idea that she'd
show up."

"She knew your mother is sick."

"Everyone in West Hope knows it. Like I said,
Sondra still has relatives around."

The rain that been pouring down all day now cas-
caded in heavy, diagonal sheets against the windshield.

"She said she's staying a few days," Lily said.

"I guess."

"Well, if you need to spend time with her, don't
worry about me. In fact, one of the reasons I stopped
by tonight was to tell you I'm going to be pretty busy
myself for a little while." For the first time in many
years, Lily no longer liked her life, no longer liked herself. She wished she was home now, cuddled with her
rabbit.

"Lily . . ." He touched her shoulder.

A tear slid down her cheek, the way the rain slid
down the windshield. "She wants to get back with
you."

"Don't be ridiculous."

"I'm not."

He said something; she didn't hear.

"What?" she asked.

"I said, 'I think I'm already taken.' Aren't I?"

There was, of course, no answer to that question, so Lily asked, "Are you still in love with her?"

He moved his arm down from her shoulder and touched her hand. "Lily . . ."

He didn't say he still loved Sondra. He didn't say he didn't. He just said "Lily" once again.

She sighed. "Ten years is a long time. I wasn't married to anyone for ten years."

"They weren't all good years."

"She wanted more from life than West Hope had to offer." Would Lily feel that way one day? Would she be content to put her traveling days behind her? Her Paris shopping and her Barcelona lunches and her Palm Beach seaweed wraps? Then it occurred to her that it had been nearly a year since she'd come back to West Hope. Aside from a few jaunts into the city, she hadn't gone anywhere. What's more, she hadn't missed the suitcases and the airports and the being-waited-on.

"I wanted a family," Frank was saying. "I wanted kids. Sondra didn't. That was the real reason our marriage ended."

Lily thought about the eighteen five-year-olds who would be at the kindergarten teacher's wedding. She could not imagine having one dependent on her. "What about now?" she asked.

136

"Well, we're not too old, you know. Did you ever want kids, Lily?"

And then it all came back to her. Billy. The car accident. The fact that her parents wouldn't have been driving back from West Point, across the Bear Mountain Bridge, if Billy hadn't spent the day with Lily. If Lily hadn't had a final exam the next day and needed to study. If her father hadn't said that he'd take Billy home, because her father did everything she'd ever asked, because she was his princess.

"Lily?" Frank asked.

"I never really thought about it," she said through quiet tears, "about having kids." It wasn't, of course, the truth, but even under the threat of Sondra, Lily couldn't tell him about Billy. It would simply hurt too much.

Lily's father had liked him; he'd said that Cadet William Sears was the smartest in his class.

Lily, of course, just thought that he was cute, but she was not quite seventeen, so that was all that mattered.

She curled up on the sofa now, the place she'd designated as her thinking spot. Frank had asked her to stay with him that night, to sleep beside him in the back room of his store.

"If nothing else," he'd said, "it will prove that Sondra won't pay me any midnight visits."

But Lily had smiled and said she was tired, and she could trust him, couldn't she?

He'd said, "Of course," and she'd kissed him good

night, feeling only slightly guilty that the real reason she wanted to go home was so she'd be rested and fully ready to entertain her sister-in-law and her purse strings the next day. So that she could have time to conjure up a clearheaded, foolproof plan to keep Antonia from Frank, and Frank from Antonia.

Lily hadn't expected that instead she'd be sitting in her thinking spot not thinking about Antonia but about Billy Sears.

It had been weeks before he noticed her.

It was in the fall, her favorite time of year, when the leaves were red and gold and made such a pretty blanket on the grounds of the academy. She'd found a spot outside the building where her father taught his class and had his office too.

She'd seen Billy weeks earlier when she and her mother went over to the campus to bring her father a textbook that he had left at home.

"Wouldn't it be easier," her mother had asked, "if we lived on the grounds like other families do?"

But her father had said no, he wouldn't leave his sister in the two-family house alone, she'd been too good to them, being there for them all the time he was in 'Nam. "It's no great sacrifice," he added, "to drive back and forth across the bridge."

One night Lily overheard Aunt Margaret tell her mother the real reason they didn't live there was because Lily's father didn't want the boys getting a good look at his daughter.

The odd thing was, as it turned out, if they'd lived

there and not across the river, Lily might never have spotted Billy Sears, might never have seen him that day when her mother stayed in the car while Lily ran inside the building to deliver her father's book. There was Billy, sitting in the front row by the door, his blue, blue eyes so focused on his work that he hardly looked up at her, though when he did, she'd swear her heart stopped beating.

Which was why, a few weeks later, after getting her driver's license, Lily made it a point to "drop by" once or twice a week, to sit on the stone bench on the lawn outside the building and wait for him to fall in love with her.

It had taken two and a half weeks, but finally she succeeded.

And then the rest had happened. And now—for the first time since then—Lily knew she was in love again, but it wasn't easy this time either.

She clutched the soft plush rabbit and stared out the window and wondered if she would break Frank's heart, the way she'd broken Billy's.

Marion agreed to make the phone calls to let people know the wedding was being postponed.

Jo sat at her desk the following morning and, with her eyes closed, spoke slowly into the phone. "Tell them September, okay, Mom? Say we'll get back to them once we know the date."

Marion paused, then asked, "Are you sure, Josephine?"

"Yes, I am sure."

She thanked her mother and hung up quickly, aware that someone had walked into the showroom. She opened her eyes and faced Andrew.

"So you're really going through with it," he said, his tone flat and unhappy.

"I have to, Andrew. If we ever hope to have a real future together . . ."

He nodded as if he understood. "Well, until then, life will go on. But speaking of a future, did you happen to save the name of that woman who called a while back, the one from the bridal magazine who wanted us to write a column for their spin-off on second weddings?"

The sudden way he'd changed the topic was disquieting. Jo turned back to her computer. "Well," she said, "I must have typed it in the phone log." She moved her mouse this way and that, then clicked and scrolled with surprising nervousness. "Andrea Hall," she said, and relayed a phone number.

She looked at him again; he wrote the information on a Post-it note.

"That's it?" she asked. "You're not going to try and change my mind?"

"About the wedding? No. I can't compete with a memory, Jo."

"Andrew, please. This isn't about Brian. It's about me, wanting my old baggage totally resolved."

His face darkened. "And what about your new baggage?"

"What?"

"The builders, for example. What do I tell the builders? They planned to begin framing the addition around the first of June."

She swallowed. She supposed they should go ahead—they couldn't leave the cellar hole just sitting there, could they?

Before she could answer, Andrew quickly tore the Post-it off the pad and shoved it in his pocket. "Never mind. I'll tell them that we'll 'get back' to them too." He marched off toward the door. "If anyone wants me, I'm going to work at home today."

Watching him leave, Jo wondered if she would regret this day and that conversation.

He wasn't going to let her get away with it. Andrew was tired of pissing around, trying to be Mr. Nice. If Jo thought for one minute she was going to be rid of him, she was wrong.

He would start by becoming the man that he could be, the man who had *presence,* as John Benson had once said, the man who had believability and power. The only thing that Andrew lacked since leaving journalism was the dogged courage to use it.

But it *had* worked in television. Surely it could work again, without John Benson driving the Andrew David Kennedy cheerleading bus.

Plunked on the overstuffed sofa in the living room of his cottage, Andrew stuck the Post-it note to his knee and punched in the numbers on his phone.

"Andrea Hall," he said. He drummed his fingers on his other knee and waited.

"Who?" the other voice inquired.

"Hall. Andrea Hall."

There was a pause, then a short laugh. "Who's calling, please?"

Andrew didn't know what was so funny, but went on anyway. "This is Andrew Kennedy. I'm with Second Chances, the wedding-planning business for second-time brides. Ms. Hall contacted us a few weeks ago. I'm calling her back." He didn't have to add that when she'd called, the women had had a good laugh because they were far too busy planning weddings to get mixed up with a magazine. Luckily, Andrew had a much different agenda, a new way to prove his worth.

Then the voice said, "Well, I'm Andrea Hall. I'm the one who called your company." She sounded a little bit too perky, which might be good or bad, but Andrew had decided to give up analyzing women.

"Have you been making progress on your magazine?" he asked, his voice taking control, his *presence* oozing out.

"Yes. Yes, we have." There was silence again, then the woman's voice turned serious. "In fact," she said, "what a coincidence you called. I am heading out of town on business. Up to Albany, in fact."

"Well, when you get back, maybe we could talk about how Second Chances might help the magazine."

"Why wait until then? Albany isn't that far from the Berkshires, is it?"

"About forty-five minutes."

"Great. When I'm finished there, in a day or two, perhaps I could drop by?"

"Sure," Andrew said. "That would be fine." He gave her quick directions to Second Chances, then they rang off and Andrew thought what a surprise it was that Andrea Hall had remembered they were located in West Hope and that, yes, it was a coincidence she'd be in the area.

Maybe his believability was even more powerful than John Benson had once thought.

20

L ily sat, braced, in the lobby of Wheatleigh—a stately, elegant, nineteenth-century palazzo. She'd thought it would be wise to be there when Antonia arrived, to greet her guest the way Antonia would expect a host to do. Lily would, of course, have preferred to stay on her sofa, curled up with the rabbit, the way she'd done all night.

She'd slept surprisingly well, considering everything at stake.

Closing her eyes now, trying to relax the iron rod that once had been her spine, Lily absorbed the quiet calm of the world of wealth around her, the kind of world in which she'd lived as Reginald Beckwith's wife. It was so clear, yet was so long ago.

"Good afternoon, Mrs. Beckwith. So happy to see you again," the concierge at Paris's Galileo or Oxford's

143

Great Milton would say. They were small, intimate hotels, the kind Reginald favored for their food and wine and privacy (*privvv-acy,* he'd said, as if he'd been born a Brit).

If Wheatleigh reminded Antonia of the places Reginald had loved, Lily might win extra points for having kept him in her thoughts.

Luckily, the season hadn't yet started, so she was able to secure three of the nineteen rooms: the Terrace Suite for Antonia, a less costly, superior room for Pauline, and another for Antonia's driver, whose name Lily could not recall.

She'd made the reservations, so naturally she would pay the bill, despite that the world it represented no longer belonged to her. Which was rather humorous, because though Antonia would expect the splendor of Wheatleigh, she'd have a cardiac arrest if she knew that her room cost a thousand dollars a night.

Wait, Lily thought, a half smile tugging at her mouth. *Cardiac arrest? Would that be such a bad idea?*

"Would madam care for a cool drink?" The young man who had valet-parked her car was standing next to where Lily sat, grinning one of those not-quite-happy, European grins. He was lean and impeccably groomed and spoke with a Parisian accent that seemed like the real thing.

"*Non,*" Lily replied. "*Merci.*" She supposed it was just as well that he'd interrupted her fun-but-perilous thoughts. Even Lily, after all, wouldn't want Antonia dead. Who then would be left to challenge Lily's patience?

The young man nodded and disappeared under an ornately carved archway that led down a hall or into another room or a closet, for all Lily could tell. She wondered if staying out of view was a tactic used to make the guests feel as if Wheatleigh were their home.

Her thoughts then drifted to the fact that the hotel would be a perfect place for an exquisite second wedding. Through the tall windows beyond the sleek black piano, Lake Mahkeenac would make an ideal setting for wedding photos. The pool of still water, known as the "Stockbridge Bowl," was enveloped by the clear blue sky and bright green Berkshire hills—not austere mountain peaks, but friendly, round balls that looked like scoops of pistachio ice cream tucked into a luscious banana split.

"There are twelve different kinds of fish in the bowl," Frank had told her one sunny day last autumn when they'd driven to the lookout point on Route 183. She remembered the rainbow trout and the brown trout, the blue gill and the yellow perch, because they were colorful. And the black crappie, she thought with an inward laugh now. She'd teased him about the coarse, manmade-sounding name, and accused him of making it up.

Frank had laughed, which Lily loved seeing him do because she suspected he hadn't done that enough in his life. Later they'd driven to the West Hope bookstore, where he showed her the guide to the

Appalachian Trail that mentioned the dozen fish, including the black crappie. She had stood on her toes and kissed him right there in the store, and Frank had blushed because the old woman in a cardigan behind the cash register was watching.

Those were the moments Lily felt most at peace, when she laughed alongside Frank, when she was unguarded, uninhibited, just plain Lily being Lily. Something about Frank's manner made her always feel at ease.

She supposed, however, that Antonia would not understand. Any more than she would be impressed with Lily's Stockbridge Bowl fish trivia.

Folding her hands, Lily shifted right, then left. Then she fixed her gaze on the front entrance and continued waiting for the crunch of big Mercedes tires to grate the white stone driveway, and for the trill of Antonia's nonmelodic voice to call out Lily's name.

An hour later, just before lunchtime, the black car pulled up to the door. Lily knew it was the largest-model Mercedes made and had a tan interior, and that Antonia replaced the car every two years with an identical one. The woman, after all, loathed change of any kind.

Lily cleared her throat and willed herself to stand, as the young man appeared again and opened the front door.

"Antonia," Lily said. It was then Lily remembered that, with Jo calling off the wedding and Sondra showing up, she hadn't given another thought to what to do with her sister-in-law.

Antonia answered with a nod and hauled her squat self from the backseat, tossing the beady-eyed end of her vintage fox fur stole across her shoulder. "I hope they have lunch," she said. "We're famished."

Well, lunch would take care of the first hour or so.

"The main dining hall is on your right," the young man said. "I'll take your cases to your suite."

"Jonathan will tell you what's what," Antonia said.

Jonathan, apparently, was her driver's name. He was tall and appeared to be a rather youthful forty-five or fifty, Lily guessed. He nodded a nod of comfort if not deference.

"Pauline," Antonia continued, addressing the middle-aged, well-groomed woman, "please go with the gentlemen and unpack my bags. I'll see that trays are sent to your rooms." She swept past them and entered Wheatleigh. Her respite in the country, apparently, was under way.

Lily quickly fell in step behind her, half-wishing now that instead of Wheatleigh she'd selected a motel out on Route 7, where wire racks in the lobby held colorful brochures about attractions, places to explore if you were from out of town.

The Norman Rockwell Museum, Lily thought.

MOCA—The Massachusetts Museum of Contemporary Art.

Chesterwood, maybe. Was that open for the season yet? It was definitely too early for Jacob's Pillow ballet

147

or the Berkshire opera. Or Tanglewood, yes, too early for Tanglewood.

And way too soon to navigate back roads and peep at autumn leaves—they had to get through summer first and about a million weddings.

Oh, Lily thought as they entered the dining room, what on earth was she going to do now that Antonia was here?

"I know of women who've come up here to Laurel Lake Spa," Antonia remarked after they'd been seated and a waiter snapped a fine linen napkin onto her lap.

The spa! Why hadn't Lily thought of that?

"What a waste of money," Antonia continued. "As if a mud bath and a facial can take years off one's life. Besides, I rather like to eat more than a broiled lamp chop and a carrot stick for dinner." She then ordered the poached cod with mustard-seed crust and Lily said she'd have the same, but it was not until Antonia dove into a baguette with fresh cream butter that Lily had one of her trademark brainstorms—this one, no doubt, sent as a psychic gift from Reginald into her "pretty little brain," as he'd often called it.

Lily smiled. "My friends are eager to meet you," she said. "In fact, they're planning a dinner in your honor. A gourmet dinner, actually. Our Elaine has become quite a chef." It had been their idea, after all, to have Antonia come for a visit. "Be her friend," Elaine had prodded. Well, for that suggestion, surely Elaine wouldn't mind whipping up an entrée or two; surely Elaine's father would help.

148

"How nice," Antonia said, "but they needn't go to any trouble. I'll be content to sit out on the terrace and catch up on some reading."

At first Lily thought the woman was merely being sarcastic. Then she realized that was perhaps how Antonia spent most days: sitting, reading, existing. She felt an odd twinge of compassion. "It's no trouble, Antonia. My friends really want to."

"When?"

When? The rod stiffened her spine again. "Well, I think they said tonight."

Antonia sipped from the glass of fresh lemon water that, like the young man, seemed to have magically appeared. "All right," she said. "If they insist."

"Pauline and Jonathan are welcome too."

The woman set down her glass and did not meet Lily's eyes. "I think not. I'm sure they'll enjoy an evening to themselves."

Lily couldn't disagree with that.

"What time?" Antonia asked.

Lily blinked a long, deliberate blink, as if only then realizing what she'd gone and done. "Well," she said, "seven, I guess." Then she wondered how she would tell the others and if this would really work.

"Please," Lily begged Elaine, because what else could she do?

She'd left Antonia to her book, claiming that she'd offered to help prepare the meal. Which was why Lily now stood in the doorway of the kitchen of Elaine's

149

catering business, next door to Second Chances. She tried to ignore the look of woe Elaine wore.

"I'm sorry," Elaine said. "But, Lily, I'm exhausted. We're all exhausted." She leaned against one of the shiny stainless counters that Andrew had helped her buy and Frank had helped install. Frank had gutted another room for Elaine too, creating a real chef's pantry with tons and tons of shelves. He'd been so good to all of them—surely Lily wouldn't have to say this was the least they could do in return, the least they could do so Lily could marry him and they could live happily-ever-freaking-after.

"Please, Lainey," Lily implored. "Antonia will be so impressed when she sees us all together. Andrew can tell her stories about his journeys all over the world. Your father can regale her with tales of Saratoga. And I'm sure she'll be charmed by Sarah and Sutter. She's always given generously to American Indian causes."

"Lily," Elaine said. "I can't. And, anyway, my father and Larry are playing cards with Jo's mother and Ted tonight."

Lily found it inconvenient that so many new characters had come into their lives: Elaine's father, Bob McNulty, now had a wife he called Larry; Jo's mother, Marion, had married Ted Cappelinni, the West Hope butcher. So many new people; so many more lives needing to interact.

"Hell's bells, everyone can come!" she said. "Antonia will see what a wonderfully stable life I have!"

150

Elaine frowned. "I don't know, Lily. What about Frank? Are you going to include him too?"

"Well. No."

Moving to the Sub-Zero refrigerator, Elaine took out a bottle of water and quickly drank from it. She wiped her mouth on a paper napkin that was gold-embossed *Gladys and Jim*. Lily wondered if they'd ever again use napkins that didn't advertise their work.

"You don't know if Sarah and Sutter have any plans," Elaine continued. "And what about Jo and Andrew? They're hardly speaking."

"Maybe what they need is a night out with the rest of us. A chance to have a little fun."

"Oh, Lily, I don't know. I'm so tired. Besides, where could we have it?"

"Your house would be perfect."

"My house? But we've been so busy, Lily. I haven't cleaned—"

"Elaine," Elaine's father called out, as he stepped from the chef's pantry Frank had built. "Shame on you. Of course we'll do this for our Lily. In fact, Larry and I can go over now and clean your house."

"But Dad—" Elaine protested, and Bob McNulty put his finger to his lips to shush her.

"No," he said. "Lily's family, after all."

Then Elaine grimaced and Lily smiled, grateful that she'd always been nice to Bob McNulty and that he'd always been one of those sweet men, like Reginald, who seemed to enjoy feeling as if they were protecting her.

21

I t's too bad Frank isn't here," Andrew said as he passed the tray of foie gras over to Sarah. Lily wanted to kick Andrew under the table, but she feared she'd nail Antonia, not him.

"Who's Frank?" Antonia asked. She'd worn an old (of course) tweed suit. In the buttonhole of her lapel, she sported a tiny yellow rosebud no doubt plucked from the crystal vase in her Wheatleigh room. The rosebud had moved up and down as she heaved her entire full bosom behind the words *Who's Frank.*

A hush thunked across Elaine's dining-room table; the guests grew rigor-mortis-like, with forks and spoons and wineglasses halting in midair.

Andrew cleared his throat. "Frank is a good friend of ours," he said. They'd been talking about Antonia's place on Madison Avenue, about its lineage and the fact that her building was listed in the New York City register of historic places. "He has an antiques shop. I'm sure he'd be interested in hearing about your place."

The guests returned to life; dinner activity resumed.

"Antiques dealers only want to profit from what you own," Antonia said, and Lily stood up.

"More veal, Andrew?" she asked, because it was safer than popping him in the nose.

"Sure," he said.

"Why don't you help me get it?" She narrowed her

152

eyes into tiny blue slits, carefully drilling their meaning into him.

"Oh," he said, standing up. "Sure."

She spun on her heel and marched into Elaine's kitchen. Once safe behind the door, she hissed, "What are you doing? I thought you were my friend." Just because Jo had said she had a headache and didn't show up at Elaine's, just because Andrew seemed to have somehow screwed up his life, that didn't give him the right to screw up Lily's too.

"I'm just being friendly."

"Friendly, my ass. You want me to tell her about Frank, don't you?"

Andrew sighed and leaned against the counter. "Lily," he said, "I don't care what you do. Though sooner or later you might realize that games are best left to the kids."

Her lips pulled together into a firm, pink circle. "It's my life, Andrew."

He smiled, then brushed a runaway curl off her forehead. "Then you shouldn't have invited the rest of us, Lily." As he turned to leave, tears crowded her throat.

"Wait," she said with a whimper that was genuine.

He waited.

"I don't know what to do. I invited her to come to West Hope to try to be her friend. And now I don't know what to do with her, Andrew. Please don't tell me again that I should introduce her to Frank. I'm not going to do that. But I don't know what to do with her either. I really need your help. This is important to me."

With a short sigh, Andrew said, "I don't know, Lily. Why not take her to Tanglewood? You have the kindergarten teacher's wedding to plan out there. She might get a kick out of being part of the ordeal. She might enjoy being 'backstage.'"

Well, of course, Andrew had no way of knowing how Antonia loved the ballet and the opera and that being "backstage" might be just what the West Hope doctor ordered.

Lily skipped one and a half times and threw her arms around him. "Oh, forgive me, darling Andrew, I take what I said all back. What a marvelous idea." She planted a light kiss on his left cheek, then his right, and, with spirits lifted, she raised her head and pushed back through the door into the dining room. Just as she did, someone must have sucked the air out of the room, because standing at the far end of Elaine's table was Frank Forbes himself.

"My mother," Frank said, looking at Lily. "She's gone."

Well, she knew he couldn't possibly mean that his mother had pulled herself up from her bed and left town to go to Pittsfield. Lily stood there a moment, trying to breathe in the airless room.

Elaine was standing beside him. She put her arms around him, gave him a big hug.

"Oh, Frank, I'm so sorry," Elaine said, then Sarah

154

was behind her, echoing her words, then Jo's mother, Marion, who had known Eleanor Forbes most of her life, because they'd both been born in West Hope and it was, after all, a small town.

The men, of course, reserved their emotion. Ted, Marion's new husband, was the only one who'd known the extended Forbes family. He went to Frank after Marion, patted Frank on the shoulder, shook his head.

Lily's eyes darted from the scene to Antonia, who sat in her chair, looking somewhat bewildered and slightly annoyed.

"I'm glad you're all here," Lily heard Frank say. "I stopped by the shop. Jo was working late and told me where to find you." Apparently Jo did not tell him why they had gathered or why he hadn't been invited.

Lily considered that she might be angry with Jo for revealing their location but decided she couldn't fault her friend. Frank's mother, after all . . . *oh, gosh,* she thought, tears coming to her eyes despite the awkward silence of the situation.

Frank's eyes moved over to Lily, and she knew she must walk the seven or eight steps it would take to get to him, to console him, to show him that she cared. In order to reach Frank, however, she'd have to pass by Antonia's chair.

She tried to send him a smile but knew that was not enough. His return gaze was hopeful, wondering, waiting. Elaine's dining room grew oddly silent once again. Then Lily sucked in her lower lip and slowly took one step with her right foot, another with her left.

"I'm sorry to interrupt your dinner," Frank said to everyone there. Then he took a step toward Lily, then another, and soon they met right behind Antonia, who stared straight ahead as if this were someone else's party and she were merely part of the flocking on the wallpaper.

Finally, Lily and Frank embraced, and Lily said, "Come into the kitchen," as if this were her house and not Elaine's. "I'll fix you a drink."

"I can't stay," he said. "My father's at home with the next-door neighbors, the Hardings. They've been so kind through all of this."

Lily stroked his arm, his face, his eyes. "My poor, poor darling," she said.

"I would have called," he said, "but I wanted to get out of the house. I wanted to see you. And everyone, I guess."

Lily remembered enough about death and dying to know that in those first few minutes, those first long hours, as reality set in—or at least tried to—no one should be accountable for the things one said or did or the things one didn't say or do.

"Will you come with me?" Frank asked it so abruptly that Lily wasn't ready with an answer, did not have an excuse. Though what excuse could she possibly have?

"Well," she said, her mind spinning with questions and answers that could or would follow, "of course. You go ahead. I'll be along in a few minutes."

It was a small frown, but Lily noticed.

"Or now," she said. "Would you like me to come with you now?"

"Yes," he replied. "I would."

She nodded, feeling her brain shake back and forth in her skull, rattling around in there as if trying to make some sense fall into place. Then she bit her lip again, took Frank by the hand, and led him back to the stunned crowd in Elaine's dining room.

"Andrew," she called, "be a dear and see Antonia back to the hotel. I'm going to run along with Frank and help out with the arrangements." Then she looked at Antonia and said, "Sorry to call the night short, but I'm planning to take you to Tanglewood tomorrow. I think you'll enjoy it. Good night."

As she walked toward the front door, Lily turned and lifted her small hand, waving to the group as if she were embarking on a long-awaited trip.

22

S he's quite a girl, our Lily," Andrew said as he drove the back road that wound through the hills toward Wheatleigh. He'd lived in West Hope several years and had never known about—had never even heard of—the place, it was that exclusive, it was that *divine,* Lily had said.

"Yes, well, my brother was quite fond of her."

"Reginald. Yes. The girls all liked him. And Lily mentions him often. I think he meant a lot to her." He was trying to say the kinds of things Lily might want him to say, not necessarily the things that he thought should be said. But this was the least Andrew could do, after the flak he'd already created and now with the sadness of Frank's mother's death, which was not Lily's fault.

He wondered sometimes if he'd spent so much time with women that there was a small chance he'd begun to think like them.

From the corner of his eye he noticed that Antonia was eying him suspiciously. "So who are you, anyway?"

Andrew laughed. "Me? Just a friend. A guy who respects what the women have done with Second Chances. A lot of people say they want to have their own business, but these women have done it. In fact, they're actually successful."

She turned back and looked out the windshield. "You look familiar," she said.

"Ah," Andrew replied. "Well, I confess, I was once on TV. A journalist. I was known as Andrew David. I worked mostly in New York and Washington, sometimes out of the Mideast."

Antonia nodded knowingly. "Lily thinks all I do is go to the opera and the ballet. But I also have a passion for current events. As did my brother. That must be why I recognize you."

Current events? How long had it been since Andrew had watched the news? He'd become so wrapped up with the women, with Cassie, with Jo . . .

"You haven't been on for a while," Antonia said.

He shook his head. "No. I moved away from the rat race to raise my daughter in West Hope."

Antonia nodded again, as if she understood.

Andrew kept driving, thinking it was curious that Lily didn't like Antonia and that Antonia seemed . . . well, so suspicious of Lily. He wondered if they had ever given each other a real chance.

"Well, you seem civilized enough," Antonia continued. "Though I can't imagine why anyone would drive one of these." She patted the dashboard of Andrew's old Volvo.

Andrew laughed. "Prerequisite for a college professor. That's what I moved here to do." He didn't mention that he wasn't doing that now because Winston College didn't seem to want him back.

"So you gave up the television cameras for a higher, more noble purpose."

"That and the fact my former wife left me for another man and I was embarrassed and in pain and needed to run away."

Her eyes were back on him. "You're civilized and honest too. Well, that's unusual in a man. Did you ever marry again?"

He didn't expect the tightness in his throat or the twist of the muscle around his belly. "Not yet. But Jo— you didn't meet her tonight; Marion is her mother— well, Jo and I are engaged. We're getting married in the fall. September, I think."

"You might want to sound a bit more excited about your wedding date when talking with your bride."

"Yes," Andrew said, "well, we haven't set the date yet." He drove past the red cottage that had once belonged to Nathaniel Hawthorne. Elaine had said the hotel was around the bend from there, which was a good thing, because Andrew was now eager to end this conversation. "Wheatleigh is up here on the left," he said. "Are your accommodations okay?"

Antonia laughed. "Lily went out of her way to be sure they were the best. As I knew she would."

He turned into the long road that served as a driveway.

"I also know more about Lily than she wishes I did," the woman continued. "For example, I know she has an ulterior motive for inviting me here, but I'll be damned if I've figured it out yet. Can you give me any hints?"

Andrew smiled and pulled into the circular, white stone driveway around the lighted fountain. "I've never been good at reading a woman's mind. Especially a woman like Lily." *Or Jo,* he wanted to add but did not.

A young man appeared and the passenger door to Andrew's car crunched open.

"Well," Antonia said with a wink, "I hate to admit it, but women can be sneaky. If you hear anything concrete, please keep me in mind. Otherwise, I'll have to get to the bottom of this charade on my own."

Andrew drove home, his mouth still set in a smile. It wasn't until he let himself inside that he remembered that Frank's mother had died.

Mothers, he thought. *Parents.* He tossed his keys onto the kitchen counter and sat down at the table, wondering if he was the only one who thought about his parents more often since they'd been dead than when they were alive.

They'd never had much time for Andrew, or he for them. They were busy physicians, after all. He was just a kid.

He looked up at the black cat clock that graced the kitchen wall, its black eyes moving back and forth, its black tail swaying with the passing of time. No one but Cassie knew that clock had been in the kitchen of the penthouse where Andrew was raised, that it was part of a fond memory of sitting at the counter watching his mother knead the bread she baked on Saturdays, staring at the back-and-forth of the cat's hypnotic "tail," waiting for the time to pass, the bread to rise, then rise again.

It wasn't that Andrew had any bad memories of his parents; he just didn't have many memories at all. One that remained, however, was watching his mother bake bread, smelling the warm, homey aromas, feeling the kindness emanate from her, because the bread would be delivered to their less fortunate patients.

His mother and his father, after all, were good people.

They'd started off "right," buying a Manhattan penthouse when they first opened their practice. As the years went by, however, they became more caught up in saving the poor than the wealthy of the world. They mortgaged and remortgaged the penthouse several times to sustain their work from the tenements of Manhattan to the shanties of Third World countries. At one point they had Andrew, a "late in life" baby, their only child.

Throughout his childhood Andrew somehow expected they would see him for the clever child he was. But their humor became minimal and their compassion was stretched too thin by others, and by the time Andrew was in high school, he had stopped trying to create the close-knit family that perhaps was not meant to be.

But, yes, they were good people, respectable, respected. They had both worked until well past seventy, lived past eighty, then died less than six weeks apart.

He'd been sad for the loss, but the truth was, they hadn't been very close. If he'd become a doctor he might have salvaged some intimacy on some level, but the good Drs. Kennedy had little in common with a television news guy who flew under the high-profile wing of their neighbor John Benson.

Still, they were his parents and he'd felt sad when they died, though he supposed Frank Forbes felt a lot sadder now.

The clock ticked, the cat's eyes and tail went right, then left.

They would go to the funeral together.

Or would they?

He thought about Jo. Would she want to go to Brian's mother's funeral? Would she think that Brian's impending trial had hastened the woman's death? Would she feel guilty about that, as if the woman would not have died if Jo hadn't had Brian arrested?

He dropped his face in his hands. "Argh," he said. Then he remembered what Frank said: "I stopped by the shop. . . . Jo was working late . . ."

She was working late? She hadn't gone home with the headache she'd claimed to have?

"Women can be sneaky," Antonia had said.

He sighed again and stood up. Then he noticed the pink sheet of paper on the table, scribed with bright purple ink.

Dad, Going to sleep at Marilla's. Kisses, Cassie.

He touched the edge of the paper, his smile returned. At least there was one person in the world that he could count on, teenage crazies notwithstanding.

Then Andrew realized that this would be a night he could spend with Jo, with Cassie out of the house, with the big bed waiting just for them. But instead of going to her, Andrew decided that he'd go to Marilla's. Maybe he could wrangle his daughter into coming home. She'd been spending too much time at her girlfriend's, not enough time in the company of at least one parent who thought she was the greatest thing on earth.

Besides, he reasoned as he took a last look at the clock, grabbed his keys, and headed out the door again, time passed much too quickly to waste it trying to make things happen that maybe weren't meant to be.

One of Marilla's brothers leaned against the front door-jamb. He wore a faded T-shirt and tattered jeans. A cigarette did a slow burn between his pointer and middle finger. Andrew guessed the kid was all of sixteen.

Andrew stood straighter, more erect. "What do you mean they're not here?" he asked.

"They're supposed to be at your house."

"My house? No. Cassie said they were staying here."

"Nope. Not here."

"Then where are they? And where's your mother?"

"Look, Mr. Kennedy," the kid said, inhaling a deep drag. "I don't know where the girls are. My mother's out. On a date. She won't be home till late."

Marilla's mother was not one of Andrew's favorite people. She'd had three sons (fathered by different men) before Marilla and was rumored to spend more time looking for a husband than at her job as a checkout clerk at the local IGA. But Cassie had convinced him the woman was harmless and that, more importantly, Marilla needed a friend. So he'd allowed the friendship because Marilla seemed like a nice, shy girl, and who was he to condemn a child because of whispered stories about her mother? He supposed he should have been a better parent.

"If you find them," the boy continued, "tell Marilla she's grounded." He took another drag then closed the door in Andrew's face.

Andrew stood there a moment, wondering what on

164

earth he had been thinking to have allowed Cassie to visit that secondhand-smoke-riddled, unchaperoned environment. But instead of pounding on the door, instead of threatening to call the cops, Andrew took a deep breath, regained his balance, and knew that there was only one person who could help him now.

"Cassie is missing," he said when Jo opened the door. "Please. Please help me find her."

Jo froze for a moment, the fright that sparked in her clear green eyes matching the fright that sparked in his.

And then, because she loved Cassie too, because she loved him and he surely did love her, Jo grabbed her jacket from the back of a kitchen chair. Without a word she locked the door and followed him toward his car.

23

Whenever anyone died it all came back to Lily in a horrid rush: the police at the door, the description of the tuna-fish can, the damn smell of lilacs.

Frank was on the telephone in the kitchen of the Forbes family home, while Lily sat in the parlor, trying not to stare at the rectangle of dust on the dark hardwood floor where the hospital bed for his mother had been. His father sat next to Lily and explained that Frank and Mr. Harding removed the bed right after the ambulance had left, right after Eleanor had gone.

She took his hand, held it in hers. "I am so sorry, Mr. Forbes," she said.

"Please," his tired voice whispered, "call me Ralph."

"Ralph," Lily said.

From the other room, Frank's low voice carried. "Just a little while ago. . . . Yes, it was a blessing. . . . The church will take care of the arrangements."

Lily didn't remember making any calls. She supposed Aunt Margaret had done it.

"May I get you something, Ralph?" she asked. "Coffee? Tea?"

"Brandy would be nice. Eleanor let me have it once in a while. After she took sick I sneaked it sometimes. I think she knew it, but she never scolded me."

Lily patted his hand.

"It's in the dining room," Ralph added.

She stood and went into the other room. On the ancient sideboard a crystal decanter of brandy stood, its bronze liquid gleaming, as if it had been waiting for Ralph and for this moment. Next to the decanter was a single snifter. Lily's hand trembled a little as she began to pour.

"Thank you," Frank said, coming up behind her. "Thank you for doing this. For being here."

She set down the glass. She turned around, wrapped her tiny arms around him, felt his envelop her. "This is so sad," she said.

"It will be fine," Frank replied. "She doesn't hurt anymore. Worse than her physical pain was the pain of knowing that her 'boys' were watching her suffer. She

166

called us that," he added. "She called us her 'boys.'"

Lily wondered if that included Brian but didn't ask.

"And Dad will be fine," Frank said, reassuring himself. "He'll be lost for a while, but he will be fine. He's a strong man."

"Like you."

Frank didn't answer.

"What can I do?" Lily asked. She slid from his hug, touched her fingers to his cheek. "To make this easier for you?"

He smiled. "Just be here for me. I know that might sound insignificant, but, believe me, it's not."

And then Lily remembered that she couldn't be here and be with Antonia too. The muscles in her back, her arms, her legs all tightened. "Will you hold a wake?"

"No. Just the funeral. Probably Thursday morning. Mother never liked much of a fuss."

Thursday morning, she thought. Tomorrow was Tuesday. Which meant she could spend tomorrow with Antonia, couldn't she? Frank wouldn't need her, would he? But then, what about Wednesday? She bit her lip, stopped herself from crying out.

"I know this is a busy time for you," Frank said, as if reading the anguish as it danced across her face, "what with that woman here. Who is she, anyway?"

Ah, she thought. *That woman.* Her front-tooth caps dug more deeply into her lower lip. What had she said to Antonia in front of Frank? What had she said to Frank?

"Is she a new client?" he asked.

167

She said, "Yes, in a way," because she didn't know how else to respond. She might be good at scheming, but she was lousy as a liar.

"I heard you say you'll go with her to Tanglewood tomorrow," Frank continued. "Is she part of the kindergarten teacher's wedding?"

"Well, in a way," she said again.

He smiled. "So you can spend the night here."

Lily blanched. "Here?"

"Well," he replied, "yes."

Besides the other complications, Lily had never been in a house where someone had just died, at least not to her knowledge. Would strange things happen? Would the lights dim or the curtains flutter or would doors close of their own accord?

"It would be a comfort to me," Frank said. "And to Dad." His eyes became small pools of sadness.

"Oh, Frank," she said, taking his hands.

"You'd have to stay in the guest room, though," Frank said, nodding toward the parlor. "So Dad won't be upset. Please, Lily?"

"Well," Lily said, her thoughts colliding again, "I suppose . . ."

"It would be great, Lily. Then you'd be here tomorrow when everyone starts coming."

She blinked. She turned back to the sideboard and picked up Ralph's glass. "What do you mean?"

"The minister, the funeral director, the church ladies, you know."

No, Lily didn't know. She'd been through this only

three times in her life: when her parents died and she'd been too young and too grief-stricken and too guilty to remember; when Aunt Margaret died and had pre-arranged it all; and when Reginald died and Lily had been overtaken by Antonia, who took care of everything without consulting Lily.

As for Frank, he'd obviously forgotten that she had plans tomorrow. "But," Lily tried to speak very gently, "you know I have to work tomorrow, Frank. That I have to pick up that woman and go to Tanglewood." She said the words *that woman* as if Antonia was a stranger. She wondered if Frank's mother now knew the truth about Lily Beckwith, if she had some sort of universal insight now that she was on the "other side."

"You can't change that until the afternoon?"

Just as Lily looked back at him, the small pools of sadness spilled down his cheeks. She reached up and dabbed his tears. "Oh, honey, I'm so sorry. I'll stay here tonight. But why don't I just scoot out in the morning and take care of business. I'll be back before you know it."

She hated what she was saying, hated the deceit. She hated herself even more when Frank so trustingly said, "Okay, Lily. Thanks."

Jo was grateful that Andrew let her drive, that he admitted he was too upset to get behind the wheel. The busier she could be, the less time she'd have to feel guilty that she had not warned Andrew that Cassie was changing, hiding things from him, growing up maybe

169

too fast. The less time she'd have to let worry overtake her, the way it had overtaken Andrew, who was rigid and pale and who swung sharply from utter silence to bursts of short sentences:

"Why did she lie, Jo?"

"Where the hell is she?"

"Why hasn't she called?"

He held on to his cell phone as if it were his lifeline. No one would guess that Andrew was famous for leaving his phone at home or at the office or in the pocket of a jacket that he'd worn three days earlier. It was another way, he supposed, in which he was a lousy parent.

They went directly to the police station, where Jo asked for Russell Thomas, Elaine's former brother-in-law. Jo had known Russell and Lloyd, Elaine's ex-husband, most of her life, because they'd all grown up together: Russell, Lloyd, Frank, Brian. And Jo.

Sergeant Thomas was not in, he worked days, the man behind the old desk said.

"Call him. Please," Jo said. "This is an emergency. A child is missing." Then she remembered Marilla. "Two children. Girls."

"If it's two, they're probably together somewhere. Run away maybe. One's what you have to worry about. One girl missing and we'll put out an Amber Alert."

Jo glared at the man.

"I'll call Russell," he said, and picked up the phone.

She wanted to call Elaine. And Sarah. Then her

mother. She would not bother Lily, who had enough to worry about right now. Jo wanted to call the others for support, but she supposed if she was going to be Cassie's stepmother she needed to learn how to handle these situations with Andrew. On their own. No other opinions interjected.

Oh, God, she thought, *this is so hard.*

While they waited for Russell to arrive, Jo dropped coins into the vending machine that stood at the far end of the room. Andrew paced, then sat, then paced again. Jo watched as a small cup filled with coffee, doubtful Andrew would drink it.

"We need to speak with Marilla's mother," she said, carrying the paper cup to the bench where Andrew had sat down again.

"She's on a date," Andrew hissed as he took the cup. "Her son has no idea where they are. If the mother cared, she wouldn't have left him in charge, would she?" He stared up at the ceiling, his words not really succeeding at blaming anyone but himself.

"Andrew," Jo said, sitting beside him. "Maybe the girls are fine. Maybe this isn't the first time. All those other nights . . . when Cassie said she was at Marilla's . . . when you and I were together . . ."

His head rotated like the girl's head in *The Exorcist.* "What?" he asked, as if to say, *How dare you?*

"Well," Jo said, her body stiffening, "all I'm saying is maybe the girls have done this sort of thing before. . . ."

Andrew stood up, threw his full coffee cup into the tin wastebasket. Brown liquid splashed against the putty-colored wall. "So Cassie lied to me, is what you're saying. Well, I'll believe it when she tells me. And not before, okay?"

Jo leaned back against the wall and wished she'd never kept anything from Andrew, wished she hadn't tried so hard to be the perfect stepmother that she surely wouldn't be.

24

Lily spent the night with her eyes open, braced, listening for Eleanor's soft bumps to permeate the night. She stayed on a small twin bed tucked under the eaves in the guest room that had once been Eleanor Forbes's sewing room and now smelled faintly of damp wool and cedar. She lay on her left side, face toward the wall, so she wouldn't have to look at the wire dress form that stood in the corner, the shape, no doubt, a replica of Eleanor's dimensions. She had been taller than Lily thought.

When her parents were killed, Lily had slept until noon the next day.

"She's in shock," she'd overheard the doctor say to Aunt Margaret. "It's nature's way of protecting her from the pain."

The doctor was wrong. Lily might have slept, but she'd still felt the pain, still felt the thud of each wrecking-ball word that had swung into her stomach, leaving a raw and empty hole.

"They're . . . both . . . dead."

Thud.

Thud.

Thud.

Billy telephoned the next morning. Someone at the academy had told him about the accident.

"I can't talk to him, Aunt Margaret," Lily had cried. "Please, don't make me talk to him."

He was at the funeral, amid the flags and the formations and the damn gray, cold stone buildings. Lily clung to Aunt Margaret and tried not to look at Billy. How could she look at him when it was his fault, their fault, for loving each other?

Two days later, Billy showed up at Aunt Margaret's house. Through the closed back door, Lily said she could not see him, not then, maybe not ever. If they hadn't wanted to be together, if they hadn't had sex that afternoon in the shed behind the garage . . . if, if, if.

Lily thought she'd never be able to have sex again, surely not with Billy. Without sex, they couldn't have the kids they'd talked about. It would be Lily's penance, if there was such a thing.

Billy came over half a dozen times and called nearly twice that. But Lily wouldn't see him, she wouldn't talk to him. Within weeks the visits and phone calls tapered off, then ended.

In the meantime, Lily skipped her period. The next month she skipped it again. When the third time came around, Lily stood in her underwear at the full-length mirror in her bedroom. She studied her belly, decided it looked swollen, wondered what to do. That's when Aunt Margaret had walked in.

"Are you?" Margaret asked.

Lily quickly dropped her hand. "Am I what?"

"Pregnant?"

It had amazed Lily that her aunt was that perceptive, until the woman said she noticed that the number of Tampax in the bathroom cabinet hadn't dwindled lately.

Lily started to cry and Margaret made an appointment with Dr. Moore. Margaret said this was too important to leave up to "chance" by using one of those new home pregnancy tests.

Pulling the cedar-smelling blanket up to her quivering chin now, Lily realized it had been years since she'd allowed herself to think about Dr. Moore's office, about the small, square waiting room that had been packed with women and round bellies, women whose eyes all seemed fixed on Lily, who had looked so much older than she was.

Aunt Margaret had waited in the car.

When Lily was called she took a plastic cup into the ladies' room and emerged with a urine sample. Later that day, a nurse from Dr. Moore's office had called and said, "Negative."

Lily was both relieved and disappointed. Three days later, she packed her bags for college. The night before she left, Lily started her period. It had lasted her "normal" four-and-a-half days, as if nothing had happened.

She'd never missed a period since then, had never figured out what it was all about, though she suspected it was some kind of female hysteria. Or just simply "shock," as the doctor had said.

As daylight sneaked into the room, Lily rolled onto her other side, facing Eleanor's mannequin. She wondered what Frank's mother would have thought of Lily if she'd known all her truths. Then she wondered what had ever happened to Billy, and if he'd ever known that Lily was sorry.

With those last thoughts, Lily closed her eyes and finally went to sleep, saying a quiet prayer of thanks to Eleanor for her silence through the night.

"You guys are weird."

Cassie's voice woke up Andrew, then Jo. Both had fallen into exhausted sleep, still sitting in anticipation on the sofa in Andrew's cottage.

Andrew stood up quickly, as if he and Jo had been caught making love, which they had not. It would have been difficult to make love from opposite ends of the overstuffed relic.

"Cassie," he said, shaking off the sleep. "You're home. Oh, God."

"Well, yeah. I need school clothes. For today."

She quickly headed toward the stairs. Andrew glanced at Jo, then back to his daughter. "Where have you been?"

Cassie stopped mid-step. "I slept over Marilla's." She continued up the stairs, her back toward her father.

"No," Andrew said sharply. "Where have you really have been?"

She paused again.

Jo wanted to say something. She wanted to leap from the sofa and say it was okay, Cassie was safe, which was all that mattered. Wasn't that what Andrew had said over and over throughout the night, that if only Cassie was safe, he could deal with the rest?

But watching as he stood there, hands raking his hair, Jo knew that it wasn't her place, would never be her place, to interfere.

"Cassie?" he called.

Cassie's little-girl shoulders began to shake.

That's when Jo felt an ache that crawled down to her toes. She thought about Cassie's makeup and the short shirt and the attitude. And, for the first time, Jo wondered if this was all her fault—not for trying too hard to be a perfect stepmother, but for being there at all, for being the sole reason Cassie's life was going to change.

25

Jo told Andrew she was going home to get ready for work, though he hardly noticed as he moved toward Cassie, toward the stairs.

Slipping from the cottage, Jo took her cell phone from her purse.

"I know it's early, but please come get me," she said to Elaine. "I'm at Andrew's and don't have my car."

Then she leaned against Andrew's Volvo there in the driveway and breathed a moment, in, then out, averting tears that wanted to fall.

She looked back to the cottage, to the small window set into the backdoor, to the Cape Cod café curtain that wouldn't let her see what was happening inside, wouldn't let her hear what Andrew was saying or how Cassie was responding.

Turning her head slowly away, Jo called the police station. Cassie Kennedy was fine, she said, she had returned home, apparently it had been a misunderstanding.

Then Jo closed her eyes and quietly waited for Elaine.

"Honey," Andrew said as he sat next to Cassie on her small bed, in the room where she'd grown from a little kid into a twelve-year-old young lady who, God help her father, now wore a bra and eyeliner and skirts that were too short. "Tell me what's happened. Tell me what's going on." He didn't, however, really want to talk; he would have preferred to cry along with her for everything that was happening in both their lives, for the things he understood, and the things that he did not.

She sniffed. She shrugged. "It's no big deal, Dad."

He glanced at her vanity, which had a string of photo-booth pictures tucked into the mirror: Cassie and Marilla making goofy, kid faces; Cassie and Marilla trying to look sophisticated, "Like movie stars, Dad," she had said; Cassie and Marilla stuck in the dark tunnel of puberty between growing up and grown.

He did not look at the poster of Patty.

"Honey," he said, "it is a big deal when my twelve-year-old daughter stays out all night and lies about where she was."

She sniffed again. "We didn't do anything bad, Dad."

He was not too stupid to know that what was "bad" thirty years ago when he was her age was not considered bad today. "Call me old-fashioned, but in my book, lying is bad."

"Well, yeah."

Then silence fell, not really a standoff, just the pregnant (*Ha,* Andrew thought, *now, there's a word I'd rather not consider*) pause of two generations not knowing who should speak next or what should be said.

Finally, Cassie spoke. "It's Dillon Parker, Dad. He's in eighth grade and he is so cute."

The air that whooshed into Andrew's lungs carried thoughts and images of an angry, primal nature. "Eighth grade?" was all that he felt safe to ask.

"He's very smart," Cassie said, almost like a proud parent.

Andrew tried to remember how "smart" he'd been in the eighth grade, but he only could remember a few movie dates with Alicia Henderson and a few clumsy breast-grabs in the back row of the theater. He tried not to shudder visibly.

"Honey," he said, "he's two years older than you are. That's too much at your age."

She shrugged again. "It doesn't matter."

"Yes, it does."

She shook her head. "No it doesn't, Dad. Dillon doesn't know I exist."

If Andrew was confused before, he was completely adrift now.

Cassie sighed. "Dillon lives at the camp on the lake. His father is the lake superintendent. Marilla and I camped out across from their house to . . . well, just to see Dillon, if we could. If it makes you feel better, we didn't. We think his bedroom is upstairs in the front of the house, but it's a log cabin and it's pretty dark out there. It was too hard to see."

Andrew did not know when his mouth had dropped open, but when she was finished it was hanging there like a flycatcher in the horse barn where Cassie used to love to go, before her passion for horses waned in favor of boys, specifically Dillon Parker. "You camped out?" Andrew somehow managed to ask.

"Marilla's brothers have lots of sleeping bags. We took a couple."

"And you lay there . . . on the ground . . . watching this . . . this boy's house?"

"Well, not exactly. We stayed in one of the cabins that has a good view."

"One of the cabins?" His voice was squeaking now, as if he had suddenly become puberty-stricken too.

"We took the lock off and went inside. We figured it was safer in there than outside. There are bears in these hills, Dad." She said the last sentence as if she were a park ranger cautioning a tourist.

"Well," Andrew said. "You shouldn't have done that. You shouldn't have done any of it." He knew his words were inadequate, but he was too stunned to say anything else.

"But, Dad," she said. "It gave you another night alone with Jo, didn't it?"

An uncomfortable chill crawled up Andrew's spine. He stood up. "Get ready for school, Cassie. After school you're going to come straight home. I don't know what your punishment will be yet, but it will be a whopper, and I don't mean a trip to Pittsfield to Burger King."

He left the room and headed downstairs, wondering what—if anything—Jo had to do with this.

In the morning, Lily ran to Bruegger's and bought bagels and cream cheese for Frank and his father. It was the closest she could come to domesticity, given the events ahead of her that day.

After unwrapping their uninspired breakfast and plunking it on the kitchen table, she planted a light kiss on Frank's forehead, then dashed back out the door. She jumped into her little Mercedes and sped off toward home to shower, change, and pick up Antonia and try to act as if everything were fine, as if her lover's mother hadn't just died the evening before, as if she hadn't spent the night at his somber house.

By the time she arrived at Wheatleigh, Lily was exhausted. She felt like she was juggling both a spouse

180

and a lover and trying to be true to both. Infidelity, she supposed, came cloaked in different packages.

Antonia was in the breakfast room, alone at a table. She was dressed in boxy charcoal pants and a matching jacket that had silver buttons emblazoned with someone's family crest, not hers. She was eating what looked like a poached egg and smoked salmon, which would no doubt be added to the room charge Lily would pay. Lily supposed she was lucky she hadn't run into Pauline and Jonathan at the bagel shop, as they'd no doubt been directed to fend for themselves.

"Would you care for an egg?" Antonia asked, as if this were her home and her cook was on duty.

"No," Lily said. "Thanks. Did you sleep okay?"

"Fine. How is that man? The one whose mother died?"

"Well, you know. Death is always unpleasant."

"Yes, isn't it," Antonia said as she picked at another forkful of egg.

Lily glanced at her watch. If they spent the morning at Tanglewood, maybe she could dump Antonia back at the hotel, then get to Frank's in time to serve lunch to the minister and the church ladies or whoever was there. She could tell Antonia she'd join her for dinner, then tell Frank she was coming down with a cold or something. Better yet, she could say she had cramps. Men were always so willing to let you have your way when you said you had cramps, as long as you didn't discuss it.

She put her hands in her lap and tried not to let on

that she was in a hurry and that she wished Antonia would hurry the hell up.

"What a lovely room," Lily said, calmly, slowly.

"Yes. And the service is perfect. You never see a servant unless one is needed. There's no hovering, no brash need to entertain their guests in that despicable way that's become so popular in the States."

Lily did not comment that it had been years since Antonia had left "the States" even for a short vacation.

"Well," she said instead, "as soon as you're finished . . ."

Antonia nodded and continued to take her sweet time.

"You left," Andrew said when he finally surfaced at Second Chances.

"Yes," Jo replied, eyes fixed on her computer screen. "I decided it should be between the two of you." She sighed and turned around. "Is Cassie okay?"

"She's fine. I'm the one who doesn't know what to do." He pulled a chair close to Jo's desk, then related all Cassie had said. "Maybe you were right all along," he added at the end. "Maybe the fact that we've been sleeping together has bothered her. I thought she was so cool with everything. But the way she said she'd given us a night alone . . . as if it justified that she'd stayed out all night, that she'd been spying—or trying to spy—on that boy."

Suddenly Sarah stood in the doorway that led from

her studio into the showroom. She tossed back her long hair, folded her arms across the beaded tunic that she wore. "I'm going to do something I never do," she said. "I'm going to meddle in someone else's business."

Jo laughed, grateful that Sarah had overheard their conversation and might help put this new responsibility into some sort of perspective.

"You two are obviously having some problems," she said, "what with the trial coming and all, and with canceling the ceremony and reception—which, by the way, I agree with. All along, however, Cassie has been your biggest supporter, Andrew, and your biggest cheerleader, Jo. She's done everything to act as if this marriage is the greatest thing since Green Day—who, in case you didn't know, are a tattooed bunch of rock stars she's probably in love with too.

"Unfortunately," she continued, "Cassie is smack in the middle of being twelve, and my bet is she's as confused as the two of you about all this and what it means for her. As cool as my son was when Jason and I split up, it's taken him a few months to trust Sutter in my life—in *his* life.

"Anyway, on top of everything you're moving into Jo's house and Cassie will lose her room. Does either of you remember what your room meant to you when you were a kid? It was your place, your space, the one ten-by-twelve or fourteen-by-sixteen or whatever piece of real estate that belonged to you and only you. It was your haven.

"So now Cassie is losing her dad to another woman and she's losing her space too, and she's trying like hell to be grown up about all of it.

"My guess is, however, that her fear needs somewhere to go, so camping out across the street from a boy who doesn't know she's alive is as good a way as any to try and be in control of some part of her life."

She smiled at the two of them and gave them a short salute. "So please forgive me, but I couldn't stand to listen to your speculations any longer."

With that, Sarah disappeared into her studio, leaving Jo and Andrew to look at each other.

They might have cried or hugged or something, but just then the bell rang over the front door and in walked a man in a gray suit.

"I'm looking for Josephine Lyons," the man said. Jo smiled and said that was her, and before she knew it he had withdrawn a wallet from his pocket, produced an ID, and said, "I'm Harlan Wilkes with the Suffolk County DA's office. I'd like to talk with you about your testimony in the case against Brian Charles Forbes."

26

L arceny over two hundred fifty dollars can mean up to five years' imprisonment in this state," Harlan Wilkes said as he and Jo sat at a table in the back of the luncheonette two doors down from Second Chances. "Or two and a half years with a twenty-five-thousand-dollar fine."

They had walked the fifty or so paces from the shop, though Jo did not think she could recall the trip. She only knew that Andrew had offered to come with her. She'd said, "No thanks, I can handle this."

Jo lifted the mug of hot tea now; it was heavy in her hand. "That's all?"

"Well, yes."

She thought about it for a moment. What had she expected? That Brian would go to jail for life? "But that's per complaint, right?"

"Ordinarily, yes."

"Ordinarily?"

"Well, yes. But in this case, there's just your complaint."

"No," she said, shaking her head, wishing that Andrew, Sarah, anyone else were here, someone who could think more clearly about this. "There was my complaint and two others. The investigator found four other women who Brian bilked. Two said they'd come forward."

Mr. Wilkes shook his head. "They withdrew the charges. In fact, one of the complainants is still his wife, you know. He left with her when his bail was posted."

The luncheonette suddenly grew cold and dry. "His bail?" she asked.

"Yes. Didn't you know? Brian Forbes was released right after Christmas."

No, she hadn't known. She wanted to ask why no

185

one told her, but suddenly Jo felt tired, drained.

The attorney removed a file from his briefcase and rifled through papers. "It says in the papers that he stole over three hundred thousand dollars from you."

She flinched. "Yes. Over a period of several months."

"And you have records of the transactions."

"Yes. Most of them." She hadn't kept track of the few hundred dollars here and there that she'd popped into Brian's pocket when he was "short of change." She pressed the mug to her lips, hating the way the facts would "sound," the he-did-this and she-did-that parts of the Brian–Jo scenario that did not account for emotions or feelings or, God help her, love, or what she'd thought was love. "So," she said slowly as she set down her mug without drinking, "it's me against him?"

"Don't worry, Ms. Lyons. He'll get convicted." But the man didn't look her in the eye this time when he spoke.

And then she remembered that Harlan Wilkes had said Brian was out of jail, had been out of jail for months. She shifted on the old coffee-shop chair, wondering if Frank Forbes had known that his brother was free, and if Brian would show up at his mother's funeral.

"The guest count is eighty-five," Lily explained to the special-events person at Tanglewood. "Both the bride and groom have small families. Which is why they're having the children as their attendants."

"Eighteen five-year-olds," the manager reiterated with a hesitant smile.

"Oh, but they're quite delightful." She didn't think it was necessary to mention that though it had been stipulated that the venue could accommodate up to one hundred, nowhere was it specified that they all must be adults.

Antonia sighed as if she were bored and sat down on the bench in the foyer of Seranak House, where the wedding would be held.

"I'm sure it will be lovely," the events manager said. "Now tell me, how's Frank?"

"Frank?" Lily asked, her voice jumping an octave, maybe two.

"Yes. I heard his mother died yesterday."

Lily silently cursed the cluster of small towns around Lenox and neighboring West Hope. She told herself Antonia's eyes weren't gnawing the back of her head. "Yes," Lily said, "it's such a shame. The Forbes family has lived in West Hope forever."

"Well, their business certainly helped us furnish many of the fabulous antiques in different buildings on the grounds. Even the bench you're sitting on," he said, nodding toward Antonia.

Antonia raised her plump left cheek and eyed the bench on which she sat. "He's the one with the shop?" she asked suspiciously.

"Why, yes," the events manager said. "You don't know them, then?"

"Not exactly," Antonia replied, and Lily felt her stomach twist.

"Yes, well," Lily said abruptly, "getting back to our wedding."

"Your wedding?" the manager asked with a broad smile. "There have been rumors, of course . . ."

The lighting in Seranak House seemed to dim. Lily blinked and willed herself to stay upright, to stay in the moment, however bleak it was. "Yes," she said hurriedly, "the wedding of our kindergarten teacher. It's been rumored for years that she's been spending way too much time in the fifth-grade classroom!" She giggled a carefree (she hoped) giggle and launched into a monologue about her ideas for the outfits for the attendants: pink and lavender dresses for the girls, white tuxedoes with pink cummerbunds for the boys.

"And I think each girl should carry a nosegay of pink and lavender wildflowers," she blabbered. "I must remember to have Dennis come up with some samples. Have you used him for floral arrangements? He is quite magnificent."

She paused only for a second, then dared to go on, leaping into comments about the food and wasn't it adorable that the bride and groom wanted pizza bites and chocolate pudding on the menu?

By the time they were finished and returned to the car, Lily fully expected Antonia would say something like, *Okay, Lily, what's really going on between you and Frank Forbes?* but the woman merely flopped onto the passenger seat and said, "If wearing me out has been your mission, Lily, you have accomplished it. Drive me back to Wheatleigh. I want to have a small lunch, then take a long, long nap."

Which, of course, was a gift sent from the gods, because that meant Lily could go back to Frank's and not have to lie, at least not for a little while.

27

They had been too busy the rest of the day for Andrew to have any meaningful conversation with Jo, other than to hear her say, "This will be over soon."

Andrew was beginning to wonder, however, if anything would ever really be "over" when it came to Brian Forbes and his presence in Jo's life.

By six o'clock everyone but Andrew and Jo had gone home for the day. Then she stood up from her desk and announced she was going to the Forbeses' house to see if there was anything she could do to help Lily or to rescue her if she needed to get back to Antonia. She asked if Andrew wanted to go with her.

He supposed he should have gone, for the sake of their relationship, whatever that was now.

But he explained he had to deal with Cassie, then he kissed Jo good-bye and smiled like a grown-up, non-jealous man. He did not say that, though he liked Frank Forbes well enough, he'd rather not be in the same house where Brian Forbes was raised. He'd rather not have to see framed high-school pictures in the living room, or sit in a chair and wonder if Brian's sorry ass had ever sat there, or sense the presence of the man who had wrecked Jo's life and now threatened to wreck his. So Andrew said "No thanks" to Jo and hoped he'd have no regrets.

Once she was out of sight, he turned off his computer and got ready to lock up, feeling slightly guilty that he was grateful to be going home. Sometimes, lately, Andrew found himself longing to be just with Cassie, just the two of them, living and laughing the way they did before all these women came into their lives, before he went and complicated things by falling in love.

He'd known, of course, that status quo wouldn't, couldn't last, that one day Cassie would grow up and leave the paltry nest he'd created, that she'd become the beautiful, intelligent, independent, energetic creature he'd always hoped she'd be and that she'd then set off to mark her place in the world.

He hadn't planned that he'd be the one to shake up everything or that Cassie would start her adventure into adulthood when she was only twelve.

He smiled to himself. Taking his keys from his pocket, congratulating himself for not feeling the need to tag along after Jo, Andrew locked the front door and headed through Sarah's studio out to the parking lot in the back. He had just opened his car door and got inside when he heard a woman's voice call out, "Andrew? Andrew. There you are."

He paused for a moment. The voice was oddly

familiar, but not familiar enough to belong to Lily, Elaine, Sarah, or Jo.

But the instant Andrew turned, he wished that he hadn't. With everything else happening in his life right now, he really didn't need to see Frannie Cassidy, John Benson's assistant, his old mentor's right and left arm and God only knew what else, standing across the parking lot waving at Andrew as if he were a long-lost something or other.

"Frannie," he said as she approached and he remained seated. "What the hell are you doing here?"

He might have sounded harsh, which probably wasn't fair, because Frannie had always been nice to him—well, up until the "end," when things happened that she didn't, couldn't understand.

She wore black pants now and a black shirt that shrieked *Manhattan* and a big grin that was spread across her too thin, oval face. "I told you I'd come." Without hesitation she circled the car and hopped in on the passenger's side. Unlike Antonia, she made no surly comment about the age or the state of his vehicle. "It's great to see you again," she said. "You look terrific, by the way."

He remembered the time she told him she hoped that Jo dumped him; he remembered how loyal she'd been to John.

Andrew sighed. "I don't care what John wants," he said. "The answer is no, Frannie. No matter what he thinks, the man is out of my life." He did not add that

191

John's wife, Irene, was gone as well.

Frannie, however, just sat there, grinning. "My name isn't Frannie," she said. "Well, not for the purpose of this meeting anyway. My name is Andrea Hall, and I believe you called?"

Andrew frowned.

"Andrea Hall!" Frannie repeated. "Remember? The woman you talked to about starting the magazine for second-time brides?"

He turned his face out the side window. "Oh, Christ," he said. "It was a setup."

She swiveled to face him. "No, Andrew, it wasn't a setup. I really wanted to start that magazine. I still do."

He shook his head. "Sorry. Not interested." John Benson, of course, must be behind this, and purging the Bensons from his life was a vow Andrew was going to keep.

"You don't understand," Frannie continued. "I don't work for John anymore. In fact, John and Irene moved to the West Coast; didn't you know?"

"Didn't know. Don't care."

She tapped the dashboard with small, nervous taps. "You never saw the side of John that I had to endure."

Again, Andrew was silent.

"I came up with the idea for the magazine months ago. I worked up a business plan; I outlined editorial content. But when I presented it to John he said, 'No way.' He didn't want to help you or your friends. He wanted to keep you tied to his empire."

Andrew ran his fingers over the steering wheel,

acknowledging that the things Frannie was saying made sense, that John was a man who liked to think he owned people as well as things, that unless a venture had been his idea he deemed it worthless.

"What about *Buzz*?" he asked, because it had been part of his life for many months, though he hadn't bothered to look for it on the newsstands since he and the Bensons had split.

"Sold. From what I understand, the new owners are going to turn it into erotica."

"Great," he said. "Just what the world needs."

"What the world does need, Andrew, is a fun, quality magazine with a spin on second weddings. It's an idea whose time definitely has come. I wasn't going to go ahead with it; I was going back to law school. But magazines are in my blood, Andrew. And when you called me . . . well, I think we could make this work if we did it together."

He wondered if this was a bad dream, if he'd fallen asleep and this was his punishment. "Who's Andrea Hall?"

Frannie smiled. "She doesn't exist. It's just a name I made up. The number you called is my home phone. When you asked for her it took me a second to remember." Then she smiled again. "I picked *Andrea* because it was close to *Andrew*. It was kind of a dumb joke."

He couldn't argue with that.

"Please, Andrew. Will you at least let me show you the proposal? I have a room at the Hilltop Bed and

Breakfast, just outside town. It's still pretty much off-season and they're not very busy. I'm sure they'd let us work in the corner of the living room."

"Frannie . . ." he said, then let the sentence trail off. "My life is complicated now."

"Maybe it wouldn't be," she said, "if you had a real job, if you took on a project where you could showcase your real talents."

"My real talents?" He laughed. "Pardon me for not seeing what a magazine has to do with television."

"You're a communicator, Andrew. And you're really good at it."

He let her words linger there in the air of the old car. "Frannie, I'll need to think about it." More than before, Andrew wanted to be home with Cassie. More than before, he wanted his quiet life back. But had it only been days ago that he'd wanted excitement? That he'd wanted something beyond putting together weddings and working with a bunch of women, great as they might be?

He turned on the ignition. "I have to go home now, Frannie. Cassie is expecting me."

"I'll be at the Hilltop," she repeated, and got out of the car. Before closing the door, she leaned down and said, "I hope to see you in the morning. No strings attached, of course."

The afternoon had been an eddy of one doorbell ring after another, of one "Yes, hello, my name is Lily, I'm a friend of Frank's," of one casserole dish after another to make room for in the refrigerator that should have been at Frank's store, it was so old and so small.

The doorbell rang again, but this time it was Jo, who did not bear a casserole and was a welcome sight. She went immediately into the parlor, because Jo had been raised in West Hope and would know what to do.

"Hello, Mr. Forbes," Jo said, taking Frank's father's hand. "I am so sorry about Eleanor."

He nodded. "You're Josephine, aren't you? Marion Lyons's girl?"

"Yes."

Standing next to Jo, Lily feared for a moment that he would mention Brian. Instead, he said, "I remember when you were a little girl and you'd come by on summer evenings."

Jo smiled. "And sit on your front lawn and listen to the ball game on the radio."

Ralph smiled a dry, old smile. "You brought me a pennant one time."

"A Red Sox pennant. You stuck it in the grass, and all the neighbors blew their horns when they drove by."

"That was the year they almost won. Almost!"

They laughed and talked about how amazing it had been when the Sox finally won the Series in 2004.

Lily stood on one foot, then the other, wanting just to go outside, where the small talk would be done with and she could finally breathe.

Inevitably, the conversation turned back to Eleanor, and Ralph looked tired again. Lily used the opportunity to steer Jo from the parlor out onto the porch.

195

"Death should not be something so *social*," Lily said as they sat on wicker chairs. "Take these chairs, for instance. Frank hauled them from the garage and cleaned them up this morning. He said the weather was going to be summerlike and people might want to sit outside." She paused, rubbed her hand across the arm of the chair. "Isn't that like him? His mother just died and he's trying to make other people comfortable."

Jo smiled. "How is he?" she asked.

"Better than I am. I'm afraid I've never been good at being a hostess unless a caterer is involved."

"Nonsense. I'm sure you're doing a fine job."

"Well, I do know I had no idea so many people lived in West Hope. I think they've all come and gone through the back door this afternoon."

"And you have Antonia to worry about."

Lily closed her eyes. "I'm tired, Jo."

"Then call Antonia and say so. Tell her you'll see her tomorrow or the day after that. She has her assistant and her driver to keep her company if she gets bored."

Lily shook her head. "I can't do that, Jo. I have too much at stake."

Jo looked away. "What about around here?" she asked suddenly. "Have there been any surprises?"

"Surprises? Such as what?" She leaned her head against the back of the chair and closed her eyes. Maybe if she just slept for half an hour . . .

"Brian," Jo said. "Has Frank's brother shown up?"

Lily laughed and opened her eyes. "Excuse me, Ms.

Lyons, but that family member happens to be indisposed, as you well know."

"No," she said. "No, he's not. Brian has been out on bail since right after Christmas. I found out today."

The early-evening early-spring air rode with a chill up onto the porch. "Really?"

Jo nodded. "I didn't know if Frank knew. I didn't know if Brian was . . . well, if he was here."

"Oh," Lily said, "that would be awful."

"Frank hasn't said anything about him?"

"No. Not a word."

Jo nodded again. "It's not as if I'm not going to face him sooner or later. But I assumed it would be in the courtroom in a couple of weeks."

"Oh," Lily repeated, "this would be awful. You don't suppose he'll find out about Eleanor, do you? You don't suppose he'll show up?"

Jo smiled a half smile, then said, "Well, it shouldn't matter to you or me. Eleanor was his mother, after all." Then she stood up. "Now, say good-bye to Frank and go have dinner with Antonia. I'll stay here and help out for a while. But if I were you, I'd get home early and try to sleep."

"No," Lily said, "I'll come back here tonight. Frank seems to like it when I'm in the house."

28

I thought you liked Jo."

"Dad, come on. Of course I do."

"Don't you want us to get married?"

"I want you to be happy."

"What about you? Would it make you happy?"

"I'm a kid, Dad. Kids don't have any say in the matter."

"That's not completely true."

"It's mostly true. And you know it."

"But I don't understand. You're the one who kept telling me to propose."

"I thought it would make you happy."

"It did. But things are different now. They've become . . . well, difficult."

"Because of the trial?"

"How do you know about that?"

"Lily told me that's why Jo postponed the wedding. Because her old boyfriend is some kind of a thug."

"A thug? Well, that's a good word."

"So is that why it's postponed?"

"Did you think it was because of you?"

"No."

"Are you glad we postponed it?"

"I don't know."

"Jo's a good woman, honey. And she likes you a lot."

"I know."

"But you aren't sure now if I should marry her?"

Cassie didn't respond for half a minute. Then two big tears plopped into her lap. "I don't know, Dad. I don't know how I feel about anything anymore."

"Oh, honey," Andrew said, and he wrapped his arms around his daughter and held her the way he'd held her when she was three or four and was afraid of the dark.

The next morning Andrew decided to work on the blog before getting ready for work. Later there wouldn't be time. It would be a busy day as they geared up for the kindergarten teacher's extravaganza, with two smaller weddings in between. Lily would no doubt be tied up with Frank or Antonia; Jo and Sarah would pick up the slack; Elaine would be busy cooking things that seemed to take far too long to prepare. Not for the first time, Andrew wondered why weddings couldn't be private, solemn occasions instead of the costly productions they were.

Not that he'd even hint at that question while he composed the blog.

He wondered if Frannie would think blogging was a good idea and if it should be incorporated into an online version of the magazine that she seemed so desperate to get under way. Maybe it should be confined to the Second Chances Web site.

As he popped open his laptop at the kitchen table, Andrew was certain of only one thing: Frannie was right. The magazine would be a success, just as the business of planning second weddings had taken off. Frannie had worked for John long enough to know the ins and outs of magazine publication. Andrew knew it wasn't much different from TV news: share with the audience things they don't already know that will enrich their lives and make them feel satisfied that they "tuned in."

Most important, he remembered from his journalism days, was to share things the audience could relate to, especially issues from real lives.

Real lives like his and Cassie's, he supposed.

No matter what their ages, Andrew typed, keep a special eye on your kids. They might appear to like or even love your spouse-to-be, but this is going to be a major change in their lives too. It's only natural for them to feel a sense of loss. They're losing a part of you that had been reserved for them.

Be careful that reality doesn't get ignored in the excitement of the wedding plans.

He stared at the screen and wondered if that would be perceived as too scary, too anti second wedding. Frannie would perhaps have an opinion.

She was a professional, after all.

Someone who understood the marketing and communication of media-savvy ideas.

Someone who had the enthusiasm to help erase Andrew's feelings of boredom, of needing something productive in his life again, something challenging.

In that moment Andrew knew that on his way to Second Chances, he would stop at the Hilltop B&B, that he would listen to what Frannie had to say. It would cost a small fortune in start-up money, but maybe Frannie had an idea about that too. He might as well pursue it.

After all, it wasn't as if Winston College was beating down his door; it wasn't as if he even could be sure that one of these days he'd be someone's husband again.

Grace Koehler had soft gray hair and soft gray eyes and the gentle nature of a seasoned innkeeper. She welcomed Andrew and said Ms. Cassidy was in the front room and had been hoping that he'd come.

Which confirmed that her visit yesterday had not been a dream.

There was fresh coffee on the table where Frannie sat wearing her trademark black attire, though it looked like a different outfit. Next to the coffee, two maroon-color binders sat as if waiting to be opened and their pages unfurled.

"Good morning," Andrew said, and sat down across from her.

"Andrew," Frannie said, "we can do this, you'll see." She handed him one of the binders without asking if he wanted coffee.

They decided they'd go to the funeral as a group—Elaine, Sarah, Lily, Andrew, and Jo, or at least that's what Lily said when Andrew finally arrived at work. "Safety in numbers," Lily said, which probably meant if she went with all of them the world might not notice that she was attached to Frank, which made little sense because it wasn't as if Reginald's beastly sister would show up.

"Sorry I'm late," he said, ignoring Lily's comment and settling into the remaining chair where the group was clustered in the Second Chances showroom. "I've been working on a new venture for our business." Thankfully, no one corrected him by saying that he was not a partner in the business, that he was, technically, only the receptionist.

"Oh," Lily nearly swooned. "Another venture? Can it wait until after the funeral? Or until Antonia is gone? I can't put one more thing inside my head right now, not one."

"How long will Antonia be here?" The question came from Sarah, whom Andrew would have thought might be the least interested.

"I have no idea," Lily said. "I've hardly seen her. I can't imagine what she thinks."

"She thinks you're up to something," Andrew said, and all eyes turned to him. "Well, that's what she said to me. I think she's going to stick around until she finds out what it is." He watched as Lily's cheeks went from pink to pale.

"But we had a nice dinner last night," she said. "I took her to Northampton, to that tavern in the old hotel. She even let Pauline and Jonathan come. We went in the big Mercedes."

Andrew wasn't sure what any of that had to do with anything, except he knew, with Lily, one never could be sure.

"Well," he said again, "that's what she said to me."

Then he felt bad, because Lily looked as if she was going to cry.

"Lily," Sarah said, "why don't you just tell her about Frank? God, I can't believe you're doing this only because of money."

After a painful moment, Lily said, "Maybe it's not just about the money. Believe it or not, none of you knows everything."

Then she stood up, took her keys from her purse that had probably cost more than Andrew made in a semester at Winston College, and tearfully marched out of the showroom.

"Andrew," Elaine said, "you shouldn't have said anything."

"Oh, please," Sarah said. "It's about time someone brought this up. It's absurd, don't you think? The way she's dragged all of us into it, expecting us to cover for her, expecting us to be part of her charade?"

Then Sarah stood up and went into her studio, and Elaine left to go back to her kitchen, and Jo and Andrew were alone. Andrew said, "I didn't mean to cause a Third World War."

Jo said it didn't matter, but by the way she went right back to work, Andrew had a huge suspicion that it did. Worst of all, he'd never had the chance to tell them about Frannie and about the commitment he'd made for the magazine.

Later in the morning, the kindergarten teacher and her

203

groom-to-be stopped by to look at sample arrangements of the wildflowers, which was a problem because there weren't any. Lily had forgotten about it.

"Her fiancé's mother died," Jo said. "I'm sure you understand."

Like many brides and grooms, they did not really care, because their only interest was themselves and their day. It wasn't as if they knew Lily. It wasn't as if they knew Frank or his mother, because they'd each lived in West Hope only a few years.

"Can't you reach her on her cell phone?"

"I'm afraid not," Jo replied. There was no point in revealing that though, unlike Andrew, Lily had her cell phone with her at all times, she rarely turned it on. She felt the instrument was for her convenience, when she needed to speak with someone. "If someone wants me," she'd said more than once, "they can leave a message." Jo found it annoying and somewhat controlling but decided there were worse ways to be.

"Will you be ready for the children Monday?" the bride asked, her lips pursed with expectation. "Lily said they could come in for fittings and rehearsals."

It was the first Jo had heard about it, but she said, "Absolutely. I'll double-check it myself. And I'll call you later. Perhaps I can have the flower samples here tomorrow afternoon—after Mrs. Forbes's funeral."

"Well," the groom said, "the day after tomorrow will be fine. Won't it, honey?"

The bride hesitated, then nodded. "Call me, please. Hiring wedding planners was supposed to make this easier on me." She smiled through tight lips and Jo got the message. It marked the first time that she'd sensed any doubt from a Second Chances customer, and it did not feel good.

"Tell Lily I'll run interference for her tonight," Andrew said to Jo just before they closed up for the night. "I'll take Antonia out for dinner. It's the least I can do, after upsetting her so much." The truth was, in addition to hating that he'd upset Lily, he felt sort of sorry for Antonia, stuck out there at Wheatleigh with no apparent entertainment. Besides, he reasoned, spending the evening with Antonia would get him out of going to the Forbeses' house.

"I will," Jo responded. "And I'll also let her know that after Eleanor's funeral, we really need her to get back to work. Lily gets sidetracked sometimes."

"Don't we all," Andrew replied, trying to sound nonchalant but doubting that he did. He hadn't yet asked Jo to reset a wedding date; she'd probably say she still wanted to wait until after the trial was behind her, and he didn't want to hear it. He didn't want to hear anything with the name *Brian* attached to it. In the meantime, he'd sidetrack himself by starting the magazine.

29

S he seemed delighted to be in the company of a
male.

Andrew had brought Antonia to the Stone
Castle for dinner. For the occasion the woman wore
bright red lipstick, a sparkly blue dress, and a triple
strand of pearls. He thought the dress might be a little
fancy for the castle, but Martha Holland, the castle's
owner, was too kindhearted to flinch. Just as she was
kind enough not to mention Andrew and Jo's "postponed" wedding plans.

Antonia set her sequined purse on the table next to
the forks. "What is my sister-in-law up to, Andrew, that
she bullied you into being in charge of me tonight?"

He smiled. "First of all, Lily didn't bully me into
anything. This was my idea."

Antonia nodded and sipped from her water glass,
leaving behind a crescent-shaped red tattoo.

"I knew she'd feel obligated to go with the other
women to the Forbes house tonight. Frank is our land-
lord at Second Chances, did you know that?"

"She felt obligated but you did not?"

"You know how females are about this stuff. They
think they have to help. Frank's father is still alive, so
it's just the two men. God forbid two men should be
trusted to plan anything, let alone a funeral." He
thought he sounded humorous and convincing, that
Lily would have been pleased.

"It doesn't matter. I've decided to go home tomorrow."

Just then the waitress arrived and announced the specials for the day: some kind of white fish cooked with tomatoes and olives, butterflied lamb chops with mint jelly, spinach-and-goat-cheese-stuffed ravioli. She asked if they wanted wine but Antonia said no, she had a long ride the next day. Then she ordered the fish special and Andrew asked for the free-range chicken off the menu, all the while trying to decide how to change the old girl's mind.

"Lily will be disappointed if you leave," he said after the waitress headed for the kitchen.

Toying with her pearls, which Andrew suspected she did whenever she was thinking, Antonia said, "I've been here for three days. I've barely seen Lily. And when I do, she keeps looking at her watch. She doesn't think I notice. She thinks that I'm demented, I believe. But I'm not demented, Andrew, and I don't miss much. Clearly, Lily doesn't want me here."

He had always admired a woman who could be direct. In recent years he recognized that was one reason why he'd been attracted to Irene Benson, John's wife. He twisted on his chair. "She said you had a nice dinner last night with your assistant and your driver."

Antonia laughed. "Lily thinks I treat them like they're peasants. She doesn't have a clue that Pauline and Jonathan have been in love for years. I thought that coming out into the country would give them a long-awaited chance to have some time together without the daily monotony of living under my roof."

"And it would give you a chance to see what Lily's up to too."

She laughed again. She had a hearty, engaging laugh. He wondered if Lily had ever heard it.

"It's unfortunate," Andrew continued, "that Frank's mother died right now. Lily feels obligated to help out. Once the funeral's over, I'm sure she'll be attentive. You might not believe me, but she's been looking forward to your visit."

A gray-white eyebrow lifted. "Don't bullshit me, Andrew. Lily didn't even know I was coming until the night before I got here, so she hardly had the time to look forward to anything."

It was his turn to laugh. "Lily's been right about one thing—you are formidable."

Antonia raised her water glass. "Just so we understand each other."

Andrew shook his head. "But maybe you haven't given Lily a fair chance either. Take a look at the rest of us—me, Jo, Sarah, and Elaine. We all have other people in our lives—family, you know? A mother or a father or a kid, someone we're connected to. But Lily?" He shook his head again. "Lily has no one. No one but you, that is." He hadn't thought about that until then. He'd known there was a reason they tolerated Lily's airheaded antics and her eccentricities; he hadn't realized until he said it that maybe that was why.

"Well," Antonia said quietly as she lowered her pale eyes and straightened the linen napkin on her lap. "I have no one either, except for her, of course."

Andrew reached across the table and touched Antonia's arm. "Now you have us too, if you want us, that is." Then he felt all choked up inside, as if he were a girl. His eyes darted around the restaurant, searching for the waitress. He'd decided they should have a bottle of wine after all.

30

Lily picked out a silk suit that was not quite navy, not quite black. Black looked so dreadful against her ultrapale skin. At Reginald's funeral she'd worn deep berry because it was autumn and he'd always liked her in red. She didn't remember what she'd worn to her parents' double funeral. The tranquilizers the doctor had prescribed were so strong she hardly remembered the service at all.

She might have asked for a Valium or two now, had she known that the altar would be filled with lilacs, with the pungent smell reminiscent of pain and hurt and death. She might have insisted that she come with Jo, Elaine, and Sarah like they originally planned if she'd known she'd have to sit so close to the damn purple blossoms and the memories they triggered.

But Frank had wanted her with him, and she didn't know how to say no.

Reaching the front of the old Congregational Church, Lily suddenly felt faint, light-headed. She gripped Frank's elbow more tightly than she'd intended. "Lilacs," she whispered.

"They're beautiful, aren't they?" he said. "Our neighbor Mrs. Harding volunteered them from her trees. We're so lucky that they're blooming now."

While Lily had tended to Antonia, Jo helpfully tended to the funeral flowers. Lily never thought to ask Jo what the flowers would be. And Jo would never have known the effect lilacs would have on Lily.

With damp palms now and a dry mouth, Lily stepped into the pew before Frank and his father.

The service took forever. Several townspeople, mostly women, said a few words about how gentle and kind Eleanor was, how much she had achieved for the church, the schools, the various charity drives over the years, the Heart Association, leukemia, the March of Dimes.

Lily wondered what folks had said about her mother and her father; for the first time she felt cheated that she'd been medicated to "get through it." She wondered if she'd felt as disconnected and as weak as she did now.

She tried to breathe through her mouth, but then, instead of merely smelling the fragrance, she tasted the damn lilacs on her tongue.

The minister talked about Eleanor's family life, how she raised her two sons in the town of West Hope. He did not mention that Brian was a criminal.

A lady stood up and sang "Amazing Grace." A few sniffs could be heard inside the church, then Frank gestured to Lily that it was time to leave. Thank God.

They filed behind the casket, which had been hoisted by six pallbearers from Gregorie's Funeral Home, a huge spray of lilacs draped across the top. Lily held her breath as they moved down the aisle. She might have even made it if she hadn't noticed Sondra.

As they passed the pew where Sondra stood, the woman stepped into the aisle and planted a kiss on Ralph Forbes's cheek, then another one on Frank's. The magnanimous gestures no doubt were intended to give the audience something to chat about as they nibbled the ham sandwiches and shortbread cookies that would be served in the fellowship hall after the burial in the cemetery next to the church. (Lily had wanted Elaine and her father to make a proper buffet, but Frank's father said no, this was what Eleanor had wanted.)

Lily grasped Frank's elbow more tightly. She nodded coolly at Sondra and kept her "Screw you" to herself. After all, they were in church.

They walked past Jo, Elaine, and Sarah. Andrew, however, wasn't there. She looked at Jo quizzically: Jo mouthed the word *Antonia*; Lily wanted to cry.

Then, as their small procession continued behind the casket, someone opened the tall wood doors to the outside. The spring air was warm and welcoming, until a breeze swept into the narthex, catching the scent of the flowers on the casket and pushing the sweet and sickish smell at Lily in one tsunami swoop.

Her head, her arms, her legs grew weak. She leaned her body against Frank's, and then Lily passed out.

"How much?" Antonia asked as Andrew poured more coffee from the vintage silver pot that was on the table in Wheatleigh's breakfast room.

He smiled. "If we each put up fifty thousand, that's a hundred fifty, including Frannie's share. The rest will be easy to raise from banks and investors, once they know we've made a personal financial commitment." He'd had the brilliant idea sometime during the night, an awesome way to help out Lily and Antonia and the others too, including him. Maybe Antonia would be more inclined to warm up to Lily if the old girl had a purpose in her life other than going to another damn ballet that she probably knew every step to and every boring opera to which she probably could sing every note.

He hoped the plan wouldn't backfire and Lily wouldn't excommunicate him from their small band of wedding entrepreneurs.

"You need my money," Antonia said.

"Actually, we don't. We'll do it without you. But it would be nice to have you involved. And, to be honest, it wouldn't hurt to have the Beckwith name connected to the magazine."

"Lily is a Beckwith. At least, God help me, legally."

He let the silence hang there a moment, hoping she'd recognize how foolish she had sounded, how "beastly," as Lily would say.

Antonia nibbled on a chocolate croissant, then plucked her linen napkin and dabbed the corners of her mouth. "I've never taken a single risk in my life, Andrew. I'm too old to start that nonsense now."

"Well," Andrew replied, "I'm going to go out on a limb here and say maybe it's time you started some kind of 'nonsense.' Before it's too late to enjoy it."

Her eyes moved across the room, to the ornately carved mantelpiece that framed the nineteenth-century fireplace, to the floor-to-ceiling windows that invited the formal, outdoor gardens in. "Leonard Bernstein stayed here whenever he conducted at Tanglewood," she said matter-of-factly, her chin now raised as if to let him know that she'd detached from his proposal and didn't want to speak of it again. "He took the Aviary Suite, of course, because it is the most magnificent. His grand piano came with him, and his assistants set it up in the suite's sitting room."

Andrew leaned closer to her. "Cut the crap, Antonia. You can't intimidate me the way you intimidate Lily."

Antonia laughed, then looked back at him. "Between you and me," she said, "if you were the one courting my sister-in-law, I'd have no trouble saying go ahead, marry the guy, I'll let you keep your share of Reginald's inheritance. But the fact is, I know next to nothing about this Frank Forbes, because she won't let me get close enough."

So, Antonia had figured out Lily's scheme.

The old girl winked. "I've known from the day Lily showed up in New York that she had something going on. I sent my spies to follow her—Pauline and

Jonathan, two lovers in cahoots with this old dame. They came to West Hope, then reported back to me that she was spending a lot of time with an antiques dealer. Which was why I changed my mind and decided to take her up on her offer of a visit to the country." She smiled again, then sipped from her water glass. "While she's abandoned me here, left me lounging with a book, Pauline and Jonathan discreetly resumed following our Lily. Did you know she's spent the last few nights at Frank Forbes's house?"

Andrew shook his head and decided it was not his place to deny the accusations. "He's a decent guy," he said. "We all like him; maybe you will too. But in the meantime, the magazine is business." He placed the copy of the business plan on the table in front of her. "*Second Chances,* the magazine," he said. "I think that, like the wedding-planning business, the title *Second Chances* can refer to life as well as weddings. If you want to let it."

Antonia picked up the proposal and stood up. "I'll be in my suite," she said. "Tell Lily I've decided to stay another day."

Lily had never minded being the center of attention, but then, she'd never had a million people hovering over her whispering things like "Get water" and "Give her air" and "Should we call 911?"

From the blurred edges of consciousness, Lily heard cell phones beep and ding, then a flurry of footsteps followed by hurried voices. There seemed to be confusion about the water: Should they take it from the baptismal font?

The decision must have been no, because just then she felt something plastic press against her lips. She sipped; she opened her eyes; she saw Frank crouched over her in the aisle, holding a Poland Spring water bottle to her mouth. She wanted to ask whose bottle she was drinking from but decided it shouldn't matter.

"Lily?" Frank asked.

Other voices hushed. She blinked. Her eyes gyroscoped to the knees and calves and feet that had gathered there. She noticed that the shoes were mostly polished, Sunday best.

"Oh, Frank," she said, raising herself up to a sitting position. "I am so sorry. I am so embarrassed."

"It's okay," he said. "Would you like more water?"

She shook her head.

"She's okay?" It was Ralph Forbes's voice this time.

"Yes, Dad," Frank answered.

"She's okay," Ralph said in a louder voice.

"She's okay," echoed a few times in the church.

A siren sounded softly in the distance. It grew louder, more intense, more "hurry up, it's an emergency." Lily knew it was for her.

She shook her head. "Please," she said, "I'm fine." She tried to stand but realized that the casket was right there, right there with its sickish-sweet purple lilacs waiting to be laid to rest with poor Eleanor.

"Frank? What can we do?" It was Jo, of course. Jo and Sarah and Elaine. Lily smiled. Of course they

215

would be there. They were always there for her. She looked at them a moment. Jo and Elaine, of course, had known Eleanor and might like to stay for the graveside prayers and for the tea and sandwiches made by the church ladies. Sarah had, no doubt, come only to be supportive.

"Please," Lily said. "If you don't mind, Frank, I would like to go home. Sarah, will you take me?"

31

Jo would have preferred to be the one to carry Lily out of there. She would have preferred to escape the reception after the service in the cemetery. Her mother and Ted were there. She clung, metaphorically, to them and to Elaine and wondered how soon was too soon to make a polite exit.

She had had enough of the Forbes family. She'd served dinner the other night for Frank and Mr. Forbes; she'd run interference from well-wishers; she'd made arrangements for the flowers; she'd organized the reception, because her mother had done this a hundred or more times and helped tell Jo what was what.

She wouldn't have done more if she'd been Brian's wife, or even Frank's.

Thinking about Frank, Jo wondered if later she should tell Lily how, in Lily's absence, Sondra had stepped in without hesitation and circulated among the people—the way she was doing right now—as if she still was married to Eleanor's older son.

Brian, Jo remembered, had not liked his sister-in-law.

Pulling her eyes from Sondra, Jo surveyed the fellowship hall—the small clusters of white-haired heads of mostly ladies, a few gentlemen, good people who had lived and worked together for a lifetime, who'd watched one another's children be born and raised, who had laughed and cried with one another and now were there as one of their own was buried. She wondered if they were sharing memories of Eleanor or if their conversation had moved on to the weather, to the coming high-school graduation, to the hoped-for influx of tourists, to the July 4th parade and picnic on the town green and whether they should allow the crafts vendors this year or not.

Standing beside Jo, Elaine chatted with Jo's mother and Ted. Jo held her teacup and small square napkin and knew she should join their conversation, but she really was too tired. Too adrenaline-depleted, she supposed, from worrying that Brian would show up today, a fear that had kept her rigid throughout the service, with her peripheral vision focused on the door.

She wondered if the real reason Andrew hadn't come was not to be a buffer with Antonia but to dodge the issue and the family and the possible talk of Brian Forbes. As far as Jo knew, Andrew didn't know Brian was out of jail and that he might show up if somehow he learned his mother had died.

She set the teacup on top of the napkin and held the saucer with both hands, trying not to think that soon

217

she'd be in Boston all alone, being the one and only witness at Brian's trial instead of getting ready for her wedding.

"Did you try the crumb cake?"

Jo turned quickly; there was Sarah.

"How's Lily?"

"Safe and sound and tucked into her imaginary apartment."

Sarah liked to call Lily's apartment that, because it reminded her—it reminded all of them—of an Alice in Wonderland fantasy, of cotton-candy daydreams that a little girl would have, that a little girl would imagine as her world. It might have been because the furniture all came from Madison Kids, the upscale Manhattan store that catered to the children of the privileged. Or it might have simply been because Lily was who Lily was.

"Is she all right? Do you think she fainted because of all the stress she's been under?"

Sarah smiled and adjusted the silver clip that held up her long, black, shining hair. "You mean the stress that she's put herself under? Well, she seemed okay. I suppose sneaking back and forth between your lover and his dead mother and your dead husband's sister might be stressful, though."

Jo said, "Ssshh, Sarah, stop," even though she knew that Sarah probably was right.

"Sorry," Sarah said. "It's just that secrets only end up hurting other people." She'd learned that firsthand, of course, from having been hurt by secrets herself.

Then Jo had an idea. "Sarah," she said, "I know we're busy right now, but do you think you and Sutter could come with me to Boston for Brian's trial? I think I might need a lawyer to help me handle this. And I definitely know that I'll need a friend."

"Andrew won't be going?"

"No."

Sarah wouldn't ask for further explanation. She was too considerate for that. "Well, you can count me in. I'll have Sutter check his calendar, though I'm sure he'll rearrange his schedule if he knows it's for one of us."

It was nice the way that Sutter, like Frank, like Andrew, had blended into the small band of former college roommates and seemed both amused by their antics and respectful of their personalities and goals. She wondered if Elaine would ever let Martin into their circle too.

Jo's eyes moved back to the group of mourners, most of whom were finishing their sandwiches now, returning their empty teacups, tightly wrapping little cookies in small, white napkin squares. "Thank you," Jo said, glad, once again, that she had come home to West Hope, glad that, no matter what might end up happening between her and Andrew, she had friends again, the way Eleanor Forbes had friends until the end.

Lily knew Antonia would be expecting her. She supposed the woman had grown tired of playing three-handed canasta with her driver and Pauline, that she had inhaled and exhaled enough damn country air to last the rest of her lifetime, that she was thoroughly pissed that Lily had dropped her, left her to be entertained by Andrew, a man she didn't know but at least had been a city boy and still had traces of urban polish.

Staring at the phone that sat on the end table, Lily didn't know why she couldn't bring herself to reach across the plump, pink cushion resting on the sofa, dial Wheatleigh, and ask to speak with Antonia.

She could tell her she had fainted at Frank's mother's funeral.

She could say it had been too hot in the church, that she hadn't had breakfast, that she'd been working too hard lately and needed a day to herself, that perhaps they could meet later for dinner.

She could tell Antonia all those things, but if she didn't reach for the phone, she wouldn't have to say a word.

Lily closed her eyes and wondered how Frank was doing, if he'd ever forgive her for causing a scene. Then she thought about the lilacs, she thought about her parents, and then about Billy, Cadet William J. Sears.

He was from Litchfield, Connecticut, from her side of the Hudson, from a quiet, moneyed town that often sent boys to private school. Billy had gone to Deerfield Academy in Massachusetts, had been in the same class as the boy who became King Abdullah II of Jordan.

After the Deerfield lacrosse team had traveled to

West Point to compete in a tournament, he decided he wanted to go there. Once, when they'd picnicked along the Hudson, he told Lily he'd been awed by the history and the grounds and that he'd wanted to be part of what he felt made America great. He said he wanted to prove that being from a rich family did not mean he was spoiled or snobbish or ungrateful.

How she had loved him. Not because of his uniform, not because of his huge blue eyes. She'd loved him because he thought she was beautiful, or so he'd said, and because he wanted to do something meaningful, something that would help others, maybe even change the world.

She'd loved him because he loved her, because he would love the children they would have someday, because together they would carve a purposeful life. She'd loved him because their love was real, not like the "happy, giddy things" of the fantasy world that her mother and Aunt Margaret had created to sustain them through the Vietnam War. Lily and Billy had a real life and they were going to have a real future.

After the accident, however, Lily regressed to her childish cocoon, where all things were safe, where there were no worries, no problems, no pain.

She had stayed there many years.

And yet, she realized now, none of it had been safe. Not her first or second marriage, not even life with Reginald. And though she'd felt safe with Frank, the lilacs did her in. The time had come, she knew, to learn how to smell the flowers without running away. It was time to face her past and the damage that she'd done.

Without another waver, Lily finally reached for the phone. But she did not call Antonia or Wheatleigh. Instead, she dialed long-distance information for Litchfield, Connecticut.

A William B. Sears was listed in Litchfield. Lily paused and let the operator connect the two lines, past and present.

"Hello?" It was the voice of an elderly woman.

Lily closed her eyes. "Hello," she said slowly. "I'm trying to locate William J. Sears. He was a cadet at West Point, the class of 1981." Her throat had grown so dry, she was surprised her words came out.

Silence followed, then, "Who's calling, please?"

"Just an old friend. My name is Lily. I've been wondering whatever happened to Billy. How he's doing, if he's okay." She was amazed with her clarity of thought, her vigilance of nerve.

"He doesn't live here."

Lily wove her fingers through the fake fur of the plush rabbit that was perched on the couch. "Did he?" she asked. "Ever?"

The woman sighed. "I'm Billy's mother. He has several acres right on Route 8 in Mount Rose. Just north of Winsted."

She didn't know Mount Rose. But she knew that Winsted was south of West Hope. An easy ride, not far. She drew the rabbit to her breast. "How is he? How is he doing?"

"He teaches sixth grade. His wife teaches third."

His wife. Well, of course Billy would be married. Did she think he had pined for her, waited for her to reappear in his life? "Oh," she replied. "That's nice." Then she realized he'd become a teacher—perhaps his way to save the world.

"I can tell him you called. He comes here on Sundays. He brings the whole family."

Family.

He brings the whole family.

"No," Lily said, "that's okay. I just wondered if he was okay." She knew she was repeating herself. But she didn't know what else to say.

"Well, good-bye, then."

"Wait," Lily said. "He has a family, you said. He has children?"

"Yes. Five."

Five children. Billy Sears had five children who could have been, might have been, hers.

"Oh," Lily said, "that's nice."

"Three girls, two boys. The oldest is twenty, the youngest is ten."

"Well," Lily repeated, "that's nice." She quickly calculated: Billy had had his first child when Lily was barely out of college; she'd been through two marriages and was on her third when he'd had his last.

She could have had five children and several acres up in Mount Rose. But she had been Lily, too scared of love, just too damn scared. It had been so much easier to hide behind piles of money and lots of servants and a dream wardrobe to die for.

She might have said good-bye to Billy's mother, or she might have just hung up. Then Lily stayed on the sofa, hanging on to the rabbit, quiet tears gently spilling, until long after the sun had set, when there was a knock on her door and Frank's voice called out to her.

32

L ily," he said as he entered the room, "what are you doing sitting in the dark?"

She quick-wiped her cheeks as he snapped on the lamp, the Mad Hatter lamp whose shade was a top hat and whose base was a giant pocket watch. Lily wondered if she'd have to give up those things now that she planned on growing up.

Frank looked tired, his face lined and drawn, his usually cheerful eyes now faded and sad. He sat down beside her.

"I'm so sorry," she said. "I'm so sorry that I caused a scene."

He shook his head. She took his hand; it was cool and dry.

"Do you feel all right?" he asked, though his eyes didn't meet hers. "Did you call a doctor?"

"I'm fine," she said. She wanted to tell him about the lilacs, about her parents' funeral.

"I would have come sooner," Frank continued, "but I was so busy. There were so many people . . ."

She wanted to tell him about Billy Sears, that he was a teacher, that he had five children who might have been hers. She wanted to tell him she never meant to act so spoiled; she wanted to say that she'd only been scared.

"So you're sure you're all right?"

"Yes," she replied. "It was the crowd, I guess. The closeness of everyone."

He nodded. Then he said, "Lily, I'm going to take Dad away for a few days. I think a short vacation will be just what he needs."

Before today Lily would have thought it was a great idea. She would have thought about the time it would give her to spend with Antonia, to try to convert her into a friend. But sitting there on the couch, she'd grown tired of the old Lily, the shallow, scheming, airheaded Lily. And the plain truth was, she wanted to be with Frank.

"I know we're busy at work," she said, "but maybe I could go with you. I'd enjoy some quiet time with you and your dad."

Frank turned to face her, surprise on his face. "Well, I didn't think—"

She shushed him. "I'd like to, Frank. Really, I would. I could try to cook, and your father could teach me to play cards or something and we'd have a good time. I'd even listen to the ball game. Become a Red Sox fan." She remembered that, as a child, Jo had shared such innocence, one neighbor to another. Lily wanted to learn to share things too. To share life and love and just plain hanging out, without judgment or expectations.

Frank turned his eyes away from her again. "Thanks, Lily, but I don't think it would work." His voice was lower now; his shoulders had dropped too. "We're going to Lake Mahkeenac."

If he had only looked at her, she wouldn't have sensed that something was being left unsaid. Lily pulled her hand from Frank's. She put the rabbit on the floor and stood up. "Are you renting a cottage?" she asked. "You could teach me how to paddle a canoe. . . ." She hoped her intuition was off base, that she was merely being sensitive after her stressful day.

"No," Frank said finally. "It won't work, Lily. We'll be using the place that belongs to Sondra's family."

Sondra.

Oh.

Her.

Lily nodded mechanically. She paced to the window and stood there in the silence, looking out across the town green. She wondered if Mount Rose had a green with little cement sidewalks and a gazebo where the local bands played on hot summer nights. "Well," she said, hating that she knew the answer to her next question, "does that mean Sondra will be going too?"

His response came way too slowly. "She knew my mother most of her life, Lily. Please understand, she's only being kind."

She turned back to him. He looked absurd, really, a grown-up man with thinning hair and middle-aged-though-muscled arms from hauling around antiques, sitting there among Lily's stuffed animals on pink, fluffy cushions. "Do you plan to sleep with her?" she asked abruptly, because suddenly Lily needed to know if her world was going to shatter the way she sensed it was.

Frank stood up. "I was afraid you'd take it that way. But, no, I don't plan to sleep with her. Although, to be honest, it does feel pretty good to have a woman care about me enough to want me to be happy." He took a step toward the door.

"Frank," she said, "I want you to be happy." She moved closer to him. "And I'm ready to marry you. Just tell me when." The words surprised her perhaps as much as they surprised him. Their eyes locked, each awaiting the other's next comment.

"Lily," Frank said, "my mother has just died. Now you spring this on me. It's not fair, you know. I'm not sure what I want right now."

He didn't want to marry her after all? Lily's cheeks grew as pink as the couch. "What are you saying? You don't mean—"

He held up a hand. "I need some time away. I'll be in touch."

As he headed for the door, Lily felt an urge to lash out, to say something to make his stomach ache as much as hers did now. "I suppose this means you'll be away for your brother's trial." With every syllable and every word, she wished she could stop herself. She should have turned around, gone back to the window, looked back out across the town green. Instead, Lily said, "The trial is next week, in case you forgot. In case you care at all about what he did to Jo."

Frank didn't say a word; he simply left the apartment.

And Lily was left standing in her ice-cream-colored living room, wondering what on earth she had done, and why she'd felt the need to hurt him the way she surely had.

33

Jo knew the best thing she could do was keep busy until the trial. With her wedding plans canceled—*postponed,* she kept reminding herself—there was little to do but focus on work, on other people's weddings, not hers.

Andrew was hardly around. She didn't know where he was or what he was doing. "Babysitting Antonia" was what Elaine said the morning after the funeral, though Jo couldn't imagine what he could be doing to entertain the woman and her entourage.

Jo had just hung up from double-checking the time of Monday's fittings for the kindergarten teacher's kids, when she looked up to see Cassie in the showroom.

"Hi," Cassie said, "remember me?"

Jo got up from her desk and went over to greet her. "Cassie," she said, "this is a surprise." She tried not to show relief that Cassie was dressed in normal jeans and wasn't wearing makeup. Maybe Jo's mother had been right when she said to let Cassie be herself.

The girl smiled. "I forgot there's no school today. They're getting ready for the high-school prom. Our school's the newest so they use our gym." She glanced around the shop. "Is my dad here?"

"No," Jo replied. "I'm not sure where he is."

Cassie looked around the showroom and shrugged her shoulders. "He's with that woman, I guess."

Jo felt a spark of jealousy, until she realized the "woman" must be Antonia. "Ms. Beckwith?" she asked.

"The woman from New York. They're planning something, you know."

Jo nodded as if she knew. It was better, she decided, than explaining to Cassie about Lily and Antonia and Frank Forbes and the money. She glanced at the clock. It was only eight forty-five. "Hey," she said, "I have to ride over to Tanglewood to meet with the caterers. Would you like to come with me?"

Cassie shrugged again. "Okay, I guess. Sure."

"Great. On the way I'll fill you in on this positively crazy wedding with eighteen five-year-olds." She grabbed her purse and jacket, wanting to congratulate herself on being casual with Cassie, on seizing the chance to regain her footing with the girl who had once liked her.

"Are you and Dad ever going to get married?" Cassie asked as soon as Jo had steered her Honda out of the parking lot.

It was a warm spring morning, the kind that let you shed your jacket, the kind that promised that summer would arrive at any time. It was the kind of morning Jo had hoped for for her wedding, when Laurel Lake would be the perfect setting of spring green trees and crystal water. All of which was nice but did not answer the question Cassie asked. "I hope we will," Jo said, feeling a small heaviness descend upon her heart. "But things are a little crazy right now."

"Because of your old boyfriend?"

Jo couldn't help but smile. Andrew must have told Cassie the truth, or at least part of the truth. "Yes. He wasn't a very nice man, Cassie. He stole money from me and he's going to jail."

Her young eyebrows lifted. "Lily said he was a thug. But she never said he stole money from you."

So it had been Lily, not Andrew, who divulged part of the shady side of Jo's experience. Lily had never understood how Jo could have been swindled by a man. In Lily's world, men were supposed to *do* for women, not the other way around.

Jo nodded. "He pretended he was using the money for his business. But he turned everything into cash, then he took off."

"He took off?" Her echo told Jo that she was now captivated.

"We were in a restaurant. He got up to go to the men's room and never came back. I never knew if he'd run away or if he'd been kidnapped."

Cassie's turquoise eyes were saucers now. "Wow.

This is like a soap opera."

Jo tried to smile. "Do you know where that term comes from? A soap opera?"

Cassie looked at her blankly.

"When daytime television dramas first came into vogue, they were sponsored by the people who make Ivory soap. In fact, I think they invented the original soap opera."

"No kidding," Cassie said. "How do you know that?"

It was Jo's turn to shrug. "Too many years in public relations," she said.

"Was he in public relations too? Your boyfriend?"

She wanted to ask Cassie to please stop referring to Brian as her boyfriend, but she feared Cassie would take it as criticism and shut her out again.

"No. He said he was an investment counselor, but he really wasn't. He was a con man."

Cassie frowned. "Like Paul Newman and Robert Redford in *The Sting*? My dad is nuts about that movie."

Jo hadn't known that bit of information about the man she loved. "Sort of," she answered with a grin.

She steered the car onto Route 183 and headed south toward Tanglewood.

"So," Cassie said, "are you and Dad going to get married once your boyfriend is in jail?"

"I hope so," Jo said. "If it's okay with you."

"Well, yeah. Especially if it gets him away from that woman, John Benson's assistant."

Jo must have heard Cassie wrong. "Antonia Beckwith isn't connected with John Benson, honey. I doubt she even knows John or Irene."

"Not that older lady," Cassie said. "I'm talking about Frannie. The one who was John's assistant at the magazine. Dad and Frannie and that older lady are working on something together. I'm scared it's going to mean that we'll move back to New York."

Lily didn't know where the hell Antonia was. After a half-sleepless night, tossing and turning with the help of Billy Sears and Frank and Sondra, she had jumped into her car and driven to Wheatleigh, only to be told by the young concierge that Antonia was not in her room. Neither was Pauline or the driver, Jonathan.

"It's nine o'clock in the freaking morning," Lily said. "Where can they possibly be?"

Their belongings were still in their rooms and they had not checked out, but the big Mercedes was gone. Somehow Lily couldn't picture Antonia having breakfast at Dunkin' Donuts, with the servants no less.

She put her hands on her hips and stared at the young man as if that would help them materialize.

"I can give her a message when she returns," he said, with a Parisian accent that was nice but had begun to grate on her. They were in the Berkshires, after all, where the only accent tolerated should be Boston.

"You can't do better than that?" she demanded.

"I'm sorry, madam. I don't know what else."

She thought for a moment. Then she said, "Andrew.

232

Have you seen him? The man who's been to visit her. He drives an old Volvo . . ."

"I'm sorry, madam," the concierge said again, "I cannot help you."

Cannot. Would not. It didn't matter whether he was protecting the privacy of his guests or whether he didn't really know. She gave the young man a last, pleading look that was met with stone. She muttered "*Merci,* anyway," then left the hotel, supposing she'd have to go straight to Andrew to find out what the heck was going on.

They sat in the breakfast room at the Hilltop Bed and Breakfast: Andrew, Antonia, Frannie.

Andrew watched as Antonia made notes in a spiral notebook that Jonathan had bought for her last night.

Studying her a moment when he thought she might not be looking, Andrew was pleased that he'd read the woman right, that she really was a good old girl who deserved a second chance. Even her demeanor had changed somewhat. Today she wore a practical brown suit that was devoid of feathers or fluff and looked very businesslike, with just her triple strand of pearls. Her cap of snow-white hair and bright red lipstick even seemed a shade less theatrical that what he'd seen before.

On the other hand, Frannie, who must be thirty, maybe forty years younger, looked almost like a kid, devouring a sweet roll with one hand and tapping away at her laptop with the other. She was the vision of a

Generation X'er, forehead already marked with frown lines, eyeglasses balanced halfway down her nose, a spandex workout suit clinging to her bony frame.

It was amusing, the contrast between Antonia with pen in hand and Frannie making data entries as the two discussed the business plan, profit and loss projections, marketing strategies, as if there were no technology or generation gap between them.

Antonia glanced at her watch. "When Pauline and Jonathan get back from Staples, let's move over to Wheatleigh." She'd sent them out again this morning, for "necessities" to get this business going. "We can set up the whiteboard in the suite and combine our thoughts," she said. "The sooner we present this to the bank, the better."

It was interesting, too, that Antonia's assistant and her driver had seemed eager to get in on the new venture. Maybe they were glad to see their employer doing something productive and worthwhile, if this early stage could be considered that. Andrew stirred more cream into his coffee and wondered if the banks were going to agree.

"Once Andrew's blog is up and running, we can use it to help direct the editorial for the magazine," Frannie said. "We can make this a collaborative—instead of us simply telling brides what to do, it will be sort of a combination of how-to's in the real world."

"A reality magazine," Andrew interjected, because that was a TV spin and he understood that approach.

"Well," Antonia said, as she flipped the pages of

notes she'd already accumulated, "one thing is for certain. Between the magazine and the Web site and the blog and the business . . . we will be responsible for transforming second weddings from a mere event into an industry." She looked up and smiled through her red lips. "Sort of like the Beckwith typewriters and adding machines."

Then Grace Koehler came into the breakfast room to tell them Jonathan and Pauline were back. The three new moguls stood up and thanked her for her hospitality and said they'd see her later.

As they left the Hilltop Bed and Breakfast and formed a small caravan toward Wheatleigh, Andrew figured it would be best if he didn't wonder if the others—especially Lily—were going to approve.

Andrew wasn't home either.

Damn, Lily thought, *this isn't fair!* Not after she'd made the decision to tell Antonia to forget it, that she didn't need Reginald's money even if she didn't have Frank, because for once in her life, Lily Beckwith was going to stand on her own two, stiletto-shoed feet.

But where the heck was everyone, now that she'd grown up?

34

Andrew called Cassie on her cell phone at quarter past three. She'd be getting home from school; he should let her know where he was.

"We had the day off, Dad," Cassie said.

"Oh," he said, with a pang of bad-Daddy guilt. "Did you spend it with Marilla?"

"No. Marilla is grounded, remember?"

Part of Andrew was relieved. Part of him felt inadequate—again—because he'd not followed through with punishment for Cassie.

"Where are you, anyway?" Cassie asked.

He looked around the guest room of Antonia's ancient apartment, at the dark-wood furniture and deep-maroon oriental rugs and the heavily gilded picture frames showcasing sour faces that might have been the Beckwith ancestors of office-products fame. "Actually," he said, "I'm in New York."

The silence told him Cassie wasn't pleased. "What am I supposed to do for dinner?"

He put one hand in his back pocket and moved from the bed to the window that overlooked a small terrace. It could have been at Wheatleigh in the Berkshires, except it was ensconced by a high stone wall and not a bank of lush, green cedars and a view. "I was hoping you could have dinner with Mrs. Connor and plan to stay there while I'm gone. I called her earlier and she said that was fine."

Pause. Sigh. Pause.

"Whatever, Dad. When are you coming home?"

The pang again. "A few days," he said. "Will you be okay with that?" He hoped she'd read between the lines and know he trusted her to do as he asked, not to spend a night or two lurking in the wilderness, scoping out some poor boy's house. At least it seemed as if Cassie had learned something from that experience, whether she'd been grounded or not.

"What are you doing?" Cassie asked. "You're not with the Bensons, are you?"

She sounded more like an irritated mother than a pre-teenage daughter. "It's business, honey. I'll explain everything when I come home."

"Did you call anyone at work? At Second Chances?"

"No. But I can do that now. Unless you want to do it for me."

"No. I think they need to hear from you. I spent the day with Jo, learning the wedding-planning business. Among other things, I learned that right now Lily's wishing she hadn't agreed to have the wedding with all the little kids."

He was too startled to ask Cassie any questions. She'd spent the day with Jo? How the heck had that happened? He ran his fingers through his hair, not wanting to think about Jo now. Not wanting to have to deal with more than what he had at hand.

"Do you have your cell phone?" Cassie asked.

He blinked and turned away from the stone wall and the terrace. "Yes. You'd be very proud of me. I'm not only talking to you on it right now, but I remembered to bring my charger."

"There's hope for you yet, Dad."

"Very funny. I'll leave the phone on. Day or night, call me if you need anything."

"Sure, Dad. And you know how to get me."

237

He was glad he'd given her the cell phone for her birthday. He was glad she was more responsible than he was when it came to stuff like being available at any minute, emergency or not.

Andrew said he loved her, then clicked off the phone and straightened the collar of his shirt as if he already wore the tie he'd wear tomorrow morning at Antonia's bank. The Beckwith money enabled them to be granted a meeting with the bankers on a Saturday; the Beckwith money was therefore deserving of a tie.

Cassie hung up the phone, turned to Jo, and said, "He's up to something, all right. And I think it's going to stink."

Jo called Mrs. Connor and said thank you, but that Cassie would stay with her.

Then they went to Andrew's cottage and Cassie packed more than enough clothes for "a few days." Then they went to Jo's house, where Jo led the way to the room upstairs that would become Cassie's "sitting room" if Jo and Andrew ever married, if Jo ever let the builders finish the addition to the house so the three of them could live there, like a normal family. Whatever normal was.

"There's a bed under there somewhere," Jo said, pointing at the neat stacks of curtains and clothes and shoes from years—no, from decades—gone past. "I guess we should just pack everything up and give it to the women's shelter."

But Cassie had spotted something. She pulled out a dress and held it up. It was bright purple silky polyester with a large rhinestone buckle at the waist and enormous shoulder pads. "Was this yours, Jo?" she squealed. "Did you really wear this?"

Yes, Jo replied, she'd worn that to the annual meeting of one of her clients. It had been in the eighties and the meeting was at the Ritz. She laughed and asked if Cassie wanted to try it on.

Without a moment's modesty, Cassie slipped out of her jeans and shirt and pulled the dress over her head.

"Add these," Jo said, as she pulled a pair of sparkling, pointed-toe high heels from a shoe box that was labeled *silver*.

Cassie stepped into the shoes and wobbled toward the full-length mirror. She caught her hair in her hands and swept it to the top of her head. "You are such a wonderful client," she mused into the mirror. "Imagine that you paid me enough money to buy such a glamorous outfit."

Jo laughed and Cassie laughed and almost fell off the shoes.

"Here," Jo said, "try this one too." She held out a gold lamé drapey top with matching slinky pants.

"Oh, no!" Cassie said. "You put that one on. I want the lime-green thing."

The lime-green thing was a glittery "at home" caftan with slits from the ankle to mid-thigh.

They dressed and laughed and changed into other, more ridiculous eighties' outfits, then laughed until they were immersed in heaps of polyester and rhine-stones puddled around them on the floor.

By six o'clock they'd ransacked all the piles. While Cassie bagged the outfits for the shelter (hopefully the women would be able to update the clothes before wearing them), Jo put clean sheets on the bed.

When all was finished, she said, "I vote that we make girlie salads for dinner instead of going out."

"Sounds good to me," Cassie said. "I think I worked up a stupid appetite."

Jo laughed again. She suggested that Cassie go downstairs, graze through the refrigerator, and take out anything she could find that might taste good when tossed with lettuce and Italian dressing.

When Cassie left, Jo leaned against the wall and folded her arms. It had been a good day, a fun day with Cassie. Perhaps Jo might be a decent stepmother after all, if only this trial would come and go, if only she and Andrew could find a way to laugh again the way she and Cassie laughed today.

The call from Antonia had come earlier that day, but Lily didn't get the message until after she crawled upstairs to her apartment and wondered why, now that she'd resolved to change her life, nothing of importance seemed to be falling into place.

By that time, Lily didn't care that the woman had gone back to the city.

She didn't care that Antonia said she'd call her in a day or two.

She didn't really care if she ever heard from her again.

Antonia had come to represent all that Lily now felt ashamed of: the pursuit of money and the need for material things, which meant nothing when compared to love.

It was such an uninspired conclusion that Lily felt as if her life had become one big, fat cliché.

After having spent a frenetic hour or two looking first for Antonia, then for Andrew, and finding neither, Lily had decided she would do the only thing that she had left: She would work. It was the way she'd watched Jo survive one crisis after another. Maybe it would work for Lily too.

She began by accepting responsibility for the kindergarten teacher's wedding. She would stop thinking of it as a noisy, confusion-wrought ordeal and turn it into the most memorable wedding that Tanglewood or all of the Berkshires had ever seen, something Tiffany Lupek and the others would remember for years to come. Lily was going to stay focused on the present, not the past or future. In the process, she would try not to obsess about Frank, who was out at Sondra's cabin at the lake doing who-knew-what in the daytime and God-knew-what at night.

She worked (she worked?) all weekend(!). Saturday and Sunday, without batting a false-eyelashed eye, Lily organized the dresses and tuxedoes for Monday's fittings for the eighteen little ones, met with Dennis and his flower people to ensure the very best, harassed the musicians (they did know the theme from *Barney*, didn't they?), ran back and forth from Seranak House selecting proper backdrops for the photographer and trying to rearrange the lovely antiques inside the home (though the director kept insisting they were fine the way they were), and took the bride shopping for the attendants' gifts (silver lockets for the girls, silver cuff links for the boys—who cared if it was overkill, Lily was paying for it, wasn't she?).

All through the weekend, Second Chances buzzed.

Elaine worked with Tanglewood's caterers on the presentation of the pizza bites and chocolate pudding and grown-up appetizers for the adults.

Sarah located several dozen giant "fun" balls for hopping, bouncing, and rolling after the ceremony. They were lavender and pink, of course, and would also serve as a colorful backdrop at the altar.

Jo arranged the seating and ordered chairs and tables, though how she managed with Brian's trial set to start on Monday was anybody's guess. Cassie's presence might have helped distract her. Cassie made center-pieces shaped like the fun balls—and even came up with the great idea to have lots of bubbles and bubble wands of all shapes and sizes for the little kids (and the adults!) to wave around and add shimmering magic to the air.

Late on Sunday, Lily strolled the grounds of Seranak House. With the details of the wedding finally complete and every aspect now well under control (except, of course, for knowing how the five-year-olds would act and react to the formalities), Lily suddenly stopped in the middle of the sidewalk that curved down the gentle-sloping hill.

Despite her many trips to and from Seranak House, this was the first time that she paid attention to the view of Lake Mahkeenac.

She stood and watched, as if peering down into a snow globe whose ice had melted and yielded to the sweet pastels of spring. The water was so still, in contrast to her life.

Was Frank sitting on the dock, thinking about her?

Was Sondra there? *Oh, God,* she thought, *is Sondra there?*

"I need some time away," Frank had said. "I'm not sure what I want right now."

He wasn't sure if he still wanted to marry Lily or not. He'd been sure once, but now he wasn't.

"Mrs. Beckwith?" a voice called out from the portico of the house. "Did you think of something else?"

Lily raised her hand in a half wave and said, "No thanks, I'm fine." Then she continued walking toward her car, a lump growing bigger in her throat, her eyes now clouded by tears that at least prevented her from staring at the lake.

She could always go there, she supposed. She could cruise around and around the lake until she saw Frank's truck parked by a cabin on the water. She could bang on the front door and demand that he come out, that he come back to her.

But that would get her nowhere, just as it would get

her nowhere to drive to Mount Rose, Connecticut, and find the place where Billy Sears now lived.

She held her key up to the car door and beeped the lock. She got inside, hooked her seat belt, and stared out the windshield at the lake, wondering why her period was a full week late again, if—again—it was because she'd lost someone she'd loved.

35

Boston didn't look the same. When Sarah, Sutter, and Jo arrived on Sunday night, it seemed to have more tunnels than when Jo had lived here, a more intricate web of ramps and exits and other ways of getting lost. Sarah suggested it wasn't as much that the streets were different, but that Jo had changed.

Two hours earlier, Jo had hugged Cassie good-bye at Mrs. Connor's, grateful for the time they'd shared, the girl talk, and the hope that maybe they could be a family after all, which now seemed to depend as much on what Andrew was up to in New York as it did on her.

Trying to put it all aside, she'd hugged Cassie again, then climbed into the backseat of Sutter's BMW. Suddenly—or rather it seemed that it was sudden—there they were, sooner than she'd hoped, checking into the Holiday Inn in Brookline. Jo had hoped that staying there and not downtown might keep her detached from the hustle and the bustle and the reason they were here.

She got into bed without even opening her suitcase, then pulled the stiff sheet around her chin as if she might actually go to sleep.

Instead, she lay in the cold hotel-room bed, wishing she'd gone to dinner with Sarah and Sutter, wishing Andrew was beside her, wishing she'd never filed the complaint that had led to Brian's arrest.

It was only money, after all.

And it had been her own stupid fault, hadn't it? Maybe he had scammed her, but she'd given him her money willingly, hadn't she?

She wondered if his attorney would make her look as foolish as she'd feel once she was on the witness stand.

Was it too late to back out?

"He's done it to you, he'll do it to others," the police had told her a million years ago when Brian finally was found.

Which, of course, she told herself, was exactly why she was there.

Rolling onto her side, she studied the lights of Beacon Street filtering through the window and listened to the rumble of the T as the transit cars chugged back and forth into the city, back and forth, back and forth.

She wondered if Brian was already in town and, if so, where he was staying.

She squeezed her eyes together, surprised to feel a small tear trickle down her cheek. She thought she'd been controlling herself so well. She thought she'd become quite good at not thinking about Brian or not wondering how she would react when they came face-to-face.

Andrew hated that he was in New York and Jo was in Boston. He hated that she'd shut him out of that part of her life, though he supposed if he'd been her and Brian had been Patty, he wouldn't want Jo involved either.

Still, he couldn't shake the thought that he was supposed to be Jo's knight in shining armor, the one love of her life who would make up for all the rest.

Wrong.

He sat up on the side of the creaky bed in Antonia's guest room and reassured himself that at least when he saw Jo again he would be bearing great news: After spending the whole weekend trying to convince them, the bankers finally agreed to the start-up loan for *Second Chances,* the magazine, based on the chunk of money that Antonia had committed.

Snapping on the porcelain lamp on the nightstand next to the bed, he checked his watch: three-fifteen. In a few hours he and Antonia would go back to West Hope to spread the exciting word. They'd leave Frannie in Manhattan, where she'd hunt for the perfect editorial suite of Midtown offices; his job as Executive Editor would be handled via e-mail, FedEx, and all the other communications vehicles of the century from his cottage in the Berkshires. Or from Jo's house, if they could ever get together.

When they returned to West Hope, he would also call Winston College and call off his search for gainful reemployment. Teaching was great when Andrew had needed the change, but the rousing mire of media trenches was where he knew he belonged. A magazine for second weddings now . . . who knew where that could catapult them for the future.

He looked at his watch again, then sat there, swinging his feet like a little kid, hoping Antonia would rise early in the morning so they could be on their way.

Billy Sears was in his cadet uniform, his black hair trimmed in the standard U.S. Army flattop, his blue eyes bright with promise, his freckles stretched across his cheeks from the big grin on his face.

He didn't say anything to Lily, just held out a hefty bouquet of lilacs.

Lilacs?

"No!" she shouted. "Go away!"

He went away, and in his place stood Frank, not in a uniform at all, but in khaki Dockers.

"Where's Billy?" she asked. "I want to talk to Billy."

"You sent him away. You said you wanted me."

She woke up in a sweat. She lay there in her child's bed, her heart beating rapidly. She jumped up, went out to the living room, snapped on the Mad Hatter lamp. The clock read five-fifteen. She sat down on the sofa, next to her plush rabbit. She realized she was trembling.

"Billy," she said softly, because in that moment she needed to hear his name spoken out loud. She wondered what he looked like now—was his hair still black and short? Had his freckles blended with the patina of middle age? Did his bright blue eyes still hold promise?

Would he still smile if he saw her?

Lily supposed that later she would wonder if her actions were propelled by her foolish dream or by a supernatural force: Aunt Margaret, maybe, who might think that now was the time for Lily to set her past to rest. Perhaps the sign was from her father, who'd always liked Billy, the smartest in his class.

Maybe it was Eleanor Forbes who was trying to protect her son.

Lily supposed she would think about all of that later. Right now the only thing that she needed was to march over to her closet and decide what she would wear.

If Billy lived in West Hope he could be Cassie's teacher, Lily thought as she drove south on Route 8, past the general store in Otis, through New Boston, along the West Branch of the river, over the line into Connecticut. She'd left her apartment before most people ate breakfast, because she knew she'd need to see him before he went to school. If she waited until the afternoon she might change her mind. Besides, later that day she would have eighteen five-year-olds for fittings and rehearsals for the wedding.

She'd dressed in jeans (two-hundred-dollar Yanuk jeans that were brand-new and a little tight), an Emilio Pucci cashmere halter, and a Dior aviator jacket. If she was going to do this, she needed the support of her fashion friends.

Her real friends, of course, were the ones she would have wanted, the ones she'd come to depend on to accompany her on her adventures. But her real friends were unavailable: Jo and Sarah were in Boston, and Elaine was not the one to ask to go with her on the journey to find her long-lost love, who now was married and had five children. Five.

She pushed that thought from her mind and continued driving with controlled determination until she saw the sign: *Entering Mount Rose.*

She pulled onto the shoulder and sat quietly.

His mother said he had several acres right along Route 8. Surely she could find a rural-route mailbox displaying the name *Sears*. Surely she could find it if she continued driving, if she wanted to keep going.

Unless this was the one jaunt that Lily had conjured up, that Lily would not complete.

A farmer's tractor chugged down the road just then. He stopped and waved at Lily, who put her window down.

"You okay, miss?" the farmer shouted above the *putt-putt* of the tractor.

"I'm fine," she said. "Just resting."

He tipped his John Deere cap and *chug-chug*ged away, leaving Lily on the roadside, trying to decide what she should do.

36

J o ordered tea and rye toast without butter, which
now sat in front of her, untouched. If she was
alone, she would not have bothered with breakfast. If she was alone, she would have stayed in her
room, clutching what felt like a sack of golf balls in her
stomach, unable to deal with what was ahead.

But she wasn't alone. Sarah and Sutter were with her,
sitting across from her at an umbrella table in the
cheery, sunlit atrium restaurant at the Holiday Inn.

"Have I thanked you for coming with me?" Jo asked.

"A dozen times," Sarah said.

"A dozen and one," Sutter added.

Jo smiled. They were an ideal couple, Sarah and
Sutter, if there was such a thing. Elegantly beautiful in
that exotic, Cherokee way, burnished and clean-
skinned and soft-spoken and patient. She wondered
what it might be like to be that . . . well, *at ease* with
someone, two pieces of life's jigsaw, perfectly fit. She
wondered if she and Andrew really had what it took
and if they could manage not to let the rest of life get
in the way.

She wondered what it was like to be so secure with a
man that you didn't feel you needed to marry him to
know you'd be together always.

"How did you sleep?" Sarah asked.

On their drive from West Hope to Brookline, Sutter
had reviewed the process of what Jo could expect to

happen. Jury selection had taken place last Friday. This morning would be opening arguments. Jo would no doubt take the stand this afternoon. She tried to push away that thought and hold her stiff smile. "I slept neither well nor much. I don't know if I'm more nervous about testifying or about seeing Brian."

"You don't have to look at the defendant," Sutter said. "Keep your eyes straight ahead. When we're in the courtroom, keep your eyes on the judge. When you're on the stand, keep your eyes on the attorney asking the questions."

It was good advice, she supposed. But Sutter didn't know Brian, didn't understand the pull he'd once had on her heart.

"I'll check Brian out for you," Sarah said. "Then later I'll be able to tell you how crappy he looks, how haggard and ugly and old."

Jo laughed in spite of the golf balls in her stomach. "Maybe his hair is gray or gone and he has three double chins."

"Oh, we can be sure of it," Sarah said. "And he probably has a severe case of adult acne to boot. And no teeth. Definitely no teeth."

"And his pants will be too short."

"And he'll have gained thirty pounds."

"And he'll have a nervous twitch he can't control."

"And when the judge instructs him to stand," Sarah added, "he'll stand up and fart. Really, really loud. And his face will turn beet red."

Jo laughed.

Sarah laughed.

Sutter shook his head. "God help me if I ever get on the wrong side of you girls," he said.

But Jo kept on smiling, so grateful to Sarah for lessening her pain that she dared take a few bites of her rye toast and chew and swallow and feel pretty darn good—until Sutter checked his watch and said, "I hate to break up the party, ladies, but it's time for us to go."

"Dad! Some lady's here to see you!"

The child—a girl (was she the youngest? She didn't look as old as Cassie)—had opened the front door of the L-shaped ranch set at the far end of a driveway where the mailbox, indeed, had block letters that read SEARS. In a town like Mount Rose, Lily supposed, no one cared if someone knew your name.

She waited on the front step because the little girl had apparently been taught not to let strangers into the house. Through the window of the door, however, Lily saw into the living room, which had a big fireplace and a mantel crowded with photographs, family pictures of the kids she hadn't had.

In the distance she heard voices: "Where's your homework? . . . Here's your lunch. . . . Do you have band practice today?"

Lily shifted onto the left heel of her Louis Vuitton boots. She wondered if the kitchen smelled like eggs and bacon cooking, if Billy's wife was pouring orange juice into cartoon jelly jars.

And then Lily heard footsteps. She sucked in her

breath and held it until the face appeared—not Billy's, but a woman's.

"May I help you?" the woman asked, opening the door. "My husband is in the shower. We're running late this morning."

Lily didn't know what she'd expected, what kind of woman she'd thought Billy might have married. Someone like Lily, perhaps; someone tiny and fair, sparkling and vivacious. She did not expect a rather tall, heavyset brunette who had clear, makeup-free skin and wore corduroys in May.

"Mrs. Sears?" Lily asked.

"Yes," the woman confirmed. "How may I help you?"

"I know this is a bad time," Lily said, glancing nervously at her watch. "But I was passing through town . . ."

"Honey? Who is it?"

She wouldn't have recognized his voice; it had been too many years, and though he'd been twenty-two, apparently Cadet Sears hadn't had a real man's voice as yet.

But it was him. Suddenly standing next to his wife, his black hair now shot with gray, his freckles faded, his blue eyes, though, still bright, it was him.

"Lily?" he asked. "Lily, is that you?"

Mrs. Sears (*Joanna*, Lily had been told) said Lily should come in and have coffee, that she would get someone at school to take Billy's class for an hour or so to give them a chance to visit, it had been so many years.

The kids (Lily was introduced; she didn't remember one single name) and Mrs. Sears departed in a flash, leaving Lily and Billy sitting in the family room, where more photographs were on display, where more memories—his, not hers—had no doubt been made.

"So," he said, "I can't believe it's you."

"It's me," she said, crossing her legs. She felt a pang and wondered if it was a leftover heartstring being pulled, then realized it was the too-tight waistband of her new jeans.

"You look terrific."

"Thanks. So do you."

He drank his coffee; she held on to her mug.

"Well," he said, "what brings you to Mount Rose? Or through it, I should ask?"

She considered making something up but then decided what the hell. "I wanted to see you," she said.

He laughed. "Me? What for?"

She sipped her coffee then. "Old times' sake, I guess. I was mean to you, Billy. I wanted to apologize."

He laughed again. "God, no one's called me 'Billy' since 1981."

Like a man, she supposed, he'd dodged the part that dealt with her emotions. "I said I'm sorry," Lily repeated. She studied his face, looking for a reaction. But though she still saw sweetness there, she could not read anything else. Either it had been too many years, or she'd never really known him.

"You were the first girl I ever slept with," he said.

She smiled. "Well, I was a virgin too."

He stood up, walked to the sliding glass doors that provided a wide view of his "several acres." "So what's this about? Have you come to tell me there's a kid I never knew about?"

She winced. She hadn't expected that. She thought about the weeks she'd been convinced that she was pregnant, about the mix of relief and sorrow when she found out she was not. "No, Billy. I just stopped by to say hello." She stood up, set the coffee mug down on the table. "It's better if I go now. You have a nice life and I'm happy for you. I have a nice life too. But I wanted to say I'm sorry for the way I hurt you way back then."

She started toward the front door by herself.

"Lily?" he called after her.

She stopped, turned around.

"Thanks," he said. "I know we were young and pretty stupid, but, yeah, you hurt me for a while. Then I got over it, because that's what kids do, isn't it?"

"Yes," Lily replied, "that's what kids do, Billy."

She closed the door behind her and went to her Mercedes, wondering what had taken her so long to put the past where it belonged.

37

T he courtroom was cold.

Jo wished she'd worn her long-sleeved, powder-blue cashmere suit, but she'd opted for the nondescript beige linen dress, hoping it would render her less noticeable. She filed in behind Sutter, whose shoulders blocked her view, and in front of Sarah, who said she would catch her if she tripped and fell or if she passed out, the way Lily had at Frank's mother's funeral.

Sutter stopped, turned, and gestured that Sarah, then Jo, should step into the row on the right. It occurred to Jo that she'd be flanked by Cherokee bookends, which, for some reason, felt very safe.

The wooden bench was as cold as the air in the room. Sarah took Jo's hand, patted it a few seconds. Jo was surprised that her touch was warm.

If she had wanted to look to the left, toward the defendant's table, she couldn't have seen much because Sutter's large frame obstructed most of the view. So she stared at the front of the room as she'd been instructed, at the raised platform, at the seal of the Commonwealth of Massachusetts plastered to the wall, at the flags—one American, the other Massachusetts's single white star and Native American, with his bow and his arrow facing downward in a symbol of peace. It was hard to tell by the folds in the fabric, but the slogan seemed to be in Latin and might make reference to peace and liberty. She thought that, given the situation, a more appropriate flag might have been the one from colonial days that read *Don't Tread on Me.*

More people entered the courtroom. She recognized the police officer who had once helped her—Lieutenant Williams of the Missing Persons Bureau. She would have liked to say hello.

She also spotted the private detective, the one Frank had hired, the one who had found Brian, but she couldn't remember the man's name.

She moved her eyes back to the Seal of the Commonwealth, then sensed, rather than saw, that Brian had come into the room. She sucked in her breath; Sarah took her hand once again, leaned close to Jo, and merely said, "Zits."

This time, it wasn't easy for Jo to smile.

Then the judge came in and the bailiff said, "All rise." There were shufflings and mutterings, and Jo stood up with her eyes fixed straight ahead and her heart steeling itself to shatter and the golf balls teeing up inside her.

A moment later Sutter nudged her to sit down again, so she did.

Then a faceless attorney said, "Your honor, my client would like to amend his plea."

And the next thing she knew, Jo heard the words, "Guilty, your honor," in a voice that sounded more like it had come from Frank Forbes than from Brian.

Jo blinked. *Guilty?*

"Yes, your honor," Frank/Brian's voice said.

The judge moved some papers from one file to another, studied them a moment, then moved them back. He asked Brian some questions: Did he know what this meant, was he prepared for the consequences, had he been coerced?

Brian yes-and-no-your-honor'ed in the appropriate places, then the judge turned toward the jury box, which Jo hadn't noticed until then. He thanked them for their time and told them they could leave.

Jo's body temperature went from frigid to numb. Her eyes flashed to Sutter in search of explanation.

Then the back door to the courtroom opened again and Jo heard Brian say, "Excuse me, your honor, but I'd like to say something," and it took her a second to realize that this time it wasn't Brian's voice but Frank's, that Frank had come to Boston.

The judge asked him who he was and why he was interrupting his court.

Frank apologized again, then explained that he was the defendant's brother and he was there to offer restitution to Brian's victims.

Jo blinked again.

The prosecutor was on his feet voicing an objection; the woman (of course, it would be a woman) who apparently was Brian's attorney stood and countered with something; the judge whacked his gavel and told everyone to shut up.

Jo did not move a muscle, not even to breathe.

The next thing she knew, the judge spoke her name.

Sutter nudged her, gestured for her to stand up again. Her Jell-O legs somehow managed to bring her upright; Sutter stood beside her.

"Ms. Lyons, according to the notes, you have accused the defendant of stealing over three hundred thousand dollars from you. Because you are the sole petitioner in this case and the defendant has just pled guilty, are you willing to drop the charges against him if full restitution is made?"

She did not know how to respond. It was a scenario she hadn't expected. Her eyes darted from Frank to the judge. How could Frank Forbes come up with over a quarter of a million dollars?

"If she drops the charges," Sutter said, "would Brian Forbes be free to go?"

"Yes."

She turned to Sutter in search of an answer.

"May we have a brief recess," Sutter asked, "so my client can have a moment to consider?"

But as he addressed the judge, Sutter had stepped forward, exposing Jo's line of sight straight to Brian.

She waited for her heart to stop and her breathing to grow shallow and her entire body to break out in a sweat. His hair had not turned white; he didn't have acne and he hadn't gained thirty pounds. Brian was Brian—still good-looking, without a doubt, but no longer charismatic in the way he stood, the way he smiled. Or perhaps she now saw him through much different eyes.

Suddenly, the room was no longer cold.

Jo turned her eyes back to the judge. "No, your honor, I do not need a recess," she said. "I will not accept restitution if it means Brian Forbes will go free. He will only look for another victim. He needs to make amends to society, as much as he needs to make them to me."

The judge smiled at her and said, "Brian Forbes, having accepted your plea of guilty to one count of larceny against a person, I sentence you to five years in prison." The judge made a note on the file, then looked back at Brian. "And, based on the generous offer of Mr. Forbes's brother, I highly recommend that at least one hundred fifty thousand dollars be paid to the victim, Ms. Josephine Lyons."

38

I t wasn't my idea," Frank said to Jo as she and Sutter and Sarah walked out of the courtroom. Frank fell in step next to Jo and added, "It was my mother's. It was what she stipulated in her will. The money is coming from her life insurance."

Just then a blond woman passed them on her way out of the courtroom. She glared at Jo quickly, but long enough for Jo to understand that she was Brian's wife. Jo felt no envy, only pity.

Turning back to Frank, Jo shook her head. "I don't want the money, Frank. I can't take your mother's money as payment for what Brian did. I'm not sure if jail will change him, but I do know that letting him off

260

the hook by paying his debt would not teach him a thing."

"I agree," Frank said. "Please understand it was only a mother trying to protect her son. And please understand that I fully intend to follow the judge's recommendation and give you half."

Jo did not know what to say.

"Where's Lily?" Sarah asked Frank as they stepped through the doorway into the corridor.

"In West Hope, I guess. I've been at the lake with my dad. In my ex-wife's cabin."

Sarah's eyebrows lifted.

"Not to worry," he said. "It took her a few days, but Sondra finally got the message that I wouldn't sleep with her." He laughed a short, satisfied laugh. "She is one boring woman compared to Lily Beckwith."

Jo smiled and thought how wonderful it was that Frank and Lily might find a way to carve out a life together. Frank and Lily, Sarah and Sutter—this time she did feel envy. Adjusting her pocketbook on her shoulder and turning up her collar, Jo decided to stop feeling sorry for herself. But as the group rounded the corner to head toward the elevators, she noticed a figure sitting on a bench over by the window. She stopped walking. "Andrew," she said. "What are you doing here?"

Lily was tired but invigorated. She never realized that shedding old-boyfriend baggage could feel like losing twenty pounds.

Standing in the back room of the shop after the hectic fittings and first rehearsal of the bridesgirls and the groomsboys (as Lily now called them) was complete, she surveyed the rack of dresses and tuxedoes. They looked as if they belonged backstage on the set of *The Wizard of Oz* and comprised the wardrobe for the Munchkins.

She counted the accessories like a symphony conductor directing the different sections of his orchestra: first violin, then second, violas, then the cellos. She flitted her fingers and waved her palms this way and that, only briefly wondering if she'd hear from Frank again, or from Antonia, for that matter.

Frank, of course, was a man, so his odd behavior was not unexpected, because who knew why men thought what they thought or did what they did. If he went back to Sondra, Lily supposed that she would miss him but she would get over it, the way Billy had gotten over her.

As for Lily's former sister-in-law, it appeared that she and her entourage had returned to New York with nary a good-bye or a good-luck or a please-go-to-hell.

At least men got to the point, would tell you they were leaving, would say they didn't know if they loved you anymore.

She turned to the plastic containers from Wal-Mart and counted the little shoes and little socks as if they were tiny piccolos, just as Elaine trudged through the back door.

"I need a vacation," Elaine said, and parked herself

on the tall stool by Sarah's drawing table. "When I was a homemaker, life was so simple."

Lily double-checked her list of little-kid footwear then sighed. "When I was a diva, it was even simpler than that."

"I was never a diva. What was it like?"

"To be waited on every moment? To spend your days at the spa and your nights being seen? To have to worry only about whether Cartier would have your diamonds reset in time for the Valentine's Ball? Oh, my dear Elaine, life as a diva was so simple it was dull." There was no need to mention that her life had changed that very morning, that she'd decided Antonia could keep her money and Sondra could keep Frank and that Lily, dear Lily, would carry on.

Elaine laughed, then said, "You're awfully chipper today, Lily. Don't you ever just get tired?"

"That's another thing," Lily said, her voice in delicate singsong. "If I was tired as a diva, I would take a nap. A nap! Can you imagine?" She twirled, then grasped the side of the dress rack because she'd made herself dizzy. She laughed and shook her head. "Oh, hell's bells, Elaine. Sometimes being a working girl isn't pretty, but it beats the heck out of being a lump."

"But, Lily, you were always my hero. You don't have to work. You can sit back on Reginald's moneyed laurels."

"I'm afraid it's too late for that now."

Elaine swung her feet. "You don't regret it, do you, Lily? Starting the business?"

Lily shrugged, then resumed her counting, this time the little-girl headpieces.

"I mean, look at you and me," Elaine continued. "We changed our lives most of all. Sarah and Jo, they always worked. But our lives were different. I was a wife once. Boy, that's hard to remember. I wonder if I'll be good at that anymore."

"You say that as if you're going to give it a try."

Elaine smiled. She wiped her hands on the white chef's apron she wore over her jeans and Liz Claiborne shirt. She stood up again. "I followed your advice. I proposed to Martin."

"What?" Lily jumped up and down and clapped her little hands.

"You don't know if he said yes."

"Of course he said yes. He'd be a fool not to!"

"Well, then he's no fool. Because he did say yes. And we'll get married in the fall. A year after we should have gotten married in the first place."

"And we'll be your bridesmaids!" Lily shrieked. *"And we'll help pick out your gown! Oh, Lainey, this is divine. Our lives have come full circle!"* She danced over to Elaine and kissed her on her right cheek, then her left.

Elaine laughed. "I thought you might be happy," she said. "And though it's been nice chatting with you, I have to get back to work. My father agreed to cater the Elks Club bowling banquet, so I'm swapping foie gras and bruschetta for kielbasa and peppers."

"Whatever!" Lily a-cappella'ed, then resumed her

symphony, pointing to the box of small dress gloves that sat in the percussion section and dancing back into her world, back to her happy work.

Sarah showed up at four-thirty, just as Lily was about to lock up the shop.

"What the heck are you doing here?" Lily asked. "I thought you'd be in Boston a few days."

"The trial is over. Brian has gone to jail for five years and Jo and Andrew are together and all's right with the world."

"Wow. That was fast. So they could have gone through with the wedding after all."

Sarah laughed. "God, Lily, is that all you ever think about?"

"Weddings are what I'm paid to think about these days. In fact, they're what we're *all* paid to think about. Speaking of which, our Lainey is going to marry Martin! We'll be bridesmaids just the way we planned!"

"Well, that's really swell," Sarah said. "By the way, you might not believe this, but your boyfriend tried to get his brother off the legal hook."

Lily jangled her keys in her hand, forgiving Sarah for not getting as excited as she did about Elaine's news. The four of them were so different. She hoped that never changed. "What do you mean?" she asked, because if it involved Frank, she was more interested.

Sarah explained how Frank had showed up and tried

to make restitution with his mother's life-insurance money.

"He should save it for his new life with Sondra."

"As it happens, the judge suggested that he give Jo half. She says she doesn't want it, but Frank has insisted. As for him and Sondra, I don't think that's going to happen."

"The hell it isn't. He was with her for four days."

"No. I don't think he was 'with her' in the sense you mean."

"Oh, pooh, Sarah, what do you know, anyway?"

Sarah laughed. "I know that I only stopped by to tell you that Jo's ordeal is over and that she'll be working full steam ahead toward the kindergarten teacher's wedding. As for you, Ms. Lily, if you don't believe a word that I've told you about Frank, I suggest you march your little self across the town common, where he is busy at his shop, trying to reconstruct his life. Not that you care about his life anymore."

With that, Sarah turned on her Birkenstocks and went out the back door, leaving Lily standing there, a smile slowly pirouetting across her face.

39

He was with a customer.

Lily stood inside the doorway of Antiques & Such and listened as Frank cited "period piece" and "matching sideboard" and "Duncan Phyfe." His voice was low and not close—Lily suspected he was in the room at the far end of the store, the "Assessor's Office," he laughingly called it, because that was what it had been when the building was the West Hope Town Hall. It was where Frank now showcased his most coveted stock.

She moved to the front of the room and began to inspect the estate jewelry, which was set in a velvet-lined curio cabinet that subtly implied it was worth more than it was.

Personally, she found estate jewelry creepy.

"Whoever owned it is either dead or fallen on hard times," she'd said to Frank as she supervised the arrangement of the display back when he'd relocated his business across the street. "Knowing those things, why on earth would I want to wear something—no matter how sparkly—that has such a sad, ill-fated past?"

Frank had laughed, because it was still early in their relationship—before his mother had taken a turn for the worse, before Lily had stopped working hard to charm him, before Sondra had resurfaced. He told Lily she was too funny and he kissed her on the mouth and they made love right there amid the moving cartons in what once had been the town clerk's office.

She'd been startled by the spontaneity of the small-town, solid citizen but amused to think that they were making love where so many West Hopers had obtained a marriage license.

She studied a brooch with a large stone encased in a gaudy swirl of platinum. The color looked too deep to be ruby, so it must be a garnet. She wondered if the original owner had been someone like Aunt Margaret, who'd spent too much time and money surrounding herself with baubles instead of with people she might have loved. Lily wondered what had happened in Margaret's life to make her that way and why Lily had so readily followed in her high-heeled footsteps for so many years.

Loneliness, she supposed, was often at the root of such shallow behavior. Loneliness, sorrow, fear of waking up each morning finding yourself alone. Until now Lily hadn't realized those things were simply part of life and could even be embraced for the strength and courage that they fostered.

"I have a wonderful drop-leaf table coming in next week," Frank said, his voice growing louder.

Just as Lily was about to step forward and make her presence known, his customer said, "Set it aside for me, please."

Lily flinched; she nearly gasped. The voice, she was quite certain, was Antonia's.

She ducked behind the curio cabinet, wondering what the hell was going on.

Why was Antonia back in West Hope?

Why was she talking to Frank about sideboards and drop-leaf tables?

Squeezing her eyes shut, Lily wrinkled her nose. Her heart began to do a little dance somewhere in her throat, a cha-cha, maybe, or a lively salsa.

"If you wouldn't mind holding those pieces for me,

I'll let you know when I have a place."

"Of course. And give Don Benjamin a call. I'm sure he can help you find something suitable soon."

When she has a place? What the heck did that mean? And wasn't Don Benjamin a real-estate broker whose office was three or four doors down from Second Chances?

She should have stayed where she was, out of sight, and apparently out of mind. She should have remained in the shadows in her new state of contentment.

But that would have been sensible and, no matter how much she'd evolved, Lily was not that. Besides, she no longer cared what either of them did or thought, did she?

Sucking in a small breath and tipping up her chin, she stepped one, then two feet forward until she was in plain sight, until the conspirators' heads turned and noticed her standing there.

"Lily," Frank said.

"Lily," Antonia said.

"Yes," Lily answered, "that would be me. I didn't know the two of you had become acquainted."

Antonia laughed. "I've finally figured out why my brother liked you." Her red lips bounced around with animation. "Beneath your capricious, often annoying exterior lies a delightful, strong woman who is really quite unconscionable."

Lily could not tell if Antonia was mocking her or complimenting her.

"Antonia," she said, her flare of anger simmering to a simple need to know the truth, "why ever are you here?"

Another person might have called the woman's expression smug, but Lily recognized it as one of entertainment. "Well," Antonia remarked, "I could say I've come to meet the man who seems to have stolen your heart, but since neither of you knows that I know what's been going on, I suppose I should leave it up to you to properly introduce me. Unless, of course, you've been too fraught with worry that I shall cut off your inheritance."

She was enjoying this, wasn't she?

She was amused by the perplexed look that surely must be on Lily's face, by the butterflies that she surely knew were flapping their wings inside Lily's stomach.

"I don't want your money," Lily said so quickly and so loudly it surprised even her. "I want my life back, Antonia. I love this man." She pointed a shaky finger in Frank's direction, briefly noticing her need for a good manicure—good heavens, how long had it been? This business of working hardly left time for personal essentials.

She shook away her thoughts and returned to the moment. "I don't know if he loves me anymore, and I wouldn't blame him if he didn't. But I love him more than your money can buy, Antonia, and I'd rather have him than a hundred dollars of your cash." She sup-posed she should have said "one" dollar, not "a hundred," but Lily's monetary frame of reference wasn't like other folks'.

Antonia moved closer. "Too late," she replied with half a hearty laugh. "Like it or not, you're the closest thing I have to family, Lily Beckwith. For some reason, my brother's death seems to have forced us together. It's as if his ghost has been testing us to see if we could finally be friends." Her eyes shifted to Frank. "Lily has never known this, but I do know what love is. There was a man named Howard. He loved me very much, and I loved him. Sadly, he was killed in 1968, in Vietnam, the way Lily's father might have been. I never had another man, because I didn't want one." She looked back at Lily and said, "Now, if you both will excuse me, I shall go see if the real-estate office is still open."

Launching a last Cheshire grin at Lily, Antonia padded from the store.

Lily looked back to Frank, who stood, dumbfounded, asking, "Who in God's name was that?"

Instead of bursting into little-girl tears or dropping to the floor in a fit of melodrama, Lily closed her eyes and smiled at the absurdity of life, specifically, her life, and at the ways in which we have so much to learn from others, if we only can give them a little bitty chance.

She was back in his arms and that was all Andrew cared about.

"It's over," Jo said. "Not just the trial, Andrew. I

mean, it's really over. Seeing Brian . . . well, I realized that the fantasy is finished. There was no pull, no desire to be with him, not at all. All I could think was how pathetic he is and how wonderful my life has become. I feel as if I truly have been given a brand-new chance in life."

He could have said, *A second chance,* but thought that would sound corny. Instead, he kissed her and pulled her close, under the covers, safe in the warmth of his bed in the cottage where they'd come as soon as Frank had dropped them off. Cassie would be going straight to Mrs. Connor's after school; she wouldn't expect Andrew and Jo to be home. But Jo had said it didn't matter anyway. She didn't mind if Cassie knew that she was in Andrew's bed; she didn't mind if the whole world knew that Jo could at last proclaim that she loved Andrew David Kennedy with all her heart.

It had been a long time coming, Andrew said, and well worth the wait.

Then he added, "Frank is determined to give you the money. On the ride to Boston he told me all about it." He'd already explained that when he returned from New York and Elaine told him that Frank was going to the trial, he'd dashed from his cottage to hitch a ride with him. "Did you know Eleanor was the one who paid Brian's bail?"

Jo flinched. "What?"

"Apparently, Eleanor Forbes was the one Brian always turned to when he was really down and out."

"When he couldn't find a woman to pick up his

financial slack." She seemed to think a moment. "But that other woman," she said, "the one who was his wife . . ."

"Bled her dry, I guess. Bled them all dry."

"And I was the only one who finally understood."

He kissed her on the neck. "Because you are smarter, better-looking, and more loving than any of them could be."

Jo smiled. "So Eleanor knew all along what Brian did to me. And Frank knew Brian was out of jail all these months?"

"No, he didn't. Eleanor left a letter for him with her will that explained everything. She made him promise that what was left of her life insurance—what she hadn't borrowed against to post Brian's bail—would go to you to make up for the things that Brian had done. She also said for him to let you know that she was sorry."

Jo lay quietly, rubbing Andrew's shoulder with her gentle fingers. "How can I fault a woman for loving her child without conditions? I see that's how you love Cassie."

He kissed her and he said, "Yes, I do."

She kept rubbing his shoulder, kept reassuring him of her love. Then she said, "West Hope could use some new things for the library. Computers, software, things for the people in town. And the schools. Maybe they could use some new computers at West Hope Elementary. I'll talk to Frank about donating them in his mother's name."

He kissed her again because she was so wonderful. Then he said, "Speaking of money . . ." and out it came: the saga of Frannie and the *Second Chances* magazine and Antonia. He was more than glad that Jo said it sounded exciting but then she asked if they could please talk about it later and use this time to do something else. At which time Andrew smiled and said, "Sure."

They made love at last, then the sun set and the room grew dark and Andrew said, "Jo, let's get married."

She laughed, then traced his face with her sensuous finger. "We are getting married. September, remember?"

"No, I mean now. Without any frills. Without anyone knowing. Let's elope."

"It's funny you should say that. I always thought a wedding would be nice, with bridesmaids and flowers and a beautiful white gown. But lately there are days I feel so saturated by weddings I could scream, let alone want one for myself."

He rolled on top of her again and began to tease her throat with his lips, his tongue. "How about next week?"

"We could go somewhere exotic. Like Vermont. That way we wouldn't be gone long."

"Perfect," he said.

"But what about Cassie? Maybe she'll want to be included . . ."

"We can tell her just before we leave."

"But . . ."

"But nothing. I think my daughter will understand our need to be alone. Besides, she'll be grateful just to know her old dad's finally happy."

"I think she wants her new stepmother to be happy too. We had a really great time while you were in New York."

There would be time to talk about that later too.

"So," Andrew said, "let's write our wedding vows." Then he bounded out of bed and grabbed a pen from his dresser and a few pages from the business plan that Frannie had put together, which Andrew had hastily stashed in the corner with his suitcase of his New York clothes.

"I'll go first," Jo said. She closed her eyes and smiled. "From the first day that I saw you I had no idea we'd end up here . . ." she began, and Andrew started writing on the back of Frannie's sheet of paper titled long-range predictions. "I never dreamed," Jo added, "that one day I would trade in my name, Jo Lyons, for Jo Kennedy."

Andrew paused. He looked at her. "Kennedy? Are you sure you want to change your name?"

She smiled again. "Oh, yes. I like the way it sounds."

40

L ily stopped laughing when she realized Frank wasn't smiling.

"When?" he asked. "When did you plan to tell me that you have a sister-in-law?"

She knew then that this wasn't funny, that she'd known all along it wouldn't be funny when he found out about Antonia and the reason she hadn't said she'd marry him way back when he'd asked her.

Dropping down onto the settee where they'd made love so long ago, she lowered her eyes. "Oh, Frank, it's all so complicated."

He remained standing. He folded his arms. "I'm listening."

She sighed. She didn't know where to begin, so she started with the night her parents were killed, with the way she'd abandoned Billy Sears, with the huge hole that had been left in her heart, her soul. She told him about Aunt Margaret and how she'd done her best, but she'd lost her brother and sister-in-law and was empty too.

She told Frank about the baby that never was, how she'd somehow tried to fill the hole with new life but how God hadn't wanted that to happen.

And then she told him the rest: the men in her life who she'd kept at a shallow distance; Reginald, who'd skated the closest to her heart; the money and the fluff and the substitute stuff that had worked pretty well until now, until Frank, until the women of Second Chances had given Lily a real second chance of her own, a second chance to stop the nonsense and straighten out her life.

She told him she'd seen Billy Sears again, that she'd been underwhelmed, that she'd realized she'd wasted too many years feeling sad and guilty about him.

At the end, Lily said, "But it's all okay, Frank. I'm okay, at last. Please don't feel you have to marry me just because it's what I want now. I will truly understand if you go back to Sondra. She was your wife, after all." The tone of her voice surprised even her: It was honest and pure, no manipulation intended, no finagling of a Lily-agenda.

When she stood up to leave, Frank stepped in her path. He put his hands on her shoulders and looked straight into her eyes.

"I love you, Lily Beckwith," he said. "I love you as I never loved Sondra or any woman in my life. I would be honored if you'd marry me. As long as you promise to keep your late husband's money to yourself."

The flutter came to life inside her stomach. Then Lily suddenly knew. She just knew.

"Oh, my God," she said, as her hand flew to cover her mouth. She wriggled from his touch and darted to the door. "Will you wait here a few minutes? Just a few? Please? I'll be right back. Honest. Please."

She ran down the steps of the old town hall, then raced across the eighteenth-century town common as if the British were on their way again. She unlocked the front door of Second Chances, her hand trembling with excitement, her voice muttering, "Oh, jeez," and "Oh, wow."

She rushed through the doorway, grabbed her purse, then bolted through the showroom, past the racks and stacks of black-tie ensembles for the eighteen five-year-olds, through Sarah's studio, and out the back door.

She dashed toward her two-seater Mercedes just as a bicycle sped into the parking lot and a voice called out, "Lily!" She recognized the rider: It was Cassie.

"Can't stop," Lily shouted back as she fumbled for her car keys. "I'm having a crisis."

Cassie's tires squealed to a stop next to the car. "Me too," the girl breathlessly said. "We need to talk, Lily. Please?"

"Oh, hell's bells," Lily said, and pointed to the passenger door. "Park your bike and get in. You can tell me all about it while I drive."

It wasn't the first time Lily had bemoaned the fact that the West Hope Drugstore that had once, like everything else, been in the center of town had been usurped by the big chains and the big boxes and was no longer within walking distance from the old town hall.

41

"They didn't know I was in the house," Cassie said. "They didn't know I'd come home from Mrs. Connor's to get my new Green Day tour shirt."

Lily waved her hand. "On with it, girl. What happened?" She cranked on the ignition, slammed the shift into reverse.

"My dad and Jo. Well, they were in the bedroom."

Lily groaned, backed out of the parking space, then

jerked the shift into drive and gunned the engine. "Oy," she said. "Jo will never get over this one."

"No, Lily," Cassie continued. "It's worse than *that*. I overheard them talking. They're going to get married."

She peeled out onto the street. Lily loved Cassie, really she did, but right now she didn't need a chattering twelve-year-old at her ear.

"Cassie," she said, trying to keep her voice steady as she zipped the car up Main Street toward the strip mall outside town, "I don't know how to tell you, but this is not news."

She braked at the red light, the only one in town. With no cars around, she could have gone straight through, but with her luck Elaine's ex-brother-in-law was crouched behind the mailbox on the corner with his radar gun aimed. She thumped her fingers on the steering wheel.

"But they're going to elope," Cassie said.

The light turned green. Instead of stepping on the gas again, Lily turned her head. "What?"

Cassie shrugged. "They're going to elope. Next week. I thought you and the others might want to know."

Lily blinked. "You're kidding."

"No. It was my dad's idea, but Jo agreed. She said she is so saturated with weddings she no longer wants one of her own."

"Well," Lily said, the blood that had been pumping in her veins now creeping to a stop. "We can't let them do this. We just can't."

"They seem pretty definite."

"Well then, we'll just have to think of something to stop them." She looked back to the light. It had gone from green to red again. She looked right, then left, then accelerated.

"Lily?" Cassie asked. "Where are we going, anyway?"

"Now?"

"Yes."

Lily laughed. "Well, if you promise not to spill my secret to anyone, we're headed to the drugstore. I need to buy a home pregnancy test."

EPILOGUE

D id you get it?" Lily whispered to Cassie on the steps of Seranak House after she'd lined up the bridesgirls and the groomsboys for the kindergarten teacher's wedding and threatened them with time-outs if they dared to move.

Cassie nodded and patted the pocket of her cute ruffled skirt and pretty silk shirt, which Lily had picked out. She looked so grown-up today, with a light amount of makeup and powder-pink lipstick. "They'll never know what hit them," Cassie said.

Lily smiled, gazed up at the sky, and said quick thanks that the day was so gorgeous, that the sun was so brilliant and the sky was so blue. She inhaled a long breath, then turned to Sarah, who stood at the entrance to the aisle between the rows of white chairs and signaled *okay*. She looked toward the white tent where Andrew stood next to Elaine beside the long bank of buffet tables because he had agreed to help serve the pizza bites and hot dogs and french fries and all kinds of sugary, little-kid food. Jo's mother was there, too, with her husband, Ted. Lily had easily coerced them into volunteering too.

Lily signaled *okay* to Elaine.

She barely heard the string trio that glided from "Froggie Went A-Courtin'" to Mendelssohn without missing a note. Lily turned to the kids. "Okay," she said, "it's time."

And, just like that, eighteen five-year-olds moved with perfect, practiced precision—the girls clutching their wildflower nosegays, the boys with shoulders squared (except for Gabriel, who mischievously giggled and grinned and bowed to each row of guests). The most beautiful little girl was Tiffany Lupek, who proudly wore her short veil atop her chemo-bald head, smiling the smile of a child who'd only yesterday heard that she was now in remission, not really understanding the magnitude of the announcement but excited, no doubt, by hugs and kisses and tears of joy.

As Lily watched the children, she touched her hand to her belly, hoping her child—her boy or her girl—would be healthy and happy, knowing that whatever, she and Frank would do their utmost to be the best parents the world had ever seen.

"You have what?" Frank had said once Lily had dropped Cassie off, returned to the antiques store, run into the ladies' room, and emerged three minutes later holding the plastic wand.

"I have two pink lines," Lily said, not concealing her excitement. "I'm pregnant, Frank. *We're* pregnant. We're going to have a baby, ready or not."

The corner of Frank's mouth had begun to quiver, then his eyes grew moist with tears. "Lily," he said as he reached out, but before touching her he smiled and let out a small whimper of a cry and slid down to the floor the way she had in church at his mother's funeral.

He'd said he was overwhelmed, overcome, over-joyed as she'd cradled his head in her lap on the settee where it—the act of conception—had no doubt hap-pened.

"And now I'm embarrassed too," he said, half-sit-ting up.

She laughed and said they were quite a pair, weren't they? A couple of old fainters about to have a kid. Then she turned quiet and said she hoped he didn't mind but that she'd fibbed early in their relationship when she'd said she'd taken care of birth control but the truth was she'd pooh-hooed it because she thought God had nixed her plan for babies long ago. She didn't mention that she'd stupidly not worried about STDs because she figured Frank wasn't the type to sleep around.

"Lily," Frank said then, as he touched her cheek, "you've made me the happiest man in the world."

"And you," she replied, "you've made me the hap-piest woman."

No one but Cassie knew their secret. They'd decided

to save their news until after the events of today, until the limelight had been focused on the appropriate people. For once, Lily was glad to wait to become the center of everyone's attention.

From the back of the gathering seated on the lawn, Lily saw that the children were neatly aligned, just as they had practiced, just as Lily had wanted. She smiled with the thought that maybe she had a way with kids, after all.

Then, from the portico of Seranak House, Jo opened the front door and the bride stepped out, radiant, glamorous—all the things a wedding inspired.

She would be like that, Lily thought, when she and Frank were married.

It would not be a small wedding, nor would they elope. It would be in mid-September, which would allow a month before Elaine and Martin's second shot at their second chance. Lily would be plump, and she would be beautiful. She was going to insist on white tulle and organza and diamonds and pearls, and very special crudités prepared by Elaine's father, the master chef. Surely he would do that for her.

They would have a harpist and a full ensemble from Tanglewood and the loveliest flowers, all grown locally, of course.

The wedding would capture every essence of every wedding the women of Second Chances had planned, of every wedding to come, of every photo in their portfolio and every mention on their new website blog. It would embrace the aura of what weddings were all about: ceremony, commitment, love joined and love shared, whether the new wives and husbands were first, second, or "a hundred and first," as Frank once said.

It would also signify the rejoining of what remained of the Beckwith family. Lily, after all, had already asked Antonia to be her maid of honor. Antonia said she wouldn't miss it, especially now that she'd bought an old colonial on the road down to Stockbridge, one with lots of rooms for her assistants and a big playroom for Lily's kids.

Lily wiped a tear that somehow had sneaked out. Her marriage to Frank would be the one wedding her mother and father and Aunt Margaret would have applauded. She realized then she'd never, not once, wondered what Billy's wedding had been like. Maybe she'd been over him long before she knew it.

"The kids are perfect," Frank said as he stepped from behind Lily and slid his arms around her waist.

"Just like ours will be," she whispered. He kissed her neck, and they quietly watched the bride and the groom and the eighteen perfect children and the guests and all the bubbles that floated through the air as the I-do's were said.

Then, after the bride and groom kissed, instead of heading back down the aisle, the groom stepped forward and said, "I suppose you think the ceremony is over. Well, I'm happy to ask you to please remain seated, because our justice of the peace here has agreed to perform an added duty."

The little kids seemed content to stand there, no doubt transfixed by their teacher and her huge gown. (Except, of course, Gabriel, who'd already commandeered one of the giant balls and had hopped behind the altar.)

"Lily?" the kindergarten teacher's groom called out. "Are you all set?"

"Oh, yes, we are," she replied, and turned back to the house as Cassie scooped an arm through one of Jo's and said, "It's time, Jo. I can't wait any longer for you to be my stepmother."

Bewildered into silence, Jo let Cassie lead her toward the tent, just as Andrew was escorted in from the side by Elaine and Sarah on one arm, Jo's mother on the other.

The musicians played Mendelssohn's march again as Jo and Andrew were brought up to the altar and positioned in front of guests they did not know and a justice of the peace they had not met.

"We come together this day to join this man and this woman in holy matrimony," the justice began.

Andrew laughed.

Jo laughed.

Cassie told them both to shush, that it was legal, because they already had their marriage license and they'd written their vows and she just happened to have everything right there in her pocket.

When Andrew looked at her and frowned, Cassie said, "Sorry, I stole them." She then took several slightly crumpled pieces of paper from her skirt, handed them to the justice of the peace, and turned back to Jo and Andrew. "It was an emergency. Lily and I agreed that we simply couldn't have you elope. Besides, Lily's paying for today, remember?"

Then everyone laughed, even the people who didn't know them, even the kindergarten kids, because laughter was so infectious, especially on such a glorious day.

"Jo, please repeat after me," the justice of the peace continued. "Andrew, from the first day that I saw you I had no idea we'd end up here . . ."

And Jo was smiling and shaking her head in disbelief at the same time, and she repeated the vows that she'd written, and then Andrew did too.

Then the justice said, "Andrew David Kennedy, do you take this woman, Josephine Lyons, to be your lawfully wedded wife . . ." and Lily cried and Elaine cried and Sarah cried too, and Andrew simply smiled and said, "Oh, yes, I certainly do."

Center Point Publishing
600 Brooks Road • PO Box 1
Thorndike ME 04986-0001 USA

(207) 568-3717

US & Canada:
1 800 929-9108